An Unfortunate Christmas Murder

Hannah Hendy lives in a small town in South Wales with her brand new wife (Covid wedding!) and two rescue cats. A professional chef by trade, she started writing to fill the time on boring night shifts. She is the author of *The Dinner Lady Detectives*, which is her first novel but definitely not her last!

Also by Hannah Hendy

The Dinner Lady Detectives

The Dinner Lady Detectives
An Unfortunate Christmas Murder

An Unfortunate Christmas Murder

HANNAH HENDY

© CANELO CRIME

First published in the United Kingdom in 2022 by

Canelo
Unit 9, 5th Floor
Cargo Works, 1–2 Hatfields
London, SE1 9PG
United Kingdom

A CIP catalogue record for this book is available from the British Library.

Print ISBN 978 1 80032 651 4
Ebook ISBN 978 1 80032 650 7

Cover design by Ami Smithson

Cover images © Istock

Look for more great books at www.canelo.co

Printed and bound in Great Britain by Clays Ltd, Elcograf S.p.A.

1

For Cosy, who was a very good cat. I hope you are somewhere very sunny being fed the cake we wouldn't let you eat during your time on Earth.

Chapter One

It was another crisp winter's day in the small town of Dewstow and Margery could not help but smile to herself as she exited the car. She loved this kind of weather, when the air was fresh and burned your lungs slightly if you breathed in too deeply. The leaves on the trees surrounding the school had all fallen off and were just mush on the tarmac; everyone rushing past in their hurry to get into the building was bundled up in big coats. The sky was as grey and bland as it had been for weeks now and the wind whipping through the car park was chilling, but none of it could dampen Margery's spirits.

'Are you excited, Margery?' Clementine asked as they walked together towards the school. 'First year you're in charge of the Christmas menu and everything?'

Margery grinned back at her cheerily. Clementine looked hilarious today, all wrapped up in the ginormous scarf, the matching bobble hat Margery had knitted her years ago covering her grey hair. 'I am actually, Clem! I think this one will be the best yet. Well, it can't be any worse than the year we forgot to defrost the turkeys anyway, can it?'

Margery could not wait to get into the kitchen and start planning; she had been thinking about it since September. Half because she was nervous about it and half because Clementine had been pondering since August how early it was socially acceptable to get the Christmas decorations out of the attic.

Much to Margery's disapproval, Clementine had decided that the beginning of November was fine; they had barely put the Halloween decor away before she was already trying to smother their living room with lights and tinsel. Though it seemed that Clementine was in good company. The cleaning team had already dragged the Christmas decorations out and thrown them up all over the school. The hallways were full of wonky-looking artificial Christmas trees and frayed paper chains and the teaching staff had already started begrudgingly sending around Christmas cards.

The whole kitchen team had come a long way since Margery had taken on the kitchen manager's post the summer before, and she had somehow managed to turn their ragtag team into something resembling a well-oiled machine. It had not been an easy task by any means, especially since the former kitchen manager had been in place for such a long time. Margery knew that no one enjoyed change and she was proud of their little crew; feeding 1200 school pupils and all the teachers and business support staff every day was no mean feat. Officially titled Education Centre Nourishment Consultants, they all preferred to be called dinner ladies, except for Clementine who enjoyed being difficult.

Margery and Clementine entered the school, buzzing themselves in using the new security pass system. It had been set up by the headmaster and the security team after the nastiness earlier in the year involving the death of a colleague. Margery had been glad that they had finally decided to do something more to keep the staff and students safe than just give Gary Matthews on Security even more hours to work. Although it did mean that twice a week fellow dinner lady Seren would lose her pass and be late to start her shift.

Margery smiled to herself in anticipation as they strode up the flight of stairs to the first floor and into the canteen. The shutters were still closed, and she could not wait to open them for another fantastic day. Clementine swung the kitchen door open. Margery was not prepared for what they found inside.

The entire room was covered in a horrific mess of baked beans. They were everywhere. Smeared up the walls and all over the usually spotless stainless–steel work surfaces that they spent so much time sanitising and polishing every day. There was even a layer of beans slowly dripping off the ceiling one at a time, landing on Sharon who was sitting on the floor wailing as Karen fruitlessly dabbed at the mess with a roll of kitchen towel.

'What…?' Margery stared in horror. 'What happened?'

Sharon wailed from her place on the floor, wiping beans from her kitchen tabard. Karen gently patted her shoulder. 'It's okay, Sharon, we'll have it all cleaned up in no time. Anyway, at least it's something to post about on our Mums' Facebook group. You can say your husband spilt them, get a lot of likes and that.'

Margery's second in command, Gloria, appeared from the long corridor that led to the walk-in fridge and freezer and dry store. She was pushing the mop bucket, a very sour expression on her face, her black hair spilling out from her hairnet in disarray. 'I tried to stop him, Margery, but he insisted he could carry it all.' She gestured to the huge gastro tray that usually housed all the decanted beans for lunchtime's jacket potatoes, now upside down on the floor and obviously the cause of all the chaos. 'He slipped carrying the tub, I told him to use the trolley.'

She thrust the mop at young Benjamin, the newest Education Centre Nourishment Consultant. He hung his head in shame and joined Karen in dabbing at the beans. Margery shook her head at them all.

'I can't even come into work twenty minutes later than normal without something terrible happening!' she said, waving her hands at them. 'Gloria, get the cleaning team down here to help. Clem, grab some more kitchen roll! And where's Seren?'

'She's gone to get changed,' Gloria said, glaring at Benjamin. 'She had beans in her shoes.'

'Sorry!' Benjamin piped up from where he was scraping the mess off one of the work surfaces with a spoon.

'We'd better not tell you any secrets, Ben,' Clementine said. 'You might spill the beans!' Gloria turned to glare at her as she laughed uproariously at her own joke.

The kitchen door slammed open with a crash, stunning them into silence. They all whipped their heads around to look at who it was. Deputy head and drama teacher, Rose Smith, appeared in the room. She was as glamorous as ever in her smartly tailored trouser suit. Her silver bob was pristine with not a hair out of place, tucked back neatly behind her ears to show off a rather expensive-looking pair of earrings. She clacked into the middle of the kitchen on her high heels and the kitchen team parted like the waves of the Red Sea.

Tiny music teacher Mrs Large shuffled behind in her shadow, clutching her recorder bag. Assistant drama teacher Edward Daniels closed the door with a soft click, though how he managed it Margery did not know, as his

4

arms were full of papers. This bizarre procession stopped just short of the pool of liquid spreading outwards on the floor. Rose stared at it in disgust for a moment before throwing her arms in the air theatrically.

'Ladies, ladies, ladies!' Rose said, triumphantly.

'And very young man!' piped up Mrs Large, nodding in Benjamin's direction. She looked even more mousey than usual today in her beige cardigan and matching skirt.

Rose glowered at her before continuing. 'Now I'm sure you all remember that auditions for my… I mean… *our* Christmas concert are going to take place at three thirty today, and I expect you all to be there.'

'Or be square.' Mrs Large smiled at them toothily. Rose gave her a look that could have curdled milk. Mr Daniels smirked at them both, but quickly covered his expression with a cough.

'What if we don't want to be in your stupid Christmas play?' Clementine asked. 'What if we're busy with more important matters?'

Mrs Smith took a deliberate look around the messy kitchen, her eyebrows raised. 'Yes, it certainly looks like you're all terribly busy. Regardless, if you don't audition then you won't get a good part.'

'I don't want a part,' Clementine said, shrugging. 'None of us can sing for toffee.' All the dinner ladies in attendance nodded in agreement.

'And it's only the end of November,' Gloria said, handing Karen another roll of kitchen paper. 'You've got ages to chuck a play together.'

'Listen you…' Rose began, in a harsh tone and then seemed to remember her audience, lowering the finger she had been pointing at Gloria, baring her teeth into a grin, and starting again, slower this time. 'I need this, all right? Every year Ittonvale school put on a play so spectacular that they get the front cover headline in the *Dewstow Press*. How ridiculous is that? The school that's actually in Dewstow doesn't get a single mention. It's disgusting.'

They all nodded again at that; even Clementine murmured in agreement. Margery and Clementine had never got over their fierce rivalry with the neighbouring town of Ittonvale, not since the Ittonvale School Education Centre Nourishment Consultants had stolen all Summerview Secondary's clean tea towels while they were distracted at a summer fete. They had neither forgiven, nor forgotten.

'So, you can see how much is at stake here,' Mrs Smith said gravely. 'If we want to win this thing we have to start now. I wanted to start in September, really, to make a good go of it, but James wouldn't let me. He said it was crazy.'

She folded her arms, her face pulled into a sulky pout. Margery suddenly found herself pitying the headmaster. If Mrs Smith acted like this in public, then she must have been terrifying behind closed office doors. It was no wonder that their clandestine relationship had ended so suddenly. Margery sighed, she had so much work to do and not enough time for one of Mrs Smith's tantrums. Still, it would not do to fall out with the deputy head. Especially now in her role as the kitchen manager, the deputy head could make her life very difficult indeed.

'We'll be there,' she said. 'Just tell us when and where.'

Mrs Smith beamed at her and snatched one of the pieces of paper Mr Daniels was holding. She thrust it into Margery's waiting hands. Clementine took it from her and stared at it, her brow furrowed.

'This doesn't even say what it's for,' Clementine scoffed. 'It just says extravaganza of the year in all capitals and 3 p.m. in glitter glue.'

'Yes exactly, extravaganza!' Mrs Smith beamed at her. 'School hall, three thirty!' she said, triumphantly, gesturing for Mrs Large and Mr Daniels to follow her. 'Come along, you two.'

'But it says three!' Clementine said. Mrs Smith ignored her.

Mrs Smith exited the kitchen finally; Mr Daniels scuttled along behind her with the posters. Margery breathed a sigh of relief as she walked over to the notice board and pinned the poster up. It was unmistakably the work of former dinner lady Ceri-Ann. She had obviously spent a very long time drawing and colouring in the picture of the snowman on the unnecessarily large and mysterious poster. Ceri-Ann had left the school to do Health and Beauty Therapy at Ittonvale College but had recently decided to also branch out into graphic design, much to everyone's dismay. It was bad enough being continuously bombarded with offers of makeovers and head massages; it was even worse now that there were constant barrages of posters and leaflets to accompany them. Margery had tried to pluck up the courage to ask her to stop but she had never had the heart to, and so the paper recycling bin was almost always full.

'Do you have any fruit today?' Mrs Large asked softly. Margery almost jumped with fright; she had not realised Elizabeth Large was still behind her.

'Of course,' Margery said, pointing to the display fridge where she kept the least bruised apples and bananas from her fruit and veg order. 'What are you after?'

7

Mrs Large beamed at her. 'Ooh, I'd love a few satsumas if you have any? My husband usually packs my lunch, but I forgot to get it out of the fridge this morning!'

'Oh, well I can do you a sandwich too, if you want?' Margery asked, walking over to the fridge and grabbing out two squished satsumas. 'Just pop up to the canteen again at lunchtime.'

'Don't worry, I've got a Cup a Soup in my desk.' Mrs Large smiled again. Margery always thought of her as being as old as she and Clementine were but was reminded that Elizabeth could only be in her thirties when she smiled. Possibly because it gave her more personality than Mrs Smith's tyrannical regime over the music and drama department usually allowed. She took the fruit from Margery gratefully and put them in her recorder bag. 'How much do I owe you?'

'Gosh, don't worry about it, I haven't even got the till out yet.' Margery gestured to where Karen and Sharon were taking it in turns to sweep up beans into the kitchen's small dustpan and brush. 'I haven't had a chance with all this mess.'

'Well, good luck to you all,' Mrs Large said. 'And Margery? Don't worry about the concert too much, Rose's bite isn't as bad as her bark, it'll be a laugh. You'll see.'

Margery waved her off as she left the kitchen, closing the door gently behind her.

'Did you not charge her for those?' Gloria asked, appearing at Margery's side.

'No,' Margery said. 'It's only a few satsumas.'

Gloria did not agree, her brow furrowed, and she marched off, muttering something about not hitting this week's gross profit target under her breath.

'Come on now, ladies,' Margery said with a sigh, watching Gloria's back as she went to help Benjamin. 'Let's get this kitchen spotless and ready for lunchtime.'

-

The school hall looked a lot bigger than it usually did as they all trooped in through the double doors. Margery suspected that this was because they only usually gathered there for Mr Barrow's assemblies. It seemed very strange for all the uncomfortable plastic chairs to be stacked up at the back of the room. The only sign that the chairs were ever used at all were the scuff marks on the hideous vinyl flooring. She noticed that the stage had been brought out of storage in preparation and unfolded and slotted together in what she hoped was not as haphazard a way as it looked. It took up most of the back wall, especially with its large overhead light fixtures that were fitted to a particularly wobbly-looking metal frame overhanging the stage.

It had taken a great deal of coaxing to stop the kitchen team from putting their coats on and going straight home after work, but Margery knew she would never, ever hear the end of it if they did. Karen and Sharon were openly sulking. Gloria was still wearing her trademark cheery grin, but it was looking very forced. Benjamin just looked a bit surprised to be invited; his blond eyebrows were raised high on his forehead as though they had become stuck there. The only person who did not seem to mind too much was Seren. She was good friends with Mrs Smith, and Margery would often see them driving into work together, as though Seren was Rose's strange surrogate child.

Mrs Smith was holding court at the front of the hall. At some point in the day she had changed out of the smartly pressed suit she usually wore and was now wearing what Margery could only describe as 'drama teacher chic'. A look which consisted of hoop earrings and colourful scarfs over a long, flowing green dress. She looked more like a Christmas tree than the actual tree, which was wilting sadly in the back corner of the hall, leaning against the stage. It was the only real tree in the building and probably the cheapest the headmaster could find on the school's budget. If they'd found out that the headmaster had gone to the nearby woods and cut it down himself, no one would have been very surprised.

'Ooh, aren't the decs lovely?' Karen said in a hushed whisper, as they walked through the room. Clementine turned to stare at her in disgust at the abbreviation.

Mrs Smith had evidently already dragged out the poor cleaners and a few of the more gullible business support staff she could blackmail, as well as most of the teachers. They all sat in a semi-circle on the ugly chairs in front of the stage, as she gesticulated grandly at her script. Tiny Mrs Large sat at the piano behind Mrs Smith, nervously worrying her lip with her teeth. She looked quite demure in her plain beige cardigan, clutching her recorder and sheet music. Her mousey brown fringe concealed the top half of her face, as she seemed to cower behind it.

Mrs Smith looked up as the kitchen team arrived and scowled at them all. 'Nice of you to finally join us, Margery and etcetera.' She waved her hand at them dismissively. 'We've all been here hours, haven't we, ladies? You've missed all the fabulous ice breaker games.'

'We have names you know!' Clementine said, pointing to Benjamin. 'His name's...' She turned to him suddenly puzzled, swishing her own hands around in confusion. 'Erm... you know... the young one.'

Mrs Smith rolled her eyes and tutted. 'Don't even know your own co-workers' names Mrs Butcher-Baker, and you expect me to give you a good part if you can't remember your lines, really!'

'I don't want a part!' Clementine hissed.

Margery shushed her. 'Come on, Clem, let's just get this over with.'

They all took a plastic chair from the back of the room, carried them over and sat down heavily. Margery smiled at the other poor souls that had been half invited, half forced to attend. The brand-new cleaning team must have had to start work early and they both looked thoroughly miserable about it.

Mrs Smith put on her false smile again. 'Now that we are all here, I can finally reveal the theme of this year's Christmas concert!' She clapped her hands together in glee. 'The theme is…' She paused for a long moment and then raised herself slowly up out of her chair.

There was a long silence. Margery looked at Clementine who shook her head and scoffed at the spectacle of it. Seren clapped once and Gloria shushed her. Margery was sure she could hear Mrs Large muttering under her breath.

Mrs Smith drew in a deep breath, raising her arms dramatically above her head, flicking her silver bob behind her ears as she did so. 'Really? No one can guess?' She gestured at the Christmas tree in a dramatic swooshing motion. 'The theme is… Christmas!'

They all groaned.

'For God's sake, woman, the whole thing is Christmas themed!' Clementine yelled from her seat. 'Look at this place, it's disgusting, look how many terrible ornaments are on that sad tree!'

'Yes…' Mrs Smith said, as if Clementine were the stupidest person she had ever met. 'But it will be an entirely new Christmas concert, with all new songs written by me!' There was a cough from behind her. '…and Mrs Large.' There was another cough, Mrs Smith rolled her eyes. '…and Mr Daniels.'

'So, let's be clear. What are the students going to be doing while we're doing this show?' asked Miss Macdonald, the newest and youngest of all the English teachers sitting with the rest of the English department. 'Will they be doing it with us?' She was sitting next to Mr Daniels, who threw back his head and rolled his eyes at the suggestion.

Mrs Smith stared at her, dumbfounded. 'No, of course not! They'll have their own special assembly. Well…' She paused as if considering how to say it. 'I mean it'll be a bit shorter than the adult one.'

'You've cut the students' concert time again to fit this teacher one in, haven't you?' Clementine yelled, stabbing her finger at Mrs Smith violently. 'How long is it this year, fifteen? Twenty minutes?'

For a moment Mrs Smith looked like she might come back with a retort but then she just shook her head in exasperation. 'Well, we all know the student concert is just a formality before we get to the good concert! And it's ten minutes long this year, they're doing *A Christmas Carol* again.'

'*A Christmas Carol?* How can you do *A Christmas Carol* in only ten minutes! Even the Muppet one is an hour and a half!' Clementine roared. The hall erupted into arguing about the length a children's school concert should be, until Mrs Smith stepped forward into the circle, threateningly.

'Quiet!' she cried in her best teaching voice, and they all fell silent again. 'It's not ideal, having to do a children's play at all, but they don't care anyway! There is not a single Nicole Kidman in the student body. I should know...' She sneered nastily. '...I teach them.' Mrs Large nodded in agreement behind her.

'Now, let's get on with it,' Mrs Smith said, snatching the pile of sheet music from Mrs Large's lap and shoving it all into Margery's. 'Take one and pass it on now, chop chop!'

-

An hour later and they were all standing on the stage in a row while Mrs Smith marched in front of them, shaking the sheet music threateningly at them as they sang. Mrs Large sat to the side of the stage at the piano, wringing her hands together in terror whenever Mrs Smith was not bellowing at her to play the music. The choreography had been bad enough when Mrs Smith had demonstrated it, without it being performed by a group of people who barely had a dash of rhythm between them, Margery thought. They must look absolutely hilarious all swaying about. Margery could hear Clementine wailing tunelessly next to her the entire time and she kept having to pretend to cough to cover her smile.

'No, no, no!' Mrs Smith screeched, and they all came to a sudden halt, jostling each other. 'It's step one, two, three, pivot. Not whatever you're all doing!'

Margery found her mind wandering; there were so many better things they could be doing right now. She would much rather be at home eating Quality Street, sitting in front of the imitation gas fire.

She looked over at the large floor-to-ceiling hall windows. They were a lot creepier at night than during the day, and the air outside was thick with fog. It was hard to tell through the clouded windows, the condensation running down the frames, but she could have sworn she could see someone out there in the cold. She stared as hard as she could, feeling her brow furrow under the strain. There was a tall figure out there in the playground, she was sure of it. Margery watched them put their hand against the glass and peer inside the hall, though she could not make out any clear facial features through the haze. Maybe it was a teacher arriving to the practice session late, she thought. She hoped.

'Again!' Mrs Smith cried, Margery looked at her with a start and then back at the window. The person had gone. She stared for a moment till she was snapped back into the argument between Mrs Smith and the rest of the staff.

'You can't keep us here forever!' screeched Karen from the row behind. Margery turned around just in time to see Sharon break down in tears for the fiftieth time that day.

Mrs Smith glared at her from her place in front of the stage. 'I have the hall booked till half past eight, so actually...' She grinned widely, showing off a needless number of teeth, but there was no humour behind it. '...I think you'll find I can.'

'Phft!' Clementine scoffed loudly. 'Then we'll go home and forget all about this nonsense. I can't even remember what happened ten minutes ago most of the time, let alone this stupid dance.'

'It's easy,' Mrs Smith hissed at her. 'Even Mrs Large can do it.'

Mrs Large looked up from the piano, startled. Margery was sure she saw her brow furrow in concern for a moment, but the expression was gone as quickly as it came.

'Go on, Elizabeth... up you go.'

'Me?' Mrs Large squeaked. She lifted the sleeve of her cardigan and looked at her watch uneasily.

'Yes, come on,' Mrs Smith said impatiently. 'The sooner we all learn this the sooner we can get out of here. Come on.'

Mrs Large stood up awkwardly. Clementine's mother would have described her as being too short for her weight; Margery pushed the nasty thought away. Mrs Large's legs were shaky as she stepped forward.

'Gosh, I'm not really good at these things,' she squeaked out, gesturing to where Mrs Smith was standing in front of the stage. 'I'll go where you are, shall I?'

'Yes, all right.' Mrs Smith nodded, moving out of her way as she walked forward. 'That's a good idea, then they can all see you.'

Mrs Large looked at her watch again, but then seemed to realise that as it was only half past four, there was no way out of it. Resigned to her fate she stepped forward to where Mrs Smith had been. Mrs Smith went and sat down on the piano stool, she put her hands together and cracked her fingers before playing the first chord of the song.

'I'm not a very good dancer really, sorry all,' Mrs Large said, wringing her hands together as she peered at the waiting staff on stage. 'Maybe I'll just run through it once and then Mrs Smith can show you again?'

Mrs Smith waved a hand dismissively. 'Nonsense, you're fine. Now, let's get on with it.'

'Okay, I'll just do it quickly then,' Mrs Large said apprehensively, stepping from foot to foot. 'All right ladies, erm...'

'I'll count you in!' Mrs Smith grinned at her and sat back down at the piano. 'A one, a two, a one, two, three, four!'

It all happened so quickly that Margery's brain could not process it fast enough to comprehend what was happening. There was a loud and terrible screech and a big metal object seemed to fall from nowhere out of the sky.

One minute, Mrs Large had been standing in front of them beginning the awful dance sequence and the next she had disappeared under a mangled mess of metal and wires. All Margery could hear was the screams of those around her, as they watched Mrs Large disappear under the lighting rig as it fell from the top of the stage. Even Mrs Smith was wide-eyed, mouth gaping open, her fingertips still resting on the keys of the piano. Mr Daniels rushed forward from his seat to the pile of metal. Margery turned to look at Clementine, who was usually so proud of her unflappable first aid training, but even she was frozen, staring in horror at the spot where Mrs Large had stood.

Margery found her voice somehow, though it sounded small and feeble to her own ears. 'Quick, somebody call an ambulance!'

Chapter Two

'Here you are, it's well sugared,' young Officer Symon said, as he handed Margery the cup of tea. She took it with shaky hands, the spoon in the boiling hot cup clinking as she did so.

The dinner lady team were sitting in the canteen, Gloria and Seren on one side of a shiny, easy-wipe table and Margery and Clementine on the other. Karen and Sharon sat huddled together on the floor by the till in the chilly room.

Mrs Large had been rushed to Ittonvale Hospital by ambulance and from what they had heard through the grapevine, the paramedics' prognosis did not look good.

Clementine still looked shell-shocked. Margery noticed a distinct tremor in her hands as she took the cup of tea from Officer Symon, her face ashen. Though she had not fared as badly as Benjamin. He had fainted shortly after he had caught a glimpse of Mrs Large's unconscious body and was now sitting white-faced in Clementine's special 'sitting down to do the till when I'm feeling lazy on a Friday' chair.

Young Officer Symon gave Margery a small smile before he moved on with the tea trolley. He looked a bit less spotty than the last time she had seen him, a little more grown up and his hair had a lot less gel in it.

'I still can't believe what just happened,' Gloria said, shaking her head, more to herself than anyone else. 'Do you think Mrs Large will be okay?'

Margery shrugged back at her across the table. 'I honestly don't know.' She truly did not. In her unqualified opinion Mrs Large ought to be dead already. She supposed that only time would tell. 'She didn't look great when they pulled all the stage lights off her, did she? Hopefully we'll know something more soon.'

Gloria sighed and sat back in her chair heavily. 'Well, do we know who put the stage together? They've got to be in trouble for this. Obviously it can't have been done right.'

Clementine crossed her arms and glowered at the entrance door to the canteen. 'I knew we shouldn't have had stage lights, ridiculous. What's wrong with a few candles I said to Rose, but no, no one listens to me!'

'The whole school would have burnt down if you'd had your way, Clem,' Margery said. Gloria hummed agreeably.

'Maybe we could have used battery-powered torches,' Seren said. 'Then no one would have died and we'd save on electricity.'

'No one has died,' Margery reminded her gently.

'Yeah, don't speak ill of the dead!' Karen snapped at Seren. Sharon burst into tears. 'There, there Sharon.' Karen patted her on the shoulder gingerly. 'God obviously needed another angel.'

The canteen entrance doors slammed open and the headmaster appeared. He strode towards them, his long legs making short work of the distance. His red hair was not as sleek as it usually was. In fact, it was quite rumpled, as if he had just got out of bed. Margery assumed he must have come straight from home, judging by the sweatpants and ratty Deep Purple band T-shirt he was wearing under his long overcoat. She always found it startling to see any of her colleagues out of their day-to-day clothing, but to see the headmaster wearing anything but an expensive suit was always the most disturbing. He usually looked quite intimidating, as befitted his role. It was unsettling to say the least.

'Good evening, ladies, though there's not much good about it, is there?' he said, his mouth set in a grim line. 'Don't any of you worry, we'll get straight to the bottom of this.'

'We've heard that before!' Clementine snorted. The kitchen team all nodded among themselves.

'Well, I mean it this time,' Mr Barrow said, and Margery could hear the sincerity in his voice. 'Are you all okay? No one else hurt?'

'No, we're all okay,' Margery said, 'Is there anything we can do?'

'We could help clean the hall?' Clementine offered.

'No.' Mr Barrow shook his head. 'No, you've all done enough. Let's just get the police statements over with and then we can all go home and have a rest.'

He paced over to the big windows on the left-hand side of the room and leaned against the safety barrier.

'Terrible this, terrible, terrible,' he said, as he looked out into the darkness at the barely visible school playground, his arms folded. 'There'll be no new library books for the children now we have to replace the stage lights.' He shook his head and then seemed to remember he had an audience. 'Er, and such a shame about Mrs Large of course, lovely lady. Shame, shame. Who will take the recorder lessons now?'

'Hopefully nobody. Dreadful things,' Mrs Smith said as she entered the room with a flourish, whipping the colourful scarf she wore around her neck as she did so. Margery flinched seeing the length of material so close to the double doors as they clanged shut behind her. One wrong step and Mrs Smith would have ended up like Isadora Duncan, and there had been too much tragedy tonight already.

'He's nearly ready for you, James,' she said to Mr Barrow, gesturing towards the door. 'He's just finished taking statements from the teachers.'

Mr Barrow smiled at her, but the warmth did not quite meet his eyes. Margery wondered how things were getting on between the headmaster and his deputy head. Since the news of their affair had leaked and Rose's husband had left her, things between them had been a little strained. At the very least, it made the management meetings Margery now sat in very tense indeed.

Clementine had heard from Mrs Boch, the librarian, that Rose had dumped him unceremoniously after a weekend away. On the other hand, Margery had heard from Mrs Mugglethwaite, the woman who worked at the post office and the town's local gossipmonger, that Mr Barrow had decided to go back to his wife. She wondered if the truth would ever be revealed.

'Well, I'd better go and see who else is here.' Mr Barrow looked defeated. He had deflated like a child's birthday balloon since Mrs Smith had arrived a few minutes ago. 'Where's the rest of the staff, Mrs Smith?'

'They're all wandering about in the corridor.' Mrs Smith gave him a withering look. 'I'll show you.'

They turned and left together. Mrs Smith exited first and did not hold the door open for him. It nearly slammed in his face, but he caught it in time. He held it open so that the waiting police officer could enter the canteen.

Officer Thomas nodded to Margery and Clementine in recognition as he entered. They had struck up a strange sort of friendship with the older man after the events earlier in the year. They had even invited him and his wife to their wedding, though Clementine had viewed the invitation as a bit of a gloat at solving the police's own case for them. He wandered over to the nearest free table, putting down a pile of paper that Margery assumed were the rest of the staff's statements.

'Ah, it's the dinner lady detectives!' he said, his mouth barely moving under the enormity of the huge bushy moustache on his top lip, though Margery could tell he was smiling from the way his eyes crinkled. He continued, 'Always a pleasure, shame it's not under better circumstances.'

They nodded at the greeting. The tone of the evening too sombre for Clementine to retort about how they preferred to go by their official title of Education Centre Nourishment Consultants though Margery knew she was probably itching to. Officer Thomas gestured for them to stay sitting down as Gloria rose from her seat.

'I won't keep you all long, we just need to get a good picture of what happened here tonight so we can stop it from happening again and see if you need any further help. It was a nasty thing you witnessed.'

'Is Mrs Large going to be okay?' Seren asked. Gloria patted her on the shoulder and gave her a sympathetic look.

'I've afraid I can't tell you that. Poor woman. We've contacted her family and her husband is on the way to the hospital, it's all we could do.' Officer Thomas sighed.

'Right, is there anywhere I can take you one by one to go through this statement form with me?'

'Of course,' Margery said, rising from her seat. 'You can use my office. Well, I mean, dry store.'

'Come on then, lead the way. I'll interview you first.' Officer Thomas grabbed the pile of papers up again. 'Oh Symon, you start interviewing out here, will you? Let's get this over with. Oh, not you Mrs Butcher-Baker, I'll interview your wife first.'

'But we're practically the same person!' Clementine cried. She had got out of her seat to follow Margery like she was her shadow. 'We may as well share the same body, and we will one day when the science catches up to my ideas!'

Margery gave Clementine a sympathetic look. 'I won't be long, Clem.' She led the policeman through the kitchen and down the narrow corridor to the stores. It took her a moment to unlock the door, her fingers still trembling. She wondered when it would stop, if ever. She finally managed it and they entered. If Officer Thomas thought her office was lacking, he did not mention it, only plonked himself down awkwardly on a twenty-litre tub of fryer oil and put a new form onto his clipboard.

'Right, we can fill in your personal details after,' he said, taking the lid off his pen. 'So, what happened? Tell me everything you can remember.'

'Well…' Margery paused, trying to think. It had all happened so quickly that she had had very little time to react. 'I suppose, we were watching Mrs Large dance and one minute it was fine and the next all the lights had fallen down.'

'I see. Dancing, was it? Terrible, terrible.' Officer Thomas scribbled on the form. Margery watched from across the room at her desk, but she was too far away to see his writing. 'And before that, you didn't see anything suspicious? Everything was fine?'

Margery nodded. Everything had been fine. 'Why, what are you saying?'

Officer Thomas looked at her carefully, as if deciding what to do. He cleared his throat. 'You don't know who does the maintenance around here, do you?'

Margery did not. 'Well, the caretaker retired in the summer and we've all kind of been pitching in in the meantime.' She shrugged. 'Mr Barrow put an advert online, but he didn't have a single application.'

It had seemed strange to her at the time, and even stranger now thinking about it. The headmaster had even asked them to put an advert in the post office window but still nothing, not a jot of interest. Stranger still was that they had managed to replace Ceri-Ann, who had left at the beginning of summer, in a mere few days.

'Hmmm, I suppose it's a tough job to fill,' Officer Thomas said, stroking his moustache. 'So, you don't know who put the lights up?'

Margery shook her head. 'No idea, does the head-master not know who put it together? I'd assume he'd be the one coordinating that.'

'Hmmm,' Officer Thomas said again. 'That's the thing, he says he doesn't.'

'Oh,' Margery said in surprise. 'Well, it wasn't put together on Friday so whoever did it must have done it today. Not many people have access to the school at the weekend. We have a new security system you see, you have to have a manager's card to access the school after hours.'

They had found this out the hard way when Seren had offered to stay behind and deep clean the walk-in fridge. When she had tried to leave the building, she found herself trapped between the two exit doors of the school reception overnight and had to sleep on her coat, subsisting only on the half-eaten packet of prawn cocktail Wotsits she'd had in her pocket.

Officer Thomas nodded and continued to write, the nib of his pen scratching on the paper. She watched the inky letters form on the page and found it strangely soothing.

'But…' she continued, thinking out loud, 'someone would have seen whoever put the stage up if they did it today. Clem and I walked through the school hall in the morning, and it was already up.'

'Huh. So, you wouldn't have access to the school at the weekend then?' he asked casually, but Margery could see his brain kicking into gear slotting the pieces of the puzzle together.

'Well, if I'm honest,' she said, 'I've never tried to come here at the weekend. I'm assuming my pass would work in case of an emergency, but I prefer to spend my weekends doing nicer things with my wife. Visiting National Trust sites, that sort of thing.' He smiled at that. 'You know…' Margery continued, 'it's all computerised, it'll be able to tell you if someone used a pass on the main entrance over the weekend and probably even at what time.'

He nodded again and finished scrawling. She wondered whether she should tell him about the figure she had thought she had seen, or whether he would think she was mad. She decided not to, for now at least. No one else had mentioned seeing anything. And anyway, there were several trees on the outskirts of the playground that could have maybe waved against the window in the wind. Her eyes could have been playing tricks on her. Seeing things that were not there in the shadows.

'One last thing, Mrs Butcher-Baker.' Officer Thomas had stopped being jovial now; his gaze was practically icy in comparison to the warm welcome he had given them on his arrival. 'Do you know if Mrs Large had any enemies?'

'What!' Margery cried. 'Mrs Large? God no! Well, I wouldn't have thought so… she was quite quiet, but she was a very nice lady. I've never heard anyone say a bad word about her really. Maybe Mrs Smith once or twice, but I think that's just because they work close together. I can't tell you the number of times I've wanted to throttle Clementine for something at work. Why on earth would you ask that?'

He eyed her again as though he was trying to discern something from her facial expressions. 'We think there's much more to this than meets the eye.'

'Is that why you wanted to know so much about the caretaker? Do you think the stage was tampered with?' Margery asked. She could feel the confusion written on her face.

'We think the stage wasn't put up correctly in the first place.' Officer Thomas took off his glasses and began to clean them.

'How do you know that?' Margery asked.

'Well, stage lighting isn't really my forte, but from what the team understand the safety rigging wasn't attached to the lights. The whole thing was a ticking time bomb.'

'But surely not intentional?'

He went quiet again, putting his glasses back on. When he finally spoke, he chose his words very carefully. 'We are

25

treating this, at the very least, as a potential manslaughter investigation. Depending on whether Mrs Large pulls through, and from what the paramedics have told me...' He trailed off, leaving Margery in suspense.

'You don't think Mrs Large is going to die?' Margery breathed. It seemed abhorrent that such a thing could happen, even though she had seen the accident in real time.

'Honestly, we don't know yet, so it's doubly important we find out who put the stage up; it looks very malicious to us. Now, I'm only telling you all this as we know each other, and I trust I have your silence.'

'Of course,' Margery said at once.

'That includes any investigating you and Clementine are bound to try and do.' He looked at her in amusement for a moment. 'Please restrain yourselves.'

'I promise to try.' Margery nodded.

'Try very hard,' he said. 'Well, thank you, Mrs Butcher-Baker. I think I have enough to go on.' Officer Thomas held his hand out for her to shake. 'Will you send the next person in?'

She showed herself out and sent Clementine in to see him, sitting down once more at the canteen table, lost in her thoughts. How bizarre to be asked if Mrs Large had any enemies; she could not think of anything more outlandish. Mrs Large tended to be very quiet and kept to herself, and she brought her own lunch to eat in the staff room most days. It was a well-known fact among the dinner ladies. In fact, recently deceased former kitchen manager, Caroline, used to keep a written list of the staff that did not eat in the canteen, as though it were a slight against her personally. While they had always been on first-name speaking terms, Mrs Large was quiet enough to hang around in the background of most school events, without affecting the catering team at all.

Mr Barrow had returned at some point during her talk with Officer Thomas and was pacing back and forth by the windows. He noticed her and came striding over, sitting down opposite her at the table.

'Mr Barrow,' she said, politely.

'Mrs Butcher-Baker.' He smiled, but it was more of a grimace. 'Listen, I have a favour to ask you.'

'Okay?'

'You must promise me, you and Clementine both, that you will not try and investigate this.'

'Gosh, why does everyone think we're going to invest-igate?'

'Call it intuition.' He had a deadly serious look in his eyes; he looked almost haunted by what he was asking her not to do. 'Please.'

'Yes but…' He held his hand up to silence her.

'Please.'

'What makes you think we're going to do anything?' Margery asked finally, sagging back into her chair in defeat.

He laughed genuinely. 'Because I have met your wife, Mrs Butcher-Baker, she'll be the first on the case if this isn't sorted immediately.'

Margery did smile at that. Clementine was not known for sitting still and waiting to be told what to do, especially if there was even a hint of injustice involved. She might be quite abrasive outwardly most of the time, but Margery knew that underneath the tough exterior she cared deeply for her colleagues.

'Please, just let the police do their jobs. If there is something more to this, then they'll find it.'

'They didn't last time,' Margery accused. Margery and Clementine had inadvertently solved former kitchen manager Caroline's murder after some very amateur sleuthing and a number of disastrous incidences only eight months before.

'No, they didn't,' he said, his face falling. 'But regardless, the last time you were both nearly killed. We can't have that happen again. Promise me you won't go meddling in anything that doesn't need meddling, give the police time to sort it all out.'

'I will try.'

'And Clementine?'

Margery smiled. 'You know I have no control over Clementine.'

Mr Barrow smiled back at her. He knew as well as she did that Clementine was her own hurricane, and if she thought she could help someone, no one would be able to stop her. 'Just try, for me?'

Margery nodded and he stood, nodding back at her once before leaving the canteen again. The other members of the catering team looked on with interest.

'You all right, Margery?' Sharon called. Margery nodded. She was going to have to have an awkward conversation with Clementine when they got home.

Chapter Three

Margery struggled to get to sleep; it had not helped that they had missed their usual bedtime of nine thirty. She was overtired by the time they finally crawled under the brushed cotton duvet cover, and when she did finally drift off, her dreams were full of horrors. She had not ordered enough potatoes, so they ran out of mash at lunchtime, and Mrs Smith was screaming at her from across the canteen while Mrs Large stood next to her silently staring with big, wide, frightened eyes. Margery woke abruptly in a cold sweat at five in the morning and then tossed and turned until the alarm clock went off at seven.

It was still dark outside, but she dragged herself out of bed anyway and over to the bathroom across the hall, where she stared at her own tired face in the mirror and tried to wake up. Her once-blonde hair was almost fully grey now; what had not been grey before had turned after she had been the kitchen manager for a few months. She had thought about dyeing it, but Clementine had never felt the need to after her hair had gone white hilariously prematurely decades earlier. Margery always took solace in her bravery.

They had lived at number twenty-two Seymour Road for over thirty years now. The small two-bedroom terraced house still suited them fine. It had a reasonably sized back garden, which Clementine kept neat and tidy when Margery reminded her the lawn needed mowing. To the front, next to the pretty front garden, was a driveway, which housed Margery's car. Inside, the house was just big enough for the two women, a cat and all the assorted knick-knacks and memorabilia they had accrued over the years.

The estate was quiet. It was near enough to the main road that journeying into town in the car was not an issue, but far enough away that they were not visited by strangers often, as it was not on the town's main thoroughfare. They had got to know the neighbours over the years and were on good Christmas card terms with most. They had even more or less made up with their neighbour across the road, Dawn Simmonds, after an incident involving Margery and Clementine driving their car into her pond. All in all, it was a very pleasant place to live.

Margery splashed her face with cold water. She decided she would go downstairs, feed the cat and make herself a nice cup of tea to start the day. Maybe she would even find the time to read some of her book, or finish some of her crocheted Christmas decorations. She was currently making snowflake bunting to go down the banister of their stairs.

Pumpkin, their elderly tortoiseshell cat, wound herself around Margery's legs at the top of the staircase. She had to gently bat her away, so they did not both die falling down the stairs, or trip over the empty boxes of Christmas decorations that Clementine had helpfully got out of the attic but then left in the hallway. Somehow, they made it to the kitchen in one piece and Margery fed the cat the smelly wet cat food she loved so much, while she waited for the kettle to boil.

'Morning!' Clementine said, appearing in the kitchen suddenly and much too cheerily for someone running on so few hours of sleep. She startled Margery, who nearly spilled the tea bags all over the floor. 'Make me one, would you?'

'Clem, don't sneak up on me like that! You know I can't hear very well out of my right ear,' Margery said. 'Why are you so happy?'

'Are you joking?' Clementine said, smiling at her. 'It's the greatest time of the year, what's not to love?'

'Apart from Mrs Large and her accident.' Margery raised her eyebrows.

'Well yes,' Clementine said, awkwardly sitting down at the kitchen table. 'But I saw on my phone that it's going to snow this week. Finally! A white Christmas, it's been so long!'

She pulled her phone from her dressing gown pocket and thrust it at Margery. Margery squinted at the weather app on the screen. 'This says it's going to rain all week, Clem. That symbol is a rain cloud.'

Clementine snatched the phone back and stared at it, her face falling in disappointment. 'Oh yes, so it does. Teach me to try and read anything without my glasses on.' She sat back in her chair, sadly. 'One day.'

Margery shook her head as she got Clementine a mug from the mug tree and opened the fridge. 'Oh Christ, we're out of milk.'

'Please do not swear, Margery!' Clementine said, in mock horror still staring at her phone. 'Don't worry, it's Tuesday. The milkman will have been. Why don't you go and get it while I make us a nice bacon sandwich or something? I'd go myself but it's bloody freezing.'

Margery sighed and shuffled out through the living room to the hallway in her old, battered slippers to get the milk. She had barely opened the front door and grabbed the freezing glass bottle on the doorstep before she noticed a familiar face pottering towards her up the frosty garden path.

'Oh, hello Dawn,' she said, waving the milk bottle at their neighbour from number forty-four. 'Lovely morning, isn't it?'

'If you say so, Margery,' Dawn said glumly. She was wearing a thick winter coat and Margery felt a twinge of jealousy as she stood on the doorstep in her thin, worn dressing gown and slippers. Dawn continued, 'As you know, Sprinkles has just given birth and we are very happy about it.' Dawn could not have looked less happy if her house had been on fire, Margery thought.

'Although we still don't know who the father is.' Dawn glared at Pumpkin who had followed Margery out onto the doorstep after finishing her breakfast. 'Do you know who the father is, Pumpkin, hmmm?'

Pumpkin mewed at the sound of her name and then went back to washing her face. Dawn stared at her suspiciously.

'Oh, you mean your cat!' Margery said, the milk in her hands and the cold weather forgotten. 'Kittens! Oh well that is lovely.'

Dawn looked at her as though she had gone completely mad. 'Yes… I suppose it is. Anyway, Sprinkles did a fantastic job, there's eight of them! So, you can have two or three if you like? They'll be ready in about eight or nine weeks. I just popped over to ask when you would come and pick up yours?'

Margery stood and stared at the woman for a minute. 'Oh. Well… probably never to be honest, Dawn. Pumpkin's enough for us.'

Dawn shook her head in fury. 'I knew you'd say that! And you still haven't repaid me for my pond.'

'No, I suppose we haven't really.' Margery thought about just backing away and shutting the door on the woman, but her mother's voice in her head, telling her to be polite, stopped her. 'Sorry. Again.'

'Well.' Dawn looked at her, eyes narrowed. 'I might consider forgiving you if you both join the Dewstow church choir; we're short on members this year and we've got a jam-packed Christmas concert season coming up.'

Margery sighed internally. Why was everybody in the whole town so obsessed with Christmas concerts? You couldn't walk three feet through the town centre without seeing a poster for some amateur dramatics society or other. It had only got worse recently, especially now Mrs Smith had amped up her big plans for the school show.

'Is there anything we can do for you instead?' Margery pleaded. 'We really don't have time to join the choir this year.' *Or ever*, she thought, but managed to not say the words out loud.

Dawn shook her head, but then stopped to consider Margery's offer. 'You know what? Yeah, there is. I promised Father Brown I'd crochet some miniature robins for the church decorations, and I haven't quite got around to it.'

Margery smiled. She was a crochet whizz if nothing else. 'I can do that for you, no problem!'

Dawn beamed at her, the trouble of the kittens and the choir forgotten entirely for the moment. 'Fantastic,

Margery, he needs fifty by the end of next week. I'll drop the pattern and the yarn off later today.'

Margery opened her mouth to change her mind, but Dawn was already halfway back up their garden path, only turning before she crossed the road to wave at her. Margery waved back in confusion.

'Where have you been?' Clementine said, when Margery finally got back inside the warmth of the kitchen.

'Oh, Dawn was there waffling on. You know how she is,' Margery said and took a bite of the now-cold bacon sandwich Clementine held out for her. Clementine nodded in agreement, picking up her empty plate and taking it over to the sink. 'Do you think the headmaster means what he said to you last night?'

'About not investigating?' Margery said, through a mouthful of bread. 'Yes definitely. He was deadly serious.'

Clementine sighed as though she was hoping the answer would have changed overnight. 'I wonder how Mrs Large is, do you think we should visit her?'

Margery thought about it while she chewed her food. 'I don't know, Clem. Maybe we should wait until we know she's okay? I'm sure her family is with her now; they might not like us all turning up.'

'Or they'd love it,' Clementine said, thrusting her teacup into the air in triumph, the liquid it held sloshing over the sides. 'Imagine a visit from the dinner lady detectives, famous all over Dewstow and slightly beyond… all the way into Ittonvale!'

Margery laughed, jumping up to grab a piece of kitchen roll from the side to pass it to Clementine. 'I thought you hated being called that! You keep telling people to call us by our full title.'

'Yes well,' Clementine said as she put the cup down and dabbed at where she had spilt her tea. 'Education Centre Nourishment Consultant Mystery Solver does have a snappier and classier ring, Margery.' She stood from her chair and pushed it back under the table. 'Come on then, I'll just get dressed quick and we'll get to school. We never did go up to the storeroom to count the tablecloths yesterday, do you want to do that before work starts?'

'Definitely, thanks for reminding me. I'll be up in a minute,' Margery said, grateful that Clementine was always around to remind her of the little jobs her new role in management required her to do; sometimes she felt like she was a juggling octopus. 'Oh er... get the L plates for the car though, will you? You're going to have to start your driving lessons again, I've got a big crochet commission coming and I need to practise.'

–

Margery had to run through what each button in the car did several times and translate from what Clementine had decided they were called, while she was explaining how the car worked. Clementine had recently agreed to try and pass her driving test after many years of being chauffeured by Margery. Her practical was booked for after Christmas, though she kept threatening not to go because 'I just enjoy being driven so much, Margery'.

Clementine had passed the theory test first time, though Margery suspected that she might have smuggled in the DVSA handbook as she had not seen her study for the test at all. Margery did not believe Clementine would be able to cheat on the practical test. She had been taking once-a-week lessons with a real driving instructor and Margery had been letting her practise with her car the rest of the time. Only if Margery was in the car too, of course, to keep the whole thing proper in the eyes of the law, though if she were being honest with herself, she often wished she had never suggested it. She was nervous enough of her own driving, let alone Clementine's erratic steering and loose understanding of how and when to use the handbrake.

By the time they finally managed to get to the school, they were so much later than planned that they decided to immediately take stock of the Christmas tablecloths and other decorative items they would need for the end of term lunch. It would be a good opportunity for Margery to count the crackers and special snowman cups for squash. They wandered down the identical hallways of the school at an easy pace and up the two flights of stairs to the storeroom. The ropey old Christmas decorations seemed much less charming in the early morning light. You could almost see the fingerprints on the glass bulbs and cheap, plastic baubles.

The storage room was a disaster; everything and anything was discarded here. There were piles and piles of old English exam papers next to a box of deflated basketballs, with the plastic guns from last year's modern-day performance of *Romeo and Juliet* lying on top of them. All the departments used it as a dumping ground. The dinner ladies were certainly not innocent; an entire corner was dedicated to broken kitchen equipment and pots and pans too burnt to be recoverable, but too expensive to throw away.

Margery and Clementine managed to find what they were looking for easily enough, considering the mountains of junk. The big crate of tablecloths was thrown on top of a pile of papers at the back of the storeroom and Margery inspected them as best she could. They were as frayed as the rest of the school decorations, but there would be enough to cover each table in the lunchroom. She sighed; they couldn't afford new ones on the budget this year. The old ones would have to do. Margery always joked about downgrading all lunches to turkey dinosaurs and old cuts of meat that they had in the freezer, but it might actually come to that soon. Maybe they could do a fundraiser, she thought. Mrs Smith seemed to be able to do whatever she wanted most of the time; maybe she could use their very rocky new friendship to raise some funds for the school. It was not a bad school at all, the headmaster was immensely proud of their 'good' Ofsted rating, but it was not a wealthy school by any means.

'Margery, look at all this great stuff!' Clementine said, rummaging around in one of the many, many plastic storage boxes stacked high around the room and pulling out a box of confiscated Pokémon cards. 'I bet we can use these to play Piccalilli Paula later!'

'Clem, put that all back the way you found it please,' Margery scolded from across the room. 'Oh actually, yes we'll take them, and I can use them to fix that wobbly chair in the canteen.'

'That reminds me, Margery, where are the tools?' Clementine looked around perplexed. 'The bag's here but there's hardly anything in it.'

Margery looked to where Clementine was gesturing. Sure enough, the big workman's tool bag was almost empty, save for a gloopy-looking bottle of superglue and half a packet of thumb tacks. Margery put down the table-cloths and wandered over to it in surprise. She knew there had been much more in the bag not even a week ago when she had borrowed a screwdriver to replace a bulb in the kitchen gantry.

'Does it say who signed it out last, Clem?' She picked the heavy tool bag up and rummaged around for the sign-out sheet. It was not in the bag at all. Margery scratched her head. It was mandatory to fill the form out whenever anything was taken, and yet here was the empty bag with no sheet.

Clementine's voice broke the spell she was under. 'Oh gosh, Margery, it's nearly nine o'clock, we've got to get down to the kitchen.'

Margery looked down at the wristwatch that Clementine had bought her last Christmas; it was time to go to work indeed. The mystery of the tools would have to wait until later, though she wished they could stay and look around for them a bit longer. It seemed strange that they would have disappeared the day after the police were looking for who put the stage together. She decided that even though Officer Thomas had explicitly told them not to investigate, she should let him know about it at the earliest occurrence. The missing tools would be a great concern due to the nature of the incident. She decided to come back up with Clementine's phone after work when they had finished counting the tablecloths and take a photograph of the empty bag to show the headmaster too. Surely, he would have something to say about it, even if they were not supposed to be getting involved. They grabbed a box of tablecloths each and made their way down to the kitchen.

Chapter Four

Mrs Smith swept in during the middle of lunch service for the second time in as many days. Margery initially thought she might be coming to start a collection for a card and flowers for poor Mrs Large. Instead, she demanded that they all meet in the school hall that afternoon straight after work to pick up where they had left off with the concert. Margery could not help feeling that continuing as if nothing had happened was a bit callous, though she did not expect much else from Mrs Smith. It could not possibly have come at a more inconvenient time either; Margery had only managed to add the word 'turkey' to her Christmas menu and not much else. She was beginning to worry that the menu would not come together in time and to make matters even worse, Gloria and the others had made it quite clear that they still had absolutely no interest in being in the play. She would have to drag them there against their will again, with the promise of Secret Santa and the lure of a staff Christmas meal in the future.

As they were closing the kitchen down and getting all the frozen foods defrosted for the next day Officer Thomas strolled in through the kitchen door. Young Officer Symon followed behind him. They both looked much more business-like than they had before. Margery paused her day-labelling of the display fridge as he marched straight over to her.

'Margery, can I speak with one of your staff please?'

'Yes of course. Who?' She thought about it for a moment. 'And why?'

'You know I can't tell you that,' he said sharply. He looked down at his notepad. 'Seren Jones please.'

'Seren?' Margery asked in concern. 'Why on earth for?'

'I've already said, I can't tell you.' He was trying to be firm, but Margery could tell he was finding this interaction as awful as she was.

'All right.' She put the date label stickers down on the counter and called for Seren, who was in the back of the kitchen wiping out the inside of the raw meat fridge. She pottered over, taking off the plastic cleaning gloves as she did so. Her eyes widened with fear as she came face to face with the officer, and her steps slowed almost to a halt. Margery remembered all the issues Seren had had with the police recently after a misunderstanding in Tesco and decided to put on her best management face and step in.

'Look, I really think I ought to sit in on this conversation,' she said, in as strong a voice as she could muster. 'Seren has been through a lot recently and I'm not sure I like you whisking her away to interrogate her.'

'What did I say about not involving yourself in a police—'

Margery cut him off with a wave of her hand. 'She's a member of my team. You'll have to go through me if you want to speak to her.'

He stared at her in surprise for a moment, before deciding it was obviously not worth the trouble of fighting her. 'Fine. Come along, then.'

They went and sat down in the empty canteen at one of the plastic tables. Seren looked terrified, Officer Thomas looked worried. Margery gazed between them in concern, as did Officer Symon, who did not seem to know where to sit and was hovering behind his boss.

'Ms Jones, I'm here to talk to you regarding the missing tools in your staff storeroom,' Officer Thomas began. Margery looked at him in surprise; the police must have already realised the tools were missing. They were already taking Mrs Large's misfortune much more seriously than Caroline's; maybe they were determined to not be bested by two dinner ladies again. Officer Thomas removed a piece of paper from his clipboard and slid it in front of them both. It was the tool kit sign-out sheet. Margery squinted at it and wished she had brought her reading glasses up with her from the dry store.

'How did you find it?' she asked without thinking.

'How did you know it was missing?' Officer Thomas raised his eyebrows at her.

'I saw the tool kit in the storeroom when I was getting our tablecloths,' Margery said sheepishly in explanation. He nodded in acceptance, though he still looked suspicious.

'Ms Jones, can you explain to me why your name is the last on this sheet?' He pointed to where she had signed her name on the paper in her usual poor penmanship. She turned bright red.

'I broke my favourite mug.' Margery remembered that happening; the mug had been another victim of Karen's terrible washing up. 'I borrowed the superglue from the tool kit, and I signed it out, like you're supposed to.'

She turned to Margery, who nodded to her in encouragement. 'Were all the tools still there when you returned the superglue?' Officer Thomas asked her.

'Yes.'

'Are you sure?' He questioned her again. 'Nothing missing at all?'

'No, nothing. I remember putting it back on top of everything else,' Seren said softly. She had flushed so much she was almost purple. 'Can I go now?'

Officer Thomas looked as though he had more to say but had not quite worked out which questions to ask. Margery felt vaguely sorry for him. Dewstow was an awfully quiet town, and this was the second awful thing to happen in less than a year. Officer Thomas must have been nearing retirement age and probably had been hoping for no other big events until he had finished. 'Just a moment please, Ms Jones.'

'Whoever took the tools must have been a member of staff,' Margery found herself saying. Both Seren and Officer Thomas stared at her. 'No one else could get into the building. Security has really been upped since Caroline died.'

'Yes. I'd assume so,' Officer Thomas said.

'No, you don't understand, it really has.' Margery tried to explain. Seren cut her off.

'Last week I forgot my pass and Gary Matthews the security guard made me fill out a registration form, we've been dating for six months!'

'Have you, Seren?' Margery said in surprise. 'Oh, that is lovely news!'

'Yeah.' Seren smiled awkwardly. 'It is nice.'

'Well, congratulations,' Officer Thomas said, scratching his head. 'But none of that really helps us much. We already ran all the security cards and looked at the CCTV footage.'

'What was the outcome of that?' Margery asked.

'Mrs Butcher-Baker, let's stick to the current conversation please.'

'Fine,' Margery huffed. 'Well, if you're looking for advice on the tools, the first thing I would do is find out who has the key to the storeroom. Only managers are supposed to have one, and as we just said, Gary would never cut a key for anyone he didn't know. He barely does anything for us anymore.'

'Then how did Ms Jones...'

'I lent her the key that day to get the superglue.' Margery shrugged. 'The other thing that's worth you knowing is that all the tools are numbered and labelled. I remember because the sticker for the pliers fell off when Clementine accidentally put them through the dishwasher and Ceri-Ann printed us a new one. So, you'll know they're our pliers if they turn up because they have a massive glittery number six stuck to them.' She sighed, thinking of Ceri-Ann's disastrous graphic design work again. Officer Symon had handed Officer Thomas his notepad and he was writing down everything Margery said in a fervour.

'Anything else you can think of?' he asked.

Margery thought about it, straining her mind for anything that could help at all. 'There's only twenty tools in the case, I think. Honestly, I don't know how Kevin used to do it, he must have brought his own in.'

'Kevin is the old caretaker?' Officer Thomas paused his scribbling.

'Yes.'

43

'Get his details from Mr Barrow, Symon,' Officer Thomas said, Symon nodded. 'Every little helps at the moment.'

'The thing that's really bothering me and Clementine,' Margery continued, deciding that if they were not allowed to get involved, then the least she could do was tell Officer Thomas her side of things from a staff member's point of view, 'is that the stage couldn't have been put together by one person, there's no way. You've seen it, it's huge! It's got its own dedicated storage space behind the shutters in the hall and it's all in bits you have to slot together. There's a reason that we only get it out for the Christmas concert and the leavers' assembly in the summer term.'

'Who's the most likely to have even built it? Nobody cares about the school play, not at all,' Seren piped up. 'And there's so much to do around here, who's got time to put a stage together?'

Unless it was someone who really wanted the play to go ahead, Margery thought. Like Mrs Smith. Margery tapped her finger on her lips and pondered. The only person she could think of who would want the concert to go ahead was Mrs Smith. Possibly the rest of the drama department, though they all seemed to be as forced into it as the rest of the staff were most of the time, but Margery could not see Mrs Smith doing any hard labour herself. Let alone raising the shutters at the back of the school hall, dragging the stage platforms out one by one, and then unfolding and putting the whole thing together piece by piece to secure it in place. Then after all that was done, getting the ladder out and clambering up it to fit the light fittings. Even if she had got that far, she could not have possibly done it all alone. No, there definitely had to be somebody else involved.

'That's what we're trying to find out,' Officer Thomas said as he wrote down the last of Margery's words. 'Well, thank you both. Ms Jones, you're off the hook for now.'

'Are we free to go?' Margery said, as she checked her watch. 'We've all got to go to the next rehearsal.'

'That's still on?' Officer Thomas asked in surprise. 'Really?'

'We're as surprised as you are,' Margery said. She could see Clementine waiting for her by the kitchen door, still in her kitchen pinafore. The others must have already left to get changed.

'Well, then I'll let you get on. Margery, here's my number.' He wrote it on the notepad and then ripped the paper off to give it to her. 'Call me if you find out anything.'

They rushed off to get changed out of their kitchen clothes. Margery wondered if the police had managed to find anything else of use in their investigations. It was going to be hard to stay out of it all, she could already feel herself itching to start putting the details together.

'What was that all about?' Clementine asked as they hurried down the corridor to the school hall. Margery managed to catch her up on the way. They were dreadfully late for rehearsal and Margery hoped Mrs Smith would not be too angry at their lateness. She wished she could muster up even an ounce of enthusiasm for the play, but she felt as flat about it as the rest of the team did. All the other staff would probably have already gathered in the hall by now. They made it to the room, flinging open the double doors and almost knocking Gloria over as they bowled in.

'Where have you been?' she hissed, 'I've had to stop Benjamin escaping, and I caught Karen and Sharon trying to leave through the fire escape. You can't force us all to come and then be late, Margery, it's not on.'

'We're here now.' Margery panted, handing Clementine her asthma inhaler from her cardigan pocket. 'Come on, let's at least get good seats.'

–

They all wandered in and over to the plastic chairs by the piano. The cleaners were there. The unfortunate teachers who had been dragged into the play were there. Mrs Smith was not.

It was not like her at all. She was usually terrifyingly punctual. Margery looked around in confusion as she took a seat. Had something happened in the few hours since they had last seen her?

'We are supposed to be meeting today, aren't we?' Miss Macdonald the English teacher asked, as Margery sat down next to her. Margery nodded. Miss Macdonald's forehead wrinkled in uncertainty.

'Do you know where Rose is, Seren?' she asked Seren as she sat down next to her.

'No, haven't seen her since lunch,' Seren said, shrugging.

Margery looked around the circle of chairs at the rest of the staff. They were all wearing a similar look. The hall was in quite good shape considering what had happened the night before. The stage was still standing along the back wall, the light fittings obviously missing. Margery was amazed they had managed to get rid of all the shattered glass from the bulbs in such a short amount of time. All the twisted metal from the light rigging had been removed too. It was as though nothing had ever happened.

It felt awfully wrong to be sitting there, pretending it was all fine. That nothing had happened, let alone something as horrific as they had witnessed. Rose must be out of her mind to be continuing.

'Sorry I'm late!' Margery turned her head to look at the intruder. It was Mr Daniels, the assistant drama teacher. He rushed over, his shiny shoes squeaking on the shiny floor. He had Rose's play script under one arm and the sheet music in his other hand. He put them both down on top of the piano and turned to face them all expectantly, straightening his smart black cardigan over his crisply starched shirt and running a hand up to his neat cowlick of hair, checking it was all still in place.

'Hi everyone!' Mr Daniels gave them all a big gleaming smile, but Margery could see the nerves behind it, his shaking hands giving him away. 'I'm sure you were expecting Mrs Smith to be here, but um… she won't be making it to the rehearsal.'

There was a gaggle of voices as everyone started to talk at once. Mr Daniels raised his hands to silence them. 'But good news, we're still going to do the concert!'

Margery heard Clementine groan. 'Really? Where is she?'

Mr Daniels was still smiling, but it looked much too forced to be real. 'She's… indisposed.' He sighed, the façade falling. 'I can't tell you anything else. Come on. Let's just get on with it.'

Over the next half hour, he somehow managed to dodge any questions about Rose or Mrs Large's condition and simultaneously managed to get them all back on the stage. Margery looked over at Clementine, who raised her head and caught Margery's eye. She looked as uncomfortable as Margery felt to be back on the stage where they had witnessed Mrs Large's accident.

'Okay,' Mr Daniels said in an exasperated tone, while sitting at the piano. He had become more and more red-faced as the rehearsal went on. The hair he had so carefully smoothed into place was mussed from running his fingers through it in despair, and he had undone his tie, which now sat in a loose knot around his neck. 'Let's go from the top, then. I'll count you all in.'

He started to play the piano again, the clanging of the keys ringing out in the echoey room, and they all started shuffling about in a vague approximation of a dance. Mrs Wiggins the maths teacher wobbled as she turned to do the spin and Margery ended up face to face with her by mistake. She stepped back to move away from her and stood on Gloria's toes, who then in turn fell backward into Karen and Sharon.

'Stop, stop, *please* stop!' Mr Daniels bellowed from below the stage, the piano coming to a crashing halt. Margery looked over at him, his head in his hands, elbows resting on the keys. 'That was terrible! Now if we are going to do this, we need to do it right!'

'I don't think we should be doing it at all,' Clementine said. 'A terrible accident happened in this room not even a day ago, it's completely callous.'

There was a murmur of agreement at that, Margery looked around at the nodding heads of the staff members.

Mr Daniels ignored them and turned to the piano again as though no one had said anything. 'I'll split you up into small groups and we'll work on it separately. I'll take one group at a time and the rest of you can practise.'

Margery found herself zoning out as he spoke. She could not see how there was any way he was going to be able to make them any better before show night. Second rehearsal or not, there was a reason they all worked at the school and were not on a Broadway stage.

Her gaze wandered over to the big windows on her right that took up the whole wall. Mr Daniels had not drawn the long curtains, and it was still just about light enough that Margery could see straight out into the playground. From outside she could see someone watching them through the glass as she had the day before. Her eyes widened at the sight of them.

Margery shook her head; maybe she was imagining things. But when she looked again the man was still there. She could see him clearly today, in the better lighting. He was wearing a drab grey overcoat over a suit and holding a polished leather briefcase. The expensive kind she associated exclusively with important businessmen. She could not see his feet, the window began at knee height, but she would have been amazed if he was not wearing a shiny pair of leather dress shoes to match the rest of his outfit. Why would he be here? She did not recognise him at all, and she knew all the staff at the school after twenty years of service. Even if it was just by face and not by name. He couldn't have been a teacher. He did not have that withered, tired look long-term teachers seemed to get. In fact, he looked quite refreshed, from what she could see from the stage at least. He must have been in his late forties, but he had a full head of neatly trimmed dark hair and was just standing and staring in. It was very, very strange.

'Margery, wakey-wakey!' Clementine grabbed her hand. 'We've got to go and have our stupid and abhorrent dance lesson now.'

Margery looked at Clementine and then stared back towards the window. The man was gone, and he had left no trace that he was ever there. Maybe she was going mad. But her eyes had never failed her before. Maybe her brain had invented him out of boredom, but on two occasions? It was unthinkable. What could he be doing here? Margery tried to shake the thoughts away as she followed Clementine off the stage and over to the side of the piano where Mr Daniels was waiting for them.

'Come on, ladies.' He smiled as they approached. 'Let's get this over with. We'll get the dance down if it kills me. Now, where's the rest of your group? Hang on, I'll go and get them.' He wandered over to Gloria and Seren sitting on the cheap chairs, pretending they could not see him beckoning to them.

'Did you see that man, Clem?' Margery hissed as soon as Mr Daniels was out of earshot. 'The one in the window. He was here yesterday, I'm sure of it!'

Clementine's face lit up. 'Did you see him again, did you? Where?' She whirled around to look at the windows. There was nobody there.

Margery sighed. 'Of course, he's not there when I want you to see him. There was someone there though, I swear, Clem.'

'Don't worry, Margery,' Clementine said in a serious voice, 'I believe you.' Margery shushed her.

'Seriously, Clem,' she hissed. 'There was someone there.'

Clementine scratched her head. 'Maybe he's here to see the headmaster or something?'

'Wouldn't he have used the front door?' Margery said, as she watched in amusement as Mr Daniels tried to convince Seren and Gloria to join them. Gloria looked as though she was pretending to be very hard of hearing.

'Well, it does seem weird, doesn't it?' Clementine said, wandering over to the tall window to look out. 'Ooh, Margery, look!'

'Clem?' She joined her at the window to stare down at where Clementine was pointing. On the floor outside was a small object. Before Margery could say anything, Clementine had rushed over to the fire escape and pushed the handle, the door clanging open. She squished herself through and outside, the cold air blew into the warm hall. Margery moved to follow her.

'Mrs Butcher–Baker!' Mr Daniels yelled from the other side of the hall. 'Where are you going? We're ready for you both.'

Clementine rushed back in through the fire escape, nearly trapping herself outside before managing to crash back into the hall, partially concealed behind the curtain. They wandered back over to where Mr Daniels was trying to explain the complicated dance to Seren, who looked flummoxed.

'What was it, Clem?' Margery asked the moment Clementine turned to her to continue practising Mr Daniel's dance.

Clementine took her hand and spun her, her brow furrowed. They stopped their movements and Clementine looked around to see who was watching before she pulled her discovery out of her tabard pocket. 'It's really strange, Margery.'

Resting in the palm of her hand was a small drawstring bag. Similar to the kind the children used to carry their PE kits, but much, much smaller and not at all frayed or smelly. It could not have fitted a pair of socks in, let alone a trainer. The bag was purple velvet with a gold clasp and matching carabiner clip. Margery could not fathom what it could possibly be for. Clementine pulled the drawstring apart and peered inside, shrugging when she came up short.

'There's just some crumbs in here,' she said, her white eyebrows furrowing as she peered inside the bag.

'What kind of crumbs?' Margery asked. Clementine held them out for her to look. There was nothing remarkable about them, they could have been the sweepings from the kitchen dustpan for all she knew.

'God, Margery,' Clementine said. 'There really must have been someone there to drop this. Ghosts aren't known for carrying much about, are they? What the hell is it?'

'I told you.' Margery nodded and pointed at the bag. 'I wonder why he had it, it seems very odd.'

'Well, look, it gets even stranger,' Clementine said. She flipped the bag over in her hands, revealing the elegant gold lettering that had been stitched on neatly. 'What does that mean?'

Margery took the bag from her and looked at it closely. The letters read *MRS A.B.* in a smartly sewed font. She looked at Clementine, who was shaking her head, and then back at the bag again. She did not know what it meant at all, but she had a horrible feeling they were going to find out.

Chapter Five

'Come on Benjamin, stop sloshing it about, you're getting more food on the children than on the plate.' Gloria scolded the young man as he doled out the mashed potato from the hot counter with shaky, uncoordinated hands.

'And that quiche you made looks horrendous,' Clementine chimed in, unnecessarily, Margery thought. 'The pastry's so short it wouldn't be able to ride anything at Alton Towers.'

They had a point. When Benjamin had sent his application form in, Margery had been jubilant. With a catering qualification from Ittonvale College and oodles of cooking experience working in various pubs in the area, he had seemed like the perfect candidate on paper. He had also been very polite in person when he had arrived smartly dressed for the job interview, and all his references had been positively glowing. It was only now that he had been with them a few months that she could really see his shortcomings. Sometimes it was as though he had never stepped foot in a kitchen before, not even in his own house.

The first cup of tea he had made her had been an experience she would never forget. He had presented it to her proudly, but it had been the colour of Tippex and, inexplicably, the tea bag had still been at the bottom of the mug. She was sure that he had put the milk in before the water; the memory still made her lip curl in disgust.

'Sorry Gloria, sorry Clementine,' Benjamin said sadly. He adjusted his hairnet and went back to awkwardly spooning out the food to students. Margery could not help but like him, even if it were becoming clearer and clearer that he must have exaggerated some part of his past experience.

Sometimes, she felt privately that the young man they had all been so pleased to hire could not possibly be the same as the one she had employed. But eventually she had decided to give him a bit more time to settle in. After all, he was young, just turned twenty-one, and willing and eager to learn. She could ignore some of his bigger faults if he carried on turning up to work on time.

Anyway, something she had realised quite early on was that he was good at fixing things; he could always be counted on to replace a bulb or the blade on the industrial can opener. That was a very useful talent to have at the moment, with the school's lack of maintenance staff, and another reason to overlook his lack of culinary talent and disregard of food hygiene.

'Oh Christ, what's going on now?' Gloria said, looking over across the canteen. 'Margery you'd better get over here.'

'Gloria, please do not swear,' Clementine said, but her expression changed when she saw who she was looking at. 'What's she dressed like that for?'

Mrs Smith was weaving her way towards them, through the students in the canteen, who all jumped back to avoid her as she thundered into the room. She was wearing a scarf over her head and needlessly dark sunglasses, looking very much out of place in her attempt to look the opposite.

'Psst!' She hissed loudly at them as she arrived at the other side of the kitchen window. She leaned her arm on the Perspex display of the serving fridge, ignoring the students she was blocking, who were queuing with their trays. 'Psst Margery, psst Clementine!'

'What can we do for you, Rose?' Clementine asked politely, though to Margery's ears it sounded incredibly begrudging. 'Can we offer you a slice of quiche?'

'How did you know it was me?' Mrs Smith hissed even louder than before. She raised the sunglasses from her face to inspect the food in the serving window before her. Her mouth twisted in disgust. 'Good Lord. I know I'm no chef, but I've read a Nigella or two. You're supposed to bake a quiche, aren't you? Not boil it?'

'Ask Ben,' Clementine said. Margery shushed her.

'How many years did you steam this thing for, Ben?' Mrs Smith asked him, snapping her sunglasses back down over her eyes. 'No, no actually. Just pretend you haven't seen me.'

Benjamin turned bright red and continued to serve the food. The students in the queue had to snake out into the middle of the canteen to avoid Mrs Smith, who continued to ignore them.

'Why?' Clementine asked suspiciously. 'If you think you can sneak back here and look at our Secret Santa results, we haven't held the draw yet so you're out of luck.'

As the murmuring of disgruntled students rose, Seren came out from where she had been loading the dishwasher. She stared at Mrs Smith before rushing over.

'Rose!' She puffed as she arrived at the counter, pulling the rubber marigolds off. 'You aren't supposed to be here, you'll get into trouble!'

'Yes, yes, blah, blah.' Mrs Smith rolled her eyes. 'So be quiet, Seren, stop making a scene, for God's sake.'

'What's going on?' Margery asked, looking between the two women. Seren was twisting her hands with worry, the washing-up gloves still soapy and dripping water onto the floor of the serving area. 'Is that true, Seren?'

'Ask her!' Seren shrilled, pointing at Mrs Smith dramatically. Mrs Smith looked away and inspected her perfect nails. 'Tell them what the headmaster said, Rose.'

'No,' Mrs Smith said. 'I don't think I will.' It was Seren's turn to roll her eyes. She threw her hands in the air and stomped back into the main kitchen. Mrs Smith ignored her, but it was very forced.

'But… I mean… what happened to you, Mrs Smith?' Margery asked the woman who was currently sneering at the selection of cakes in the cold counter fridge. 'Why weren't you at rehearsal?'

'Shhh, Margery.' Mrs Smith pulled the scarf closer around her face, 'Don't call me by my name.'

'What should we call you then?' Margery asked in surprise.

'Just… keep your voice down!' Mrs Smith hissed. 'That bumbling idiot Seren is right, I'm not supposed to be here. The headmaster can't know.'

'Why?' Clementine asked. 'Is it because you broke up with him?'

'No, it is not!' Mrs Smith spluttered. 'And I didn't break up… oh just shut up.'

'We'll call you Russell then,' Clementine said. 'As your code name.'

'No, I didn't mean…'

'Or how about Mrs Smythe?'

'Well…' Margery tried to think of something to break the frosty atmosphere, before Mrs Smith leapt across the counter and physically assaulted anyone. 'Erm, any news on Mrs Large?'

'I haven't heard anything. God, poor Mrs Large,' Mrs Smith said. It was hard to tell her expression under the ginormous sunglasses, but her lips were downturned in a grimace. 'Will you get a collection going round for some flowers please? I'd do it but…'

She paused and flicked her always neat silver bob away from her face and sighed deeply. 'Anyway, more importantly, we can't speak here about…' She lowered her voice to what she probably thought was a whisper. '…Such things. Meet me at the Bell and Hope after school. Seven o'clock, sharp.'

'The Bell!' Clementine shrieked. Mrs Smith hushed her. Clementine rolled her eyes. 'Come off it, Mrs Smythe. They don't even have Frangelico.'

'I know,' Mrs Smith said, sadly. 'They wouldn't let me smoke in there either, disgusting place. But it's the only place I can think of safe enough to have this conversation.'

'Safer than, oh, say… one of our houses?' Clementine said sarcastically.

'The walls have ears, Mrs Butcher-Baker, you of all people should know that.' Mrs Smith smiled. 'And I fancy a glass of wine after all this.'

Margery nodded. 'That's fine with us, it's close enough to home that I can leave the car there and have a glass too.'

'On a school night, Margery!' Clementine teased. 'Finally letting your hair down, are you?'

Margery rolled her eyes at her. 'We can have one, can't we?'

That morning Karen had been pretending to be a bride using a big bunch of parsley as a bouquet, and Sharon and Seren had thrown rice at her while she waltzed around. Until Margery told them all to stop it and get on with the food prep, that is, then they had spent the rest of the day sulking. Clementine had been teasing her about it since. Being the boss could be hard sometimes, but Margery was glad she had Clementine to back her up. Gloria had watched, but not tried to help at all. Margery was beginning to worry that she had upset her in some way; Gloria had definitely been more frosty than usual for a while.

Behind them, Miss Macdonald on dinner monitoring duty entered the canteen to see what all the fuss was about with the queue. Mrs Smith eyed them both pleadingly.

'We'll be there.' Margery wanted to know what on earth was going on, and this seemed the easiest way. Mrs Smith nodded once and then grabbed the last slice of pizza from under the protective splash guard and sauntered off with it. They all stared after her as she strolled through the canteen and out through the fire escape. The queue pushed forward and they began serving students again.

'What was all that about?' Gloria asked. Margery shook her head. She had been the one having the conversation, and she was still not entirely sure what had just happened. Seren must know what was going on with Mrs Smith if her reaction was anything to go by.

'Christ Margery, we'd better get another pizza on before there's an uprising,' Gloria said, as they stared out at the sea of hungry teenage faces. 'Benjamin, quick! Sort it out.'

The young man dropped the ladle in the gravy, and it splashed all over the counter as he scuttled off. Gloria threw her hands up in anger and then grabbed a roll of blue roll to wipe it up with.

'Careful Ben!' she said. 'For God's sake Margery, he's doing my head in today.'

'Don't speak to him like that, be nice to him, he fixed the hot counter this morning,' Margery warned Gloria. 'And don't worry about Mrs Smith, it's just more stuff about the Christmas concert. Go and help Ben, will you?'

Gloria looked at her, eyebrows raised as though she knew Margery was lying, but then she nodded and turned to go and assist Benjamin with the pizza.

-

An hour later, when lunch was over and they were cleaning down, Gloria came back over. Margery was busy supervising the drawing of Secret Santa, which was already revealing itself to be a hellish nightmare. She did not know where Clementine thought they would buy anyone a present for under five pounds. The only shop she could think of like that nearby was Home Bargains next to the bowling alley on the outskirts of town. It had already been the cause of numerous rifts in her and Clementine's relationship. Mostly because Clementine spent all their time announcing, 'Well that's a home bargain!' at almost everything in the store.

'Margery...' Gloria said quietly, as Clementine folded the last slip of paper with a name on and put it into the binbag they were using for the prize draw. 'You can't let Ben go on like this you know, he's awful. You're the manager, you need to do something about it, and what's all this with Mrs Smith wandering in like that? She didn't pay for that pizza slice she stole either, the stock will be down one pound fifty.'

Margery thought of telling Gloria about the clandestine meeting with Mrs Smith they had planned. Every time she had tried to talk to Seren about it at lunchtime, something else had been going on. Then the big order of eggs and flour and sugar for the Christmas bake sale had turned up. Anyway, her relationship with Gloria had been a bit strained lately.

Clementine often told people that she was Margery's sous chef, but she would rather spend all her time making cups of tea and talking to members of staff from different departments than help Margery delegate. Gloria knew the job as well as Margery did, which should make her the perfect second in command, but meant in reality that they butted heads far more often than Margery would have liked.

'Right!' Clementine shrieked, wearing a moth-eaten old Santa hat she had found in the storeroom and interrupting Margery's train of thought. 'Let the games begin!'

Margery grimaced as the rest of the dinner lady team erupted in oohing; she had been dreading Secret Santa, which had always been their former kitchen manager's thing. In all honestly, she was not sure she really wanted it to continue, especially in light of recent events. It usually ended in bickering and someone only spending a pound instead of ten and someone else spending fifty pounds instead of ten. The whole thing was a hideous affair of Caroline's making.

One year, a former dinner lady, Helen Melon, had gifted Sharon nothing but a half-eaten scone and an out-of-date jar of strawberry jam, while Karen had gifted

Helen Melon a Fortnum and Mason gift hamper. They had not heard the end of it for what Margery had felt was decades. In fact, Karen still sometimes brought it up when she was in a particularly bad mood.

However, Clementine adored Christmas and was always banging on about her holiday traditions, Secret Santa being one of them, and so Margery had agreed to try it out just this one year as long as the budget was only five pounds. Most of Clementine's traditions seemed to revolve around watching cheesy Christmas films and drinking port, although in the last few years she had expanded this to include replacing everything in the house with a Christmas version of itself. The newest and most bizarre tradition of all was putting a candle on a birthday cake and wishing the new year happy birthday at midnight. Margery suspected this was just an excuse for Clementine to eat an extra birthday cake every year.

Sharon and Karen stepped forward at the same time eagerly. There was a brief wrestling match as they both tried to shove their hand in the bag at the same time, finally pulling out a paper slip each. Seren stepped forward next and ripped a hole straight through the bin bag with her over-enthusiastic hands as she grabbed a name. Slips of paper flew out everywhere.

Sharon wailed waving the paper she had pulled out in the air, bursting into tears. 'Oh no, I've got myself, I've got myself!'

Karen went to comfort her, but then looked at her own slip and screamed in panic. 'I've got myself too!'

'For God's sake, Seren!' Clementine squealed as she scrabbled around on the floor after the names. The paper pieces small and thin enough that they kept pinging away from her grasping fingers.

'Why don't you just swap cards with Karen, Sharon?' Margery suggested, gingerly patting the distraught woman on the shoulder.

'You can't do that!' Clementine cried from the floor. 'It's not Christmassy if we know who's got who, Margery!'

'Well put them all back in a new bag then and we'll try again,' Margery said.

'Oh no, we can't do that, I've got a good one!' Seren said, looking at her slip of paper gleefully.

'Have you…' Margery already knew the answer before she asked the question. 'Have you by any chance picked your own name, Seren?'

Seren nodded, smiling toothily. Margery rubbed her temples with her fingers.

Clementine had finally managed to collect the remaining names and lay them face down on the nearest prep table. 'Come and pick a name, Benjamin, quick before all the good names are gone!'

Sharon wailed even louder at that. Benjamin stayed in the corner, twiddling his fingers together anxiously. Margery sighed and counted down the days in her head until the Christmas holidays.

Chapter Six

The pub was only a half a mile walk or so from their cul-de-sac. They arrived in good time, after a brisk walk through the crisp evening air. Margery was not usually one for public houses, but she had always liked the Bell and Hope. It was the oldest pub in town, all original stone and quirky features you only found in buildings of that age. Rumour had it that the cellar underneath held a secret passageway that led straight out onto the river, once used by smugglers and the like. Margery had always been too shy to ask, but Clementine had always insisted it was true and Margery liked the stories enough to let it go.

It was wildly busy for a Thursday evening when they finally pushed open the heavy wooden pub door, half of the school staff seemed to be here. Mr Barrow was over by the jukebox, nursing a pint of frothy-looking ale while talking to Karen and Sharon, all of them wearing Dewstow Fun Runners long sleeve T-shirts and running shoes. Seren was over in the corner playing darts with Gary Matthews, the school security guard. Margery thought she even recognised a few students in the back, along with the entire English department, who by the looks of things were already four gins in. Margery and Clementine marched straight past them and into the back room, Margery hoping that they would not be noticed in the revelry. It seemed strange to her that Mrs Smith would want to meet somewhere so public, though she must have had her reasons.

They found a cosy-looking table in the corner and took off their winter coats. Clementine wandered back off to the main bar to get them both a drink, leaving Margery alone. She fiddled with the paper beer mat on the table in front of her and wondered how inconspicuous the two of them would really be, sitting on the other side of the room as everyone else they knew. The pub was dingy but not that dingy, though they were partially obscured by the Christmas tree. She lifted her cardigan sleeve and checked her watch. it was nearly half past seven and Mrs Smith had still not arrived. Clementine finally returned from the bar, clutching two glasses of wine.

'For God's sake, is the Winter Olympics on or something?' she said, plonking the glasses down on the table and putting her handbag under it before sitting down in the creaky old chair. 'It hasn't been this busy in here since the last Eurovision.'

'Where's Rose?' Margery asked, tearing at the bar mat with anxious fingers. 'She said she'd be here and she's never late. Remember when we opened the canteen three minutes late for lunch once and she threw a scone at you, you ducked and it went into the deep fat fryer?'

'Yes, all the oil went everywhere and Karen slipped, twisted her ankle and had to miss the Bath half marathon. I know, I know. Don't worry, she's over there.' Clementine nodded across from them to where someone was reading the food menu. It covered most of their head, only revealing part of a sleek, silver bob. 'I just thought we had much better seats here.'

The menu slammed down onto their table and Mrs Smith's exasperated face appeared. 'You knew I was here all along and you didn't say anything?! You're lucky I don't have a scone on me.'

'Well, the eye holes you put in that menu gave you away,' Clementine said, pointing at it and taking a sip of her drink. 'Anyway, are you coming over or not? We're missing *Casualty* for this.'

Mrs Smith made a big show of coming over to their table, the chair scraping over the worn, frayed carpet. She was still wearing her smart work suit, but she had undone the top button of her blouse; it made her look more human somehow, less of a caricature.

'Nice of you to get yourself a drink, Mrs Butcher-Baker,' Mrs Smith said, glaring at Clementine. 'I'm practically parched after all the song-writing I've been doing for the concert, and I've spent all week trying to get the art department to get their act together with the scenery. All for nothing now.'

'Can you not just repurpose a load of stuff from when you did *A Midsummer Night's Dream*? There were trees and stuff in that, wasn't there? Just pop a bit of tinsel on them,' Clementine said innocently. Mrs Smith stared at her with narrowed eyes for so long that Margery worried she had forgotten how to talk.

'Here, have mine,' Margery said, passing Mrs Smith her own glass. 'I'm not much of a drinker anyway. Why are we here Rose? Surely it's not very private.' Margery gestured towards where the English department were now arguing at the jukebox, presumably about what song should be put on next. 'And what do you mean, it's all for nothing? Where were you yesterday?'

'Thank you, other Mrs Butcher-Baker. It's nice to know one of you has manners.' Mrs Smith took the glass by the stem gracefully and slowly prepared to take a sip. Margery and Clementine waited in anticipation. Mrs Smith drank half the glass before she seemed to remember she was in company. 'We're here because I have done nothing wrong, and I want them all to know that. Why shouldn't I meet a colleague after work? And yesterday... well... I was indisposed.'

'What on earth does that mean? For God's sake, Rose, will you spit it out?' Clementine snapped, offering Margery her own glass to share. 'If we're here too long Seren will make us do karaoke and I have absolutely no intention of learning any songs recorded after 1982.'

They lapsed into a tense silence for a moment. Margery looked around the busily decorated room, thinking to herself that this must be the only place on earth that contained more Princess Diana memorabilia than her late mother's house. Mrs Smith finally broke the silence with an exasperated sigh.

'Fine. I'll tell you,' she said, rolling her eyes so far back in her head that Margery hoped she was not wearing contact lenses. 'They've put me on leave.'

'Who has?' Clementine leaned forward in genuine interest.

'Who hasn't!' Mrs Smith wailed and looked anywhere but Clementine's eager face. 'The headmaster and his cronies on the board, the *governors*.' She spat the last word as though it was a particularly nasty skin disorder. 'They suspended me! He only told me yesterday afternoon. He got Gary Matthews, of all people, to escort me from the building.' She glared over into the main room at Gary, who was still chatting away to Seren.

'You can't be serious!' Margery exclaimed. 'How long for?'

'I'm deadly serious. Until they sort it all out with the stage, he said.' Mrs Smith's face was aghast. 'They think I did it! Can you believe that? As if I'd ever do any manual labour. He said, "Think of it as gardening leave," but I already have a gardener!'

'Why on earth do they think it was you?' Margery asked.

'A very long story short, the police watched some CCTV footage from the weekend, and they've decided that I entered the school and put the stage together.' Mrs Smith snorted. 'As if I'd ever go to work on a weekend… well not that weekend anyway. I took home the marking I needed to do for the mock exam prep on the Friday, so I didn't need to go in for anything.'

Margery suddenly felt terribly guilty for suggesting to the policeman to check the security system, though she didn't know why. 'Are you sure you didn't just pop in? Surely they would have been able to check if you used your card or not?'

'No,' Mrs Smith wailed. 'I didn't! And obviously they can't prove I did or I wouldn't be sitting with you now, would I? They would have arrested me and anyway I haven't used my card for ages, I lost it.'

'Why on earth do they think it was you then?' Margery asked.

'They said it *matches my description*.' She air-quoted the last few words and then looked down at the table, utterly defeated.

'How have you been getting into work?' Clementine asked her. She looked intrigued, and Margery hoped this was not the start of one of Clementine's notoriously terrible plans.

'Seren and I drive in together, of course.' Mrs Smith shrugged. 'It makes sense to go in together since we share a house.'

'Is she *still* living with you?' Margery said, unable to keep the surprise out of her voice. She had assumed Mrs Smith would have dropped Seren like a bag of mouldy potatoes as soon as she could after Caroline's murder had been solved and Seren had somewhere else to live.

'Of course. She does all the washing and ironing,' Mrs Smith said, sincerely. 'It's like living with one of those Harry Potter goblin things.'

'So, they don't have proof it was your pass?' Clementine asked. 'Whose pass was swiped in then?'

'They wouldn't tell me.' Mrs Smith was very pale. Margery had never seen her look so worried in the decade they had known her. 'And they wouldn't tell me what looks so much like me on the footage either. I feel like they were trying to get me to confess to something, but I didn't do anything, I swear!' Her hands shook as she picked up the wine glass again. Margery watched the liquid it held slosh up the sides. 'You know I wouldn't have put the stage up myself. If I lose my job, I'll lose everything I have left. Please, I have no choice but to ask for your help.' She turned to acknowledge Clementine. 'Both of you. We'll need both the dinner lady detectives on the case.'

Margery shared a look with Clementine, who nodded back at her solemnly.

'Okay…' Margery breathed. 'If you didn't do it…'

'I didn't!' Mrs Smith wailed.

'Fine, fine,' Margery said calmly. 'So, then you must have an alibi?'

Mrs Smith stared at her wide-eyed. 'An alibi?'

'Yes,' Margery said. 'Where were you at the time they say you're on the CCTV? Surely you've told the police where you were?'

'I know what an alibi is,' Mrs Smith said softly. She had gone even whiter than Margery had ever dreamed possible.

'So, what is it?'

'I... I don't want to say. I haven't told anyone.'

'That's fine,' Clementine said, downing the last of her wine and standing up. 'Well, it sounds like a lovely drama for you to sort out. Come on Margery, let's get home and watch a nice episode of *Call the Midwife*, ooh we can watch one of the Christmas specials!'

'Ladies, you don't understand.' Mrs Smith pleaded as she grabbed Clementine by the wrist. She said the words very slowly and through gritted teeth, as if they were a pair of very stupid five-year-olds she was trying to explain the letter A to. 'This is my life's work. You've got to help me.'

Clementine rolled her eyes, but she let Mrs Smith drag her back down into the chair regardless. 'Then just tell us where you were, and we can try.'

'I was...' Mrs Smith mumbled something so quietly under her breath that neither Margery nor Clementine could hear her. They leaned forward expectantly.

'I'm sorry, what?' Margery asked. Mrs Smith would not look either of them in the eye, her jaw clenched tightly.

'I can't tell you.' Mrs Smith looked close to tears. 'I can't...'

'Then we really can't help you,' Margery said. 'We've been told not to interfere with the police case as it is.

There's nothing we can do, especially if you haven't even told them where you were.'

'I can't…' Mrs Smith hissed through gritted teeth. 'You don't understand…'

'Then make us understand,' Margery pleaded. 'For all we know you did put that stage together. There's certainly nothing to prove you didn't.'

'I don't have to explain myself to you.' They lapsed into an uncomfortable silence.

Margery thought about the mysteriously missing tools and her conversation with Officer Thomas. 'Do you have a key for the storeroom on the second floor, Mrs Smith?'

'I do.' Mrs Smith nodded, her mouth wrinkling in disgust. 'You couldn't pay me to set foot in there though, too much dust.'

'Who looks after the keys?' Margery asked. 'The head-master?'

'I'd assume so,' Mrs Smith said agreeably. 'It's probably in his office, he keeps records of all sorts of things like that since the caretaker left. He has it all on his computer, but he writes the backups down in red notepads, you can't miss them. Very organised, like me. That's why we were such a good match.' She looked away wistfully.

Margery sat back in her chair, deep in thought. That sounded easy enough to look for. She wondered if they could sneakily look for a red notepad on the next tea trolley run. They wouldn't be getting involved in the police case as such, just helping it along. She looked over at Mrs Smith, who was staring down into the empty wine glass as though if she glared at it long enough it would refill.

'We saw a man outside the hall yesterday when we were practising,' Margery said without thinking.

'Oh?' Mrs Smith leaned forward in genuine interest. 'Who was it?'

'No idea.' Margery shrugged, deciding they had nothing to lose. 'But they dropped something.'

She reached over and took the strange velvet pouch out of her handbag and put it down on the table in front of Mrs Smith, whose eyes widened at the sight of it.

'Good Lord,' she said. 'You say a man dropped this? Are you sure? Not a woman?'

Margery nodded. 'Do you know who the man could have been, Mrs Smith?'

'No.' Mrs Smith reached out and traced the lettering on the bag with her fingers. 'This definitely doesn't belong to a man.'

'So, you know who it belongs to?'

'I do.' Mrs Smith smiled at them both so weakly that the corners of her lips barely moved. 'Of course, you both know Mrs Blossom.'

'Who?' Margery and Clementine asked in unison.

'Mrs Blossom!' Mrs Smith said again with even more emphasis, looking at them both in turn, eyebrows raised. They stared back at her. Margery felt herself shrugging.

Clementine took the bag from the table and inspected it again. She had the same blank look on her face that Margery was sure was on her own.

'Oh, for God's sake,' Mrs Smith said, pointing to the bag in Clementine's fingers. 'Mrs Blossom, head of the drama department at Ittonvale school! My arch nemesis?'

They shook their heads again.

'The evillest woman in the world? No?' She shook her head at them. 'Ittonvale school must be involved in this somehow.'

'Even if that's true, what reason could she have to interfere at Summerview?' Margery could not make heads nor tails of what Mrs Smith was trying to insinuate. 'It's just a bag? It surely doesn't mean anything?'

'The initials.' Mrs Smith spoke in a hushed tone Margery had never heard from the woman before, in all their years of working together. 'This bag doesn't exactly belong to Mrs Blossom.'

'What do you mean now?' Clementine said, the exasperation clear in her voice. 'You just said it did!'

'No… I said I knew whose it was.' Mrs Smith looked around the pub to check that no one else was listening in uninvited. She lowered her voice to a whisper. 'The bag belongs to Mrs Ada Bones.'

They stared at her glumly.

'Who?' Clementine finally asked. Mrs Smith must have realised that they had no background knowledge about anything she was talking about.

'Mrs Blossom's dog.' She sighed. 'Don't ask about the name.'

'Why is it called that?' Clementine asked in bafflement.

'I said don't ask.' Mrs Smith sighed again. 'Look, are you going to help me or not?'

'I don't think we can,' Margery said. 'Not without knowing your alibi.'

Mrs Smith put her fingers to her temples and rubbed her face.

'We've known each other a long time, Margery,' Mrs Smith said finally, in a hushed whisper so quiet that Margery and Clementine had to lean in closer to hear her. 'Do you really think I could have done this? I'd never do anything to ruin the reputation of the school and more than that, Elizabeth Large wasn't just my colleague, she was my friend. Just like I thought you were.'

She stood up so dramatically that the chair almost fell backward as she grabbed for her handbag and swished away, leaving Margery and Clementine in shocked silence.

Chapter Seven

Margery found it hard to drag herself out of bed the next morning. Typically, she didn't mind going to work on a Friday; the majority of the cleaning rota and paperwork had been done by Thursday afternoon and Fridays were usually a more relaxed workday. Today was different. The weather was cold, the coffee Clementine made her was even colder, and the atmosphere in the small kitchen canteen was even frostier after Mrs Winkle the school receptionist arrived to invite them to a special school assembly.

The dinner ladies gathered at the back as they always did; the hall was even more of a squish than usual because of the stage. They were almost the last ones there. Mr Barrow had brought the school CD player out of his office and placed it on the stage, while he waited with his hands folded neatly together for the remaining classes to sit down. It was playing a cacophony of noise, which Margery knew was unmistakably last year's recorder club charity Christmas CD. Her heart sank as they listened to the very warbly version of *Jingle Bells* and she realised exactly what this particular assembly must be about. Her dread was confirmed by the look on the faces of the teaching staff across from them. Mr Barrow jumped up out of his seat as the particularly awful version of *Silent Night* started, and turned the volume down.

'Thank you all for joining me at such short notice. I am afraid to say that this is going to be a very serious assembly indeed.' He addressed the children and staff gathered and then paused and cleared his throat, looking over for a moment at the empty spot where Mrs Smith would be sitting if she hadn't been suspended. 'Unfortunately, I have some extremely bad news which some of you may have heard bits and pieces of already. I feel it's very important that you all know what has happened.' He paused again as if not wanting to say what he had gathered them to say. 'Now, as you all will know by now, our music teacher Mrs Large was badly injured at the beginning of the week and unfortunately, during the early hours of this morning she passed away.'

A collective gasp of horror vibrated around the room. Clementine grasped for Margery's hand and squeezed it. Margery was gobsmacked. She had never truly considered that Mrs Large wouldn't make it. Not really.

Mr Barrow smoothed his black tie solemnly and then continued. 'I know that this must be a shock for everyone, and I want you all to know that you will be able to have discussion sessions with your teachers when we all return to class after the assembly. Also, Mrs Wiggins is on standby if anyone would like to talk to the school counsellor. Please do not feel silly for asking questions or needing to talk, that's what we staff are here for, to support you.'

Margery looked around the hall at the teachers lining the walls. She caught sight of Mr Daniels in her eyeline. His face was almost grey, as he slumped back against the wall.

'Mrs Large was an asset to this school and a huge part of our school family, and she will be dreadfully missed.' Mr Barrow fiddled with his tie again. 'Nothing we can do will ever be able to replace her, but all we can do is remember her and all she did for the school. The choir outings and recorder club trips to France, all her work with the drama lessons and concerts, and how fantastic a teacher she was.'

He looked at something written on his hand in smudged biro. 'Mr Large has asked that any donations go to the ICU unit at Ittonvale Hospital, and they can be given to your teachers to be left in Mrs Large's office on her desk please. Also, we will be holding a candle lighting ceremony out in the playground at three p.m. today.' He nodded to Mr Evans the PE teacher, who was sitting by several boxes of tealights. 'Now, please join me in a minute's silence for Mrs Large.'

-

The kitchen team returned to the canteen in a sour and grim mood. Margery felt sick. When Caroline had died it had been upsetting, of course it had, but this was so much worse. For one, Caroline had been so, so much older and so much eviller than Mrs Large could ever have dreamed of being. Before she had died, Margery was certain that not many of the teenage students could have known the miserable elderly lady who slung Friday's stingy chip portions to them, but everyone had known Mrs Large and most had liked her, by all accounts. It was as though the whole school were mourning together now as one. Margery started the collection for the hospital among the dinner ladies, wondering again about Officer Thomas's question a few nights ago. Could Mrs Large have had an enemy? Margery couldn't think of anyone who could have disliked her enough to do such a thing.

'Can't we do something more?' Clementine asked, as she boiled the peas for lunchtime. 'Something else to raise money for them. What about if we sell her favourite lunch or something? Put all the profit towards that.'

'That's a good idea, Clem.' Margery nodded. 'Though I don't think she ate anything particular to my knowledge.'

'She used to eat a cheese sandwich on brown bread and a satsuma every day,' Seren piped up from where she was setting up the cold fridge for sandwiches. 'Mrs Smith used to laugh at her about it in the staff room.'

That did sound like Mrs Smith. Margery had not heard a word since she had stormed away from them the night before. Good riddance, she thought. There was no need for that sort of thing in their lives at the moment.

'A cheese sandwich it is.' Margery nodded grimly. She got her special marker pens and began to fill in one of the little black boards they kept for labelling unusual cakes or special offers. She had to be quite careful with what they sold pre-packaged now with Natasha's Law; another thing she was concerned about Benjamin being terrible at understanding. Gloria was right about him, as much as she did not want to admit it. She was going to have to keep an eye out for him becoming too much of a liability.

'So, have you managed to find Sharon anything for Secret Santa yet, Karen?' Margery heard Clementine ask. She turned her head to watch this exchange suspiciously.

'I didn't get Sharon,' Karen said brightly. 'And I know what you're trying to do, Clem.'

'No idea what you're on about!' Clementine retorted, but Margery watched her slip out the little notepad she kept in the back pocket of her kitchen trousers and scribble something on one of the pages. She sidled up to Margery, smirking. 'I know that Karen hasn't got Sharon because Seren has.'

'How do you know...? No, I don't want to get involved. Can you not try and ruin this for one year?' Margery tried to sound firm, but she could not keep the smile out of her voice.

'Tell me who you got,' Clementine whispered. 'So I can write it in my little book.'

'No!' Margery laughed. 'I won't, you'll have to figure it out yourself.'

'Oh, I will Margery! Don't you worry about that!' Clementine pottered off to finish what she had been doing. Margery shook her head. Seren wandered over with the sanitiser spray and cloth and cleared her throat.

'I just wanted to tell you that I know about Mrs Smith asking you to help her,' she said. Margery looked up in surprise. 'And I understand why you don't want to, but she does have a very valid alibi and I think you should reconsider.'

Seren looked terrified to be speaking so outspokenly; her hands were shaking as she sprayed the saladette fridge and began to clean it.

'We can't, Seren.' Margery shook her head. 'She won't tell us the alibi, for one.'

'Just think about it, please. For me?' Seren pleaded. Margery sighed.

-

After she had cashed the till and they had cleared everything away, Margery counted the donations. They had raised over eighty pounds for Ittonvale Hospital; she felt a swell of pride at the kitchen team. Once the word had got out about the charity sandwich, they had had a queue of students and teachers so long that it snaked out of the canteen and into the corridor. She put the money into an envelope and then put the till back onto the dry store shelf before leaving and locking the door.

'Ready, Clem?' she asked the woman waiting for her in the kitchen. The other dinner ladies had already gone home for the day. They left together; Clementine waited for Margery to lock the kitchen door and then they walked through the canteen together and out through the corridor. Clementine took out her notebook.

'So, I saw Gloria put a Lynx aftershave set into her locker this morning so obviously she has Ben for Secret Santa,' Clementine said as they walked. 'And I got Gloria so that's ruled out...'

'Clem, please!' Margery laughed. 'I'm not going to tell you who I got.'

'Just give me a little hint, Margery, go on!'

Margery shook her head again; it felt like she had shaken it so much today that it might fall off at some point. 'No, you'll just have to continue your sleuthing.'

She had been expecting a queue again, but the doorway to Mrs Large's office was empty. Inside, the desk was covered in similar envelopes to the one Margery was holding, along with a huge number of homemade cards the students had obviously been making. She checked her watch and realised that everyone must be at the candle lighting ceremony in the playground. She added their card to the top of the pile, where it slid down behind the desk.

'Ooh, watch it, Margery,' Clementine said, she ducked down to rummage under the desk for it. 'God, there's loads down here.'

Margery's eye was drawn to the poster attached to the notice board above Mrs Large's computer screen. It had the Ittonvale school logo on it. She reached out and unpinned it from the board to look at it closer, realising it was advertising Ittonvale school's rendition of *Grease* from the last summer term.

From under the desk Clementine pulled out a recyclable shopping bag full of musical notation and one of plastic recorder parts which tipped all over the floor.

'What on earth was this doing down there?' she said, as the recorder parts rolled over the floor. Margery reached down to help her pick them up and scoop them into the bag. Her hand touched something that was not a recorder part and she pulled it back as if it had burned her.

'What's this, Clem?' She breathed, looking down at the item that had rolled out along with everything else. She stuffed the poster into her handbag, unthinkingly. Clementine picked it up in puzzlement, turning it over to reveal the glittery pink number six stuck to the pair of pliers.

'It's one of the tools from the storeroom!' She dropped the pliers on the floor with a thud. 'We need to call the police.'

–

Officer Thomas arrived at the school quickly and soon Margery and Clementine were sitting next to him in the headmaster's office, along with an extremely tired-looking Mr Barrow. The pair of pliers lay on the desk between them in a plastic evidence bag. Officer Thomas had left Symon overseeing the sweep of Mrs Large's office.

'I don't understand, I thought you checked the office,' Mr Barrow said. His tone was accusatory, but the circles under his eyes made him look defeated. 'I thought you checked all of their offices.'

'Whose?' Clementine asked, her eyes widening. 'Mrs Large's?'

'Mrs Large's. Rose's. Mine,' Mr Barrow said, numbering them on his fingers. 'They checked them all.'

'Mr Daniels?' Margery asked.

'He doesn't have one.' The headmaster shrugged. 'He's always worked from the library apparently.'

'We did check them,' Officer Thomas said coolly.

'Obviously not well enough.' Mr Barrow glared at him. 'So now you're back in my school doing the job you should have done properly in the first place. Who put it there?'

'That's what we're going to find out,' Officer Thomas said. Mr Barrow gave him a scathing look.

'If we found it after the room was searched it means that whoever put the stage up is still out there,' Margery said. 'It's the perfect place to hide evidence, isn't it?'

'You seem to be very sure that it was placed there afterwards,' Officer Thomas said and then looked over at Margery and Clementine. 'For all we know one of you put it there, the perfect crime.'

Margery felt her mouth opening in surprise.

'Us!' Clementine cried. 'Do you really think we'd have called you if we'd put it there? You gave Margery your number!'

Officer Thomas looked like he was going to answer her, but Mr Barrow cut him off.

'You can't be serious.' He scoffed. 'Why on earth would Margery and Clementine be involved in this? What's their motive?'

'They've been involved in things before,' Officer Thomas said quietly.

'Yes, but this all seems to revolve around the drama department,' Mr Barrow said. 'Not the kitchen staff.'

'We can't rule anyone or any department out,' Officer Thomas said coldly. 'Not until we've got to the bottom of this.'

'You'd better get to the bottom of it.' Mr Barrow gave him a hostile glare. 'I've had to suspend my deputy head.'

Officer Symon tapped at the door of the office; it creaked open. 'We haven't found anything else, Officer Thomas, but the sergeant is asking to see you.'

'I have to go.' Officer Thomas stood and went to follow Symon. 'We will get to the bottom of this, Mr Barrow. You'll see.'

He left, closing the door softly behind him. Mr Barrow pinched the bridge of his nose with his fingertips and closed his eyes, letting out a sigh.

'Do you really think Mrs Smith did it?' Clementine asked him.

'No.' Mr Barrow shook his head. 'But what can I do? The governors are out for blood, I had to placate them somehow and she can't prove either way whether it was her on the CCTV.'

'And you'd know if she'd been here since, wouldn't you?' Clementine said. 'Since you suspended her, I mean. That tool had to be put there by someone since.'

The headmaster rubbed his chin thoughtfully. 'That's true.'

'I don't understand why Officer Thomas is so jumpy now.' Margery scratched her head. 'He was a lot calmer the other day.'

'Well.' Mr Barrow sighed and slumped back in his chair. 'I don't think it's going very well for them by all accounts.' He leaned across the desk and lowered his voice.

'I shouldn't tell you this but, there were two people on the CCTV footage, and one person was already inside. So even if Rose is involved there was someone else with her.'

'Rose said there were no cards swiped in that day,' Clementine said before Margery could stop her.

'You've spoken to Rose? How is she?' Mr Barrow asked, then seemed to remember himself. 'I mean… well she's right. There wasn't, and it's not clear who was on the CCTV. The school couldn't afford a better system when we bought it. Anyway, both people were covering their faces.'

'How did the person inside get in, though?' Margery was confused about that part of the story. 'Not through the kitchen fire escape again?'

'Oh no.' Mr Barrow looked uneasy for a moment. 'Well. Unfortunately… there's ahh… well there's a blind spot.'

'A blind spot?'

'Yes… ah… like I said, we couldn't afford a better system or a system that went all around the building.' He winced. 'There's no footage of outside the school hall. They think that's how the first person got inside.'

'Oh my God,' Margery said.

'Margery, please do not swear,' Clementine said. 'So, there's no proof it's Rose anyway?'

'Not really.' Mr Barrow shook his head. 'But I don't have a choice.'

Margery thought for a moment about telling him of the odd man she had seen twice outside the school hall. She battled with herself for a moment, but then decided that there was no point if there was no security camera footage anyway. If Seren was right and Mrs Smith was not lying about her alibi, then maybe they shouldn't have been so quick to ignore her plea for help. It must have taken Rose a great deal of effort to give up so much pride and ask. Maybe, just maybe, Rose was right about Ittonvale school being involved; it did seem strange that Mrs Blossom's dog bag would be left outside their school, by a strange man at that.

Chapter Eight

They pulled up outside Mrs Smith's house just before nine the next morning. It was still early, but neither Margery nor Clementine could wait any longer. They had thought about going straight to her house after they had finally left the school but had put it off in case the police came up with anything new. Both had regretted it instantly when they had arrived home and spent the evening talking about nothing else. Margery hoped that Mrs Smith would be up and about already. If not, she was in for a rude awakening.

They parked on the road in front of Mrs Smith's beige house; her ginormous SUV took up too much of the driveway to park alongside it without being on the immaculate front lawn. Margery had been worried she would get lost, all the houses on the newer estates looked the same to her. Mrs Smith's house looked lovely at the moment; she had obviously spent the few days she had been out of work decorating. It was wonderfully Christmassy, the tasteful lights running along the eaves of the house twinkling in the early morning gloom. They wandered up the driveway, Margery admired the large wreath displayed proudly on the front door as Clementine rang the doorbell.

'Go away,' the electronic doorbell said. 'I'm not letting you in.'

Margery and Clementine stared at it in horror. The front door swung open and Seren appeared in front of them, wearing the usual comfortable, hooded sweatshirt she wore outside of work. She gave them a weak smile.

'For God's sake, Seren!' the doorbell cried. 'Don't let them in!'

'I'm so sorry, it's linked to her phone,' Seren said, gesticulating to the doorbell. 'She's in one of her moods. Come on in. You must be freezing.'

They entered the house and took off their coats and shoes; Seren placed them gently on the shoe rack. Margery thought of the last time they had been here. They had only seen the living room with all its duck egg and grey features. She was quite excited to see the rest of it. She vaguely remembered that Mrs Smith had a Le Creuset teapot with matching mugs and wondered what other wonders from John Lewis she would own.

Seren led them down the hallway, past the large wooden staircase with its elegant rose gold garland running up the banister and into the biggest home kitchen Margery had ever seen, as large as their kitchen at work. It was so horrifyingly white that it was almost blinding, and Margery found that if she squinted a bit she could imagine she was in a snowstorm. Everything was white except for the Aga range cooker and the vast, black American-style refrigerator taking up a huge swathe of the far wall. Clementine jokily asked Seren how much they charged it in rent.

Mrs Smith was slouched on an uncomfortable-looking stool at the huge breakfast bar in the middle of the room, fiddling with her phone. She did not look any happier than she had the last time they had seen her. Things were disintegrating fast if her outfit was anything to go by.

An old, hooded sweatshirt with Dewstow Fun Runners printed on it, another of the headmaster's things, Margery supposed. She looked a lot younger than she did normally, without a dot of make-up on her face and her hair in disarray. Margery felt a sudden, motherly urge to look after her.

'Good morning!' Clementine said cheerily. Mrs Smith glared at them both. 'Christ, where are your eyebrows?'

Mrs Smith glared at her, but it wasn't quite as menacing as usual. 'I was young in the nineties and noughties. No one had eyebrows then. It's not my fault they never grew back properly.'

'Can I ask you something?' Clementine continued, seemingly undisturbed by Rose's angry outburst.

'No,' Mrs Smith said, and then continued to ignore them. She was obviously not taking her suspension very well, if the dark circles under her eyes were anything to go by. Margery had never seen her outside of a smartly pressed suit and she was finding this new side to Mrs Smith very unsettling.

'Why do you always drive that massive car to work, when you only live about six feet away from the school?'

Mrs Smith rolled her eyes. Seren pottered over with a full toast rack and a cafetière and put them in front of her. She poured Mrs Smith a cup of coffee and passed her an empty plate that matched the coffee cup.

'I couldn't eat a thing, Seren,' Mrs Smith said, taking a piece of toast from the toast rack and reaching for the preserves in the middle of the breakfast bar. 'I'm much too upset.'

'Well, just have a go,' Seren said gently, as though she was Mrs Smith's mother and not twenty years her junior. She smiled at Margery and Clementine and gestured to the breakfast bar. 'Why don't you have a seat, ladies? I'll make us all some nice warming porridge.'

'We can't get up there!' Clementine said, outraged, as they looked at the tall red stools lining the breakfast bar. She turned to Mrs Smith who was slathering butter onto a piece of toast. 'We'll slip off and die, why don't you have a nice kitchen table with proper chairs?'

'It's called having *style* Mrs Butcher-Baker! Anyway, did you really only come here to criticise my house?' Mrs Smith said, finishing with the butter and then ladling several spoons of jam onto the single slice of toast. It sagged under the weight of the toppings. 'Or how much I enjoy a short but lovely drive in a nice car?'

'Yes,' Clementine said; Margery nudged her. Seren handed her a warm bowl of porridge and a spoon; she took it awkwardly, nodding in thanks.

'Fine.' Clementine looked at Margery and rolled her eyes. 'No.'

'What absolute gibberish have you decided to ask me now?' Mrs Smith said, her mouth full of toast. 'Or have you come to tell me you won't help me again? Just to rub it in.'

'Ooh I don't think they'd bother coming here for that,' Seren said, pouring a tooth-aching amount of golden syrup onto her own bowl of porridge, 'They could have just said that in a text.'

'Quiet, Seren!' Mrs Smith said, spraying crumbs all over the counter.

'Well,' Seren said, adding a big handful of chocolate chips to the porridge in her bowl, 'it's true, we've all got WhatsApp, haven't we?'

'We do!' Clementine beamed, getting her phone out of her cardigan pocket. 'Shall we set up a group on there?

We can call it The Three Musketeers! Oh no, there's four of us... er... The Fantastic Four! No, I think that's been done...'

'I would rather drink a supermarket own-brand glass of wine than ever add your number to my phone,' Mrs Smith hissed.

'We want to help, Mrs Smith,' Margery said, ignoring Clementine, who was still waving her phone around.

'Do you?' Mrs Smith asked, wearily. 'What changed your mind?'

'Well, firstly we want to know why you and the head-master fell out, when he's clearly still in love with you,' Clementine said, through a mouthful of porridge. 'He came into the canteen the other day to buy a bag of crisps and a photo of you in a heart fell out of his wallet.'

Mrs Smith looked lost for words for once. Margery kicked Clementine gently to silence her.

'Things at the school don't add up,' Margery said; Clementine nodded agreeably. 'And last night the police accused us of finding something we'd told them about.'

'They're grasping at straws,' Mrs Smith said, folding her arms.

'Yes, exactly,' Margery said. 'If they searched all your offices and are only finding things now then you can't have done it.'

Mrs Smith held her arms up in agreement. 'Exactly.'

'Or you did do it and got someone else to put the tool there,' Clementine suggested, rubbing her chin.

'What tool?' Mrs Smith looked between them both in confusion. 'Whose side are you on, Mrs Butcher-Baker?'

Margery took the poster out of her handbag and slid it over to Mrs Smith across the breakfast bar.

'We also found this in Mrs Large's office,' she said. 'It's obviously from Ittonvale school, but we can't think why she'd have it.'

Mrs Smith sighed and took it. 'They know each other. We all know each other.'

'Who?' Margery asked.

'Mrs Blossom and Mrs Large.' Mrs Smith took the poster and smoothed it from where it had been crumpled in Margery's bag. 'So, what makes you think you can magically help now?'

'Just trust us,' Margery said. 'We haven't let you down yet.'

'To let someone down, Mrs Butcher-Baker, you have to first pick them up,' Mrs Smith said, but she reluctantly slid from the stool. 'So, you'll help me, will you?'

There was something dreadful about seeing her feet bare and not stuffed into a designer heel; she looked practically tiny now to Margery.

Margery looked at Clementine, who nodded back. 'Yes.'

'Okay,' Mrs Smith said. Margery couldn't put her finger on what exactly it was but there was a definite and immediate change in her demeanour. It was like she was standing opposite a completely different person. 'Right then. Wait there, ladies.'

'Where are you going?' Margery asked, as Mrs Smith practically leaped from the stool.

'To get ready of course! We need to get to the bottom of this!'

Chapter Nine

They arrived at Ittonvale school just after ten o'clock, the frost still thick on the ground. Mrs Smith had insisted that they drive her there because, 'They know my car'. As it was, she still stuck out like a sore thumb, sitting in the middle of the back seat. They all did, as she had made them both follow her lead and put sunglasses on. Why she thought that would work as a disguise, Margery had no idea, but she went along with it anyway to keep the uneasy peace between them. Mrs Smith still looked terrifying. She was wearing what was obviously the weekend version of one of her usual ladies' trouser suits, underneath her ginormous winter coat.

They had been waiting for what felt like an age, in almost silence except for the radio on low. Ittonvale school car park was much the same as the one at Summerview school, and the building looked very similar too. Margery was not sure what she had been expecting. She knew they were much better off financially but that did not mean the playgrounds would be made with anything other than poured concrete. The drive through Ittonvale high street had been an eye-opener. Margery always forgot how breathtakingly beautiful Dewstow's neighbouring town was, though she did not envy the residents who owned the houses with thatched roofs. The upkeep must have been horrendously expensive, as pretty as they were.

Even the lovely flower boxes on the neat high street must have been high maintenance.

'Your driving is appalling, Mrs Butcher-Baker,' Mrs Smith sniffed from where she was lounging on the back seat. 'I don't know how you think you're going to pass your exam next month, truly dreadful.'

'What are we doing here, Rose?' Clementine hissed from the driver's seat, ignoring her remark. 'We could be at home right now listening to a nice episode of *The Archers*.' Margery nodded in agreement, the oversized sunglasses on her face wobbling. 'It's the weekend for crying out loud, do you know how much laundry we have to do? If we don't have an apron to wear on Monday, it'll be all your fault.'

'Shhh. You want to get to the bottom of this, don't you?' Mrs Smith said, pulling up her sleeve to look at her watch. 'They'll be here any minute.'

'Who, though, Rose?' Clementine said, aghast. 'You can't just force us to come here and then not even tell us why! Ridiculous.'

'Well, I think we'd all be more comfortable if your car wasn't full of so much rubbish,' Mrs Smith said, gesturing around at the assorted bottles of windscreen wash and engine oil on the back seat. Margery had been keeping them in the car ever since they had run out of windscreen wash driving down a long stretch of the M5 on a drizzly day. She turned to make a retort, but Mrs Smith suddenly leaned forward to stare through the windscreen, nearly knocking heads with her. A sleek silver saloon car drove past them. Margery ducked down as far as she could in the front seat.

The car parked in one of the numbered staff spaces opposite them. The door opened slowly, and Margery found herself holding her breath. A pair of very smart high heels exited the car first, followed by the rest of the woman's ample body, which was all tucked neatly into a pink trouser suit. She stood as she shut the car door and smoothed the creases from her jacket. Mrs Smith sucked in a deep breath.

'There she is…' she hissed. 'Rhonda Blossom. Have you ever seen an eviller witch?'

Margery and Clementine shared a look. The truth was, Margery thought as she watched Rhonda Blossom help a snail from the cold pavement into a neighbouring bush, the stranger in front of her did not seem evil at all. In fact, apart from the slightly over the top outfit, she looked unremarkable. Just a teacher going to work for an extra-curricular activity, using her spare time to do something nice for the school. Margery did not dare say how she felt to Mrs Smith. Not yet anyway. After all, there was still time for Mrs Smith to prove them both wrong.

Mrs Blossom continued to totter around to the other side of the car. She opened the passenger door, reached inside and pulled out a designer handbag with what Margery was sure must be a very fluffy wig resting on top of it.

'Is that?' Margery whispered.

'Yes,' Mrs Smith breathed out, in a soft voice Margery had never heard her use before. 'That's Mrs Ada Bones.'

They watched as Mrs Blossom gently scooped the Yorkshire terrier out of the handbag and plopped her gently on the ground. The dog was wearing a matching pink outfit, the fur on its head pulled up into a tiny ponytail and secured with a bow. Margery stared after them entranced, as Mrs Blossom hefted the straps of the large handbag over her shoulder and sauntered off towards the main entrance of the school, the dog scuttling along behind her. Margery could hear Mrs Blossom's heels clacking on the concrete from all the way over the other side of the car park.

'Okay.' Clementine watched Mrs Blossom's retreating back, her brow furrowed as she took in this new and strange piece of information. 'You're telling me that your arch nemesis is this woman and a tiny dog in a matching outfit?'

'Yes.' Mrs Smith was staring down at her fingernails now, refusing to look Clementine in the eye.

'But that's a such a small dog?' Clementine said, though it was a more of a question than a statement. 'You want me to be afraid of a ridiculously small dog? Wait, why did the dog have its own bag?'

'I'm not telling you to do anything...' Mrs Smith started to say but then looked away out of the window. 'The bag is for the dog's treats.'

'Such a small dog,' Clementine said again. 'That tiny, tiny dog is an evil mastermind? It has a teeny tiny ponytail for Christ's sake!'

'I never said that!' Mrs Smith snapped, finally turning to Clementine, who was still gesticulating madly at the spot Mrs Blossom and the dog had been. 'I just don't like the dog, okay?' Mrs Smith was busily collecting her things and stuffing them into her handbag. 'No more questions now please, Mrs Butcher–Baker. Right come on then, let's go, quick!'

'Go where?' Clementine asked, aghast. 'We can't go in there, look at it! They'll kick us out for being Dewstow scum.'

'Where's your sense of adventure?' Mrs Smith rolled her eyes at Clementine. 'Don't worry so much, I have an agreement with the security. Now come on!'

'Wait, I have so many questions!' Clementine cried. 'Where did she get the matching dog outfit? Do they make them for cats?'

Mrs Smith was already out of the car and slamming the door behind her. She moved so fast she was lucky not to catch her scarf in the door. Clementine groaned in exasperation and hurried after her, and Margery had no choice but to follow them.

--

Mrs Smith's 'agreement with security' turned out to be breaking in through an unlocked classroom window in Ittonvale's science department. They had both clambered inside after her, Clementine a lot less reluctantly than Margery.

Margery had not wanted to enter at all, had wanted to go back to the car and wait for them. She did not want to go scrambling in through someone else's classroom and knocking over some other school's Bunsen burners as they entered. But she supposed she had come this far, and she may as well see it through. At least then it would all be over, and she could go back to thinking about how many mince pies they needed to make for the last day of term.

Mrs Smith opened the classroom door and gingerly peered out into the corridor. Margery wondered how many times she had been here before as she gestured for them to follow her. She certainly seemed to know her way around the building. Margery found their own corridors at Summerview Secondary still felt like a maze, even after all the years they had worked there, but Mrs Smith seemed to know exactly where to go. Hopefully, they would be able to find their way back out again. They skittered down dark hallway after hallway until soon enough they were standing before Ittonvale Secondary School's main entrance.

The reception desk on the left behind the glass looked remarkably similar to their own. The walls and carpet didn't look all that different either. The only real difference was that the glass cabinets were full of awards and trophies, and the Christmas decorations were abundant and obviously new. None of the artificial trees in the reception area had that droopy look that Summerview's did from being stuffed away in a storeroom too many times, and the fairy lights were the new LED type that twinkled in festive patterns.

They shuffled past and into the main vestibule, Margery and Clementine following quickly behind Mrs Smith up the staircase to the first floor and along another long hallway. It was windowed on both sides, Margery gazed out at the school playing fields as they rushed past. They finally arrived at a set of double doors and Mrs Smith turned to them. Her face was serious, her mouth drawn into a thin line.

'Okay, listen please, this is important,' Mrs Smith said in her best teacher's voice, with her hand on one of the doors and the other pointing a finger at them both. 'I absolutely lied when I said I had a deal with the security here, so if anyone catches us it's every woman for herself, all right?'

'Well yes, we guessed that,' Clementine said, rolling her eyes. Mrs Smith raised her finger to her mouth and shushed her. She opened the door and the three of them crept through.

They were on a long balcony overlooking the school hall. It was much grander than their own, with a proper built-in stage that had actual curtains and a heavy-duty set of proper stage lights. No risk of their lights falling down, Margery thought grimly as she peered over the safety rail. It was a lovely space, well lit, with pretty and tasteful Christmas décor all through it. Student-made paperchains ran from one side of the room to the other. There was even an actual orchestra pit, with expensive-looking instruments and wooden chairs that would not give you splinters. Over in the corner was a ginormous Christmas tree, so large that the top of it was bent against the ceiling.

'Look at that piano,' Mrs Smith whispered, a tinge of jealousy to her voice as they peered down at the baby grand in the orchestra pit. 'I bet that one isn't broken or permanently tuned half an octave flat. Do you know how hard it is to rewrite every piece of music we get given?'

'I bet they have someone who can play the piano better than you as well,' Clementine said agreeably. Mrs Smith glared at her. 'Ooh look!' Clementine said, pointing down into the hall. 'There's that dog you're scared of.'

Mrs Blossom had entered the hall with a flourish. Mrs Ada Bones was waddling along behind her, her tiny legs going double time to keep pace. They were accompanied by who Margery assumed to be the staff of the school, though their demeanour was very different than the staff of Summerview. If Mrs Smith had tried to call a weekend Christmas concert meeting, there would have been absolute outrage and possibly a case of office vandalism. Maybe even a repeat of the day the year eleven students had dragged the least favourite English teacher's Mini Cooper in through the fire escape doors of the school hall. Yet the Ittonvale staff seemed happy enough to be there. Mrs Smith caught Margery's eye and gestured at the takeaway coffee cups most of them were holding.

'Ittonvale has its own takeaway coffee shop onsite,' she muttered in explanation. Margery felt her eyebrows raise of their own accord, thinking of their own sad filter coffee machine in the canteen that was nearly always leaking water all over the floor.

'What!' Clementine cried in outrage much too loudly. Mrs Smith shushed her, but there was no need as Clementine's voice was drowned out by the chatting staff as they poured in.

'How often do you come here?' Margery hissed to Mrs Smith. 'You seem to know your way around very well.'

'We used to do our teacher training days here, back when Summerview still had some money to join them.' Mrs Smith scoffed. 'So, I know my way around if that's what you're asking.'

Margery stared downward and saw that the rows of chairs were not the uncomfortable plastic kind that they were used to sitting on. The chairs at Ittonvale were hardwood, with proper padding. Mrs Blossom even had her own director's chair that had *Head of Drama* stitched onto it in gold lettering, very similar to the bag they had found. It could have been made by the school's home economics department, Margery supposed, but somehow she thought not.

Down below, Mrs Blossom strolled over to the front of the stage, grabbing the sheet music out of her handbag. She propped it up on the music stand, as she took her place on the raised conductor's podium in the orchestra pit. Mrs Ada Bones curled up at her feet as Mrs Blossom opened the wooden case to remove her conductor's baton. The tall woman with the mole on her nose and the neatly cut blonde bob, who Margery assumed was the music teacher, sat down at the piano and cracked her knuckles. The rest of the Ittonvale staff lined up on the stage and fell into a comfortable silence as they waited for their next instruction.

There was very little preamble, Margery noticed. No having to coax anyone to get up on the stage or bribe anyone to come to the rehearsal. No stopping anyone from escaping through a fire escape. It was all very alien.

'Right, are we ready all?' Mrs Blossom asked, before she counted them in gently.

As the hall filled with the sound of music, Margery watched Mrs Smith's face turn from its usual colour to an angry shade of red. Clementine started to laugh as what they were playing dawned on her. Margery shushed her to try and save Mrs Smith's feelings, though the hilarity was not lost on her either. She looked back down at the stage and saw the Ittonvale staff performing the very dance Mrs Smith had been teaching them not even a few days before.

'That's your terrible song isn't it, Mrs Smith?' Clementine asked. Margery did not know how no one had noticed them up here yet. Clementine had never had very good control over the volume of her voice.

'Yes,' Mrs Smith hissed, through clenched teeth. Her knuckles were white on the glass balustrade of the balcony.

'Well, this is a good excuse to write something better, I suppose,' Clementine said. 'Ooh, this is all very *Bring It On*, isn't it?' Margery wished she had never let Clementine borrow her library card to rent out early 2000's films on DVD. Clementine had had her own card revoked after she had lost two Stephen King books in a row and left the entire *Chronicles of Narnia* in a plastic bag under a seat on the bus home from work.

The doors at the back of the hall opened and a man arrived and sat down in one of the chairs at the back. Margery stared at him in recognition. He put his briefcase down on the floor next to him and sat back in the chair, stopping every now and then to listen to the performance.

'Clem, that's the man I saw!' It was Margery's turn to hiss too loudly as she grabbed Clementine by the sleeve of her coat.

'What man?' Mrs Smith asked, eyebrows furrowed. 'Where?'

'There, I saw him the other day at our rehearsal,' Margery said, in explanation. 'He's the person who dropped the bag.'

'You're kidding, Margery,' Clementine said, squinting down at him. 'Who is he?'

'Do you know him, Mrs Smith?' Margery asked the woman kneeling down next to her on her left. 'Now you've seen him in person?'

'Not at all,' Mrs Smith said, her eyes wide. 'I wonder why he'd be at their rehearsal too?'

Margery had for a while now been wondering whether it was all just a big coincidence with the bag and Ittonvale, but seeing the man again brought all her suspicions back. Ada Bones certainly seemed to know him. She had left her place at Mrs Blossom's side and gone to sit on the floor next to him. He reached down to give her head a gentle pat, careful not to mess up her delicate bow.

Clementine leaned over to get a better look at him. As she did so, the sunglasses that she had propped on top of her head fell off and started to tumble to the ground.

Margery saw it happen as if in slow motion. She grabbed Clementine to drag her up; there would be no hiding behind the clear glass panels of the balcony.

Mrs Ada Bones noticed the sunglasses land immediately and rushed over, clearing the length of the hall in seconds. She yapped and growled at the glasses, and the Ittonvale staff all turned to see what was causing the commotion. Margery caught Mrs Blossom's gaze as they turned to run, her eyes widening in shock at the sight of them. Mrs Smith was the first out, crashing through the double doors of the balcony. Every woman for herself indeed.

Chapter Ten

'I told you that dog was evil!' Mrs Smith cried as Margery and Clementine stumbled after her, their shoes slapping softly on the plush carpet. Margery raced down the stairs to the main foyer as fast as her old bones could carry her; she could feel her knees giving way under the strain. They whipped through the room. Clementine very nearly knocked over one of the Christmas trees in their haste, as she spun around to look behind her. Margery caught it just in time, flinging it back upright from where it had landed in her arms as several of the baubles fell from the branches and rolled around the foyer.

It was only as they reached the main reception area that they realised that they would not be able to escape the building's security doors without a pass. There was a horrible moment where they all stood panicking in the vestibule, Mrs Smith scrabbling at the door fruitlessly, unable to escape. The doors on the other side of the room slammed open, and Margery caught a brief glimpse of Mrs Blossom as she rushed in followed by her staff.

'Stop them!' Mrs Blossom cried; Margery winced as they rushed towards them, Mrs Blossom's face set in determination as she stormed over.

The teacher on Mrs Blossom's right side tripped on one of the Christmas baubles Clementine had spilt from the tree, nearly pulling her down with her as she fell.

Mrs Blossom managed to avoid the grasping hands, but her momentum was lost. Seizing the opportunity, Mrs Smith grabbed Margery by the cardigan, nearly pulling her over in the surprise of it, and dragged her down the long hallway they had entered by. Margery stumbled as they went but managed to stay upright, her lungs burning as they rounded the corner.

'Follow me!' Mrs Smith cried, letting go of Margery. They trailed her down another corridor and into a classroom, slamming the door behind them. Mrs Smith rushed immediately to the windows and tried to pry one open, but it was no use. They were trapped. She scrabbled at it with her fingernails, but it was too stiff.

'Oh God,' Margery said, her chest heaving with panic. 'What are we going to do?'

'Margery...' Clementine wheezed, scrabbling around in her bag for her asthma inhaler. 'Please do not swear.'

'Duck down, they'll see us through the glass,' Mrs Smith hissed.

She was right. The classroom door had a glass panel along the top, and they would be visible to anybody slightly taller than average, looking in from the hallway. Margery joined Clementine, who had ducked down in front of it, the room falling into an uneasy silence as they all listened desperately. There was noise in the hallway and Mrs Smith froze from where she had been still trying to force a window open. She quickly bobbed behind the teacher's desk at the front of the classroom.

'Did you see them, Tilly?' Margery heard Mrs Blossom ask, though her voice was muffled through the heavy classroom door. 'Which way did they go?'

'No idea,' said whoever Tilly was. Margery thought that maybe she was the tall teacher who had been playing the piano, with the mole on her nose. She assumed she was Mrs Blossom's equivalent to Mrs Large and hoped she wasn't tall enough to see them through the window. 'I'll check the doors.'

Margery felt a chill run down her spine as they waited for the handle of the door they were leaning against to turn above their heads.

'Don't bother. I bet she's long gone by now.' Mrs Blossom huffed. 'Probably went out of the fire escape.'

'The fire escape!' Clementine hissed. 'Why didn't we think of that!'

Margery shushed her. Mrs Smith glared at them both from her space under the desk.

'Let's go back to the hall and start the practice again.' Mrs Blossom said. 'We've got a lot to do today without distractions.' Margery could hear the annoyance in her voice, even through the wood of the door.

'Do you reckon she's here about the sheet music?' Tilly asked.

There was silence for a moment but then Margery could hear Mrs Blossom quietly chuckling. 'Don't worry about that. What is she going to do? These are my songs, remember? She stole them from me.'

Margery and Clementine both whipped their heads around to stare at Mrs Smith, who had deliberately turned away from them, a very confused expression on her face and her arms folded where she sat on the floor under the table.

'Anyway…' Mrs Blossom continued, 'we've got to think about securing the future of the Christmas concert, double security for one. We can't have her having anything else for her awful play, can we? It's all in the execution anyway, not the script!'

'This is the exact plot from *Bring It On*!' Clementine hissed under her breath. Margery shushed her again.

Mrs Blossom and Tilly's voices disappeared down the corridor and they sat in silence for a few minutes, Margery keeping an ear to the door to check they were not coming back. When the coast seemed clear, she turned to confront Mrs Smith, who was already standing and brushing carpet lint from her clothes.

'So... you stole their play?' Margery asked, rubbing her temples with her fingers. 'Then they stole it back? And, then you dragged us here to do what?'

'If I'm honest, the song did sound better when they did it,' Clementine said earnestly. 'When we sing it sounds like a load of old typewriters falling down the stairs and don't even get me started on the dancing. Karen and Sharon look like they're being electrocuted when they get going.'

Mrs Smith leaned back against the desk, ignoring Clementine completely.

'I didn't steal the play,' she murmured from between gritted teeth. 'I don't know what she's talking about.' She closed her eyes and drew in a deep breath. When she opened them again, she seemed to have regained control of her emotions. 'And we came here to find out what's going on, Margery. Nothing more nothing less.' She looked genuinely upset; it was unnerving to Margery who before this week could never have imagined a single crack in the veneer of Mrs Smith's usually cold exterior. 'Mrs Large is dead for God's sake. Surely that's a more important detail than who may or may not have stolen a play?'

'You're going to have to do better than that, Rose,' Margery said, as she sighed and leaned against the door. 'Why should we believe you?'

'Fine. Look, just let me explain.' Her voice cracked and she cleared her throat. 'Long story short, Rhonda Blossom and I used to be co-owners together at IMDB.'

'The film review website?' Margery asked, trying and failing to keep the scepticism out of her voice. Clementine looked just as confused as she did.

'No.' Mrs Smith looked at her like she had two heads. 'The Ittonvale Musical Drama Band of course. Anyway, we had a falling out and we've hated each other ever since.'

'Oh my God.' Clementine exhaled. 'You did that performance of *The Pirates of Penzance* at Dewstow Town Hall in 1997! Remember we went to see that one, Margery?'

'We did.' Mrs Smith beamed at the memory of a former triumph. 'We were a force to be reckoned with in those days. Rhonda and Rose, the dream team. Never a dry eye in the house, and always a standing ovation! We were in a Fleetwood Mac cover band, you know.'

'Which one were you?' Clementine asked. 'Mick Fleetwood?' Mrs Smith ignored her.

'Well, what happened?' Margery asked, still confused. 'Why did you fall out?'

Mrs Smith glared at her but continued anyway. 'She got a job that I wanted.'

'What job?'

Mrs Smith was suddenly quiet for once, and Margery had a realisation. 'Ooh. A drama teacher job... but at Ittonvale school?'

Mrs Smith nodded. 'Of course. Look around you, Mrs Butcher-Baker. Think of what I could have achieved if I'd got her job here. If she hadn't stolen my lesson plan and done it first, it wouldn't have looked like I'd stolen it, would it?'

'Wait, she stole your lesson plan?' Clementine asked. 'So of course, you'd steal her Christmas concert now!'

'No!' Mrs Smith shook her head wildly. 'I didn't take their Christmas concert! We've been doing rival concerts for years now, why would I steal this one? It's not my style. I mean, yes. I've been having a bit of writer's block lately, but I wouldn't steal someone else's work, that would have made me as bad as her. What do you take me for?'

Margery examined her face for the lie but could not find one, in fact she seemed overly sincere. She sat down heavily at a nearby desk. 'What's the plan, then?'

'I still think they have something to do with the stage lights,' Mrs Smith said. 'I just don't know what, or how to find out.' She gestured at them. 'You're supposed to be the detectives, aren't you?'

Clementine made a face at that. Margery winced.

'Well, we solved that one case, pretty much by accident,' Clementine said. Margery nodded in agreement. It really had been quite accidental. They were always declaring themselves the dinner lady detectives, but it was mostly for the irony of it all. Mrs Smith's unwavering faith in them made her feel useless.

'What are you going to pay us in anyway?' Clementine asked suspiciously. 'There's been no mention of payment, has there Margery? For our services, I mean. We take PayPal now, you know, I've got the app. You'll have to let us know if you're going to pay us that way though, because I can't remember the password.'

Mrs Smith looked at Clementine as though she had never seen her before in her life.

'Well, what do you want?' she asked testily.

'We want you to go back in time and buy us loads of bitcoin when it was cheap.' Clementine laughed. 'No, wait. Ergh… erm…'

'We want to not be in your Christmas concerts any more,' Margery said. Clementine oohed.

'Yes. That.' Clementine nodded, taking Margery by the hand and looking appreciatively into her eyes. 'The whole kitchen team, not just us.'

Mrs Smith groaned. 'Fine! But only if I'm off the hook entirely, and you still have to perform in this year's concert.'

'What!' Clementine exclaimed.

'I'll need all the help I can get for this year's.' Mrs Smith shook her head. 'That's the deal, take it or leave it.'

'Fine, fine,' Margery said, shaking her head. 'Now let's get out of here, we can't get caught hanging around. We'll get arrested if they find us.'

'Or worse,' Clementine said, tapping her fingers to her lips thoughtfully, 'Made to star in Mrs Blossom's play as well.'

Mrs Smith rolled her eyes but then nodded begrudgingly. 'I suppose you're right. Come on, let's sneak out through the fire escape like they said we would. I'll be amazed if they haven't got security doing the rounds already, we've got to get out quick.'

They made their way to the classroom door and Margery put her hand on the handle. She thought of something suddenly and turned back to Mrs Smith, who was waiting behind her.

'Wait, if you didn't steal the play, then how did you end up with it?'

'Mrs Large gave it to me.'

'Mrs Large?' Margery turned to stare at her incredulously. 'Did she steal the play, do you think? Why would she do that? How did Mrs Blossom end up with it, did she give it to her?'

'I don't know.' Mrs Smith shook her head. 'I mean, she's always helped with parts of the play, the more musical bits anyway, and she's always written the sheet music for it all. But this is the first time she's given me a full play to work with. I thought she was just feeling adventurous this year, ready to join in a bit more. I know I'm always a bit of a tyrant about it, but I've always been open to other people's ideas.'

It didn't make any sense at all. Why and how would Mrs Large have taken the sheet music from Ittonvale? When would she have even found the time? Margery shook her head. It seemed very strange indeed.

They finally left the classroom and crept down the hallway, Mrs Smith leading them to the fire escape at the end of the neighbouring corridor. Margery had a horrible feeling that opening the door would set off all number of alarms, but it did no such thing. They found themselves miraculously free and rushing out into the car park.

It was pouring with rain as they hurried through. Margery shuffled as fast as she could in her sensible slip-on shoes, but by the time they managed to clamber into the car they were all soaked through. Margery slid into the passenger seat, wishing she had taken off her soggy cardigan, as water dripped from her face. She took the soggy handkerchief Clementine offered from her own cardigan pocket and tried to dry herself with it.

'Come on then, Clem, let's get out of here,' she said, wringing the water out of the fabric of the handkerchief.

'Yes, please let's,' Mrs Smith muttered grumpily from the back seat. She had somehow managed to maintain her sleek haircut under the onslaught of the weather. 'I've had quite enough of this place for a decade, let alone a day.'

'You're the one who dragged us here!' Clementine said, turning around to chastise the woman sitting behind her. 'And we can all see how well that turned out, they've probably got people watching for us on the way… oh… look, look who it is!'

Margery turned to see what she was pointing at. Walking as fast as they could through the rain to an expensive-looking car parked behind them, was the man in a smart suit they had seen at Summerview's and now Ittonvale's rehearsals. She recognised him instantly. He was carrying the briefcase they had seen in the hall in one hand, holding an umbrella in the other. Under that arm he also held Mrs Ada Bones, who looked very upset that her own smart outfit was getting wet. Clementine gasped next to Margery.

Margery squinted into the rear-view mirror at him as he set Mrs Ada Bones down so he could unlock his car. He shook the excess water from his umbrella and then popped both it and the dog inside on the passenger seat. 'Gosh Clem, I wonder what he was doing here.'

'Or where he's going,' Mrs Smith said darkly, as they watched him clamber into the car.

He reversed out of the parking space and pulled off slowly into the wet car park. The tyres almost leaving an imprint on the concrete for a split second in the flash flood, water flicking from the wheels as he manoeuvred slowly.

'Probably planning to sneak around at another school, Margery.' Clementine nodded seriously. 'Him and that ugly dog Mrs Smith is scared of.'

'Hey, I'm still here!' Mrs Smith barked. 'Well, what are you waiting for? Get after him, let's find out where he's going.'

'All right then.' Margery flinched as Clementine cracked her knuckles together and then began backing out of their own parking space, as though she were starring in a James Bond film and not merely a middle-aged dinner lady. 'Let's follow him.'

'Oh no you don't.' Margery grasped Clementine's hand weakly, trying to get her to stop. 'We've had enough trouble lately as it is.'

'Come on, Margery!' Clementine said, looking over her shoulder as she manoeuvred the car out of the space. 'We've come this far, haven't we? Aren't you even a little bit interested in where he's going or what he was doing at the school the other day?'

'Of course I am,' Margery said. She looked over at Clementine, whose face was set determinedly as she peered into the rear-view mirror. 'But this isn't a good idea.'

'It's a splendid idea!' Mrs Smith said. 'Don't be such a wuss, Margery!'

'Yes, come on, Margery!' Clementine scoffed at her again. 'We won't let him see us, we'll just find out where he's going and then go home. Anyway, I've got a special detective pass, remember?'

'Ceri-Ann made that for you on her computer!'

'Exactly.' Clementine nodded. 'And I laminated it to keep in my purse for when it's needed.'

Margery sighed. She was clearly outnumbered. Clementine and Mrs Smith together were a terrible combination. She made sure her seatbelt was buckled as Clementine began to follow after him.

Chapter Eleven

Clementine drove the car, in what could have possibly won the record for the world's slowest pursuit. Almost as slowly as the day former kitchen manager, Caroline, had crashed her mobility scooter into the glass window of the fish and chip shop on Dewstow high street.

Clementine had her tongue stuck out in concentration as they followed behind the car rolling leisurely through the car park. It reached the school exit gate and slowed for a moment before pulling out onto the main road. To Margery's distress, Clementine waited mere seconds before shifting into a higher gear as they accelerated after him in a squeal of tyres.

'Slow down a bit, Clem!' Margery shrieked. She found herself stamping down on the brake pedal which did not exist in the passenger side of the car.

'Oh yes of course, don't want him to know it's us do we!' Clementine smiled. She was enjoying this far too much for Margery's liking.

'Well, he'll definitely know we're following him if you crash into the back of his car!'

Clementine snorted at that, but she did slow down ever so slightly, just as the car in front of them seemed to take off like a rocket. It zoomed away towards the roundabout at the end of the road at an alarming rate, water slamming up into the air at the force and splattering down onto their windscreen. Clementine increased the speed of the windscreen wipers and they swished back and forth haphazardly. Mrs Smith had pulled herself up through the middle of the front car seats so she could see better, like she was the navigator for this horrendous mission.

'Speed up for God's sake, Mrs Butcher-Baker,' Mrs Smith snapped. 'Don't listen to your wife, she's an idiot, we're about to lose him!'

'Oh Christ,' Clementine said, changing gears with much more force than Margery thought was warranted, accompanied by a crunching sound the car did not usually make. 'Just when you think you've got used to second gear, off you go into third.'

Margery grasped at the passenger side roof handle desperately and clutched it for dear life as the car picked up speed. They rolled right around the roundabout after the silver car; Clementine barely stopped to check the road was clear before they were already swinging around it and pulling out onto a different road. They bowled down the hill after the man. Margery felt her stomach drop as though they were free-falling on a roller-coaster; the radar speed sign they passed showed that they had reached an ungodly speed of thirty-two miles per hour. They were still picking up the pace in an effort to keep up.

'For God's sake, Clem!' Margery squealed in uncon-cealed fear. 'Slow down! You'll kill us all. This road is a forty mile an hour limit!'

Clementine turned to quickly flash her a nervous look, but continued anyway, her knuckles white where they were clutching the steering wheel. The car engine roared. Behind Clementine's head, Margery could see the scenery whipping by through the driver's side window. The wind and rain had been battering the trees on the skyline as it was. She could barely see them as they flew past, now approaching a set of traffic lights at the bottom, a river of water flowing from the car's wing mirror and along the window. To her surprise, they had left Itton-vale completely and were headed at full speed the short distance back to Dewstow. She had been so sure he would be headed to a destination nearer the school. He flew through the traffic lights in his car, just as they went amber and then red. Clementine slammed on the brakes hard. The car skidded to a violent stop. Margery felt as though they might all fly through the windshield.

'Christ!' Mrs Smith cried from the back seat as she was flung forward and then landed back hard. 'We'll lose him, Clem!'

'I know!' she said. 'But I can't go through a red light, I don't even have a real licence yet. We can't risk getting points!'

The lights changed and Clementine moved the car again, but it was too late. They drove around in the rain for a while longer looking for him, but to no avail.

–

Margery's nerves had been in tatters by the time they got home. Clementine's speedy driving through the town centre had not helped one bit. It seemed that now she had worked out third gear it was all she could do. They had dropped Mrs Smith off at home on the way; her house had only been around the corner from where they had lost the man at the traffic lights. Margery felt very much as though they had wandered into enemy territory and the battle lines were drawn far too close to theirs.

They had immediately had dinner and gone to bed when they arrived home, though Margery had felt far too rattled to eat. After concocting the entire debacle, Mrs Smith had washed her hands of the whole thing, telling them it was their job to sort as detectives.

Margery rolled over in bed and into the empty space that usually contained Clementine, who must already be up and downstairs. She had woken a few hours before to Clementine spooning her as she usually did, so she could not have been gone long. Pumpkin, who had obviously decided that a lady spending more time in bed was fantastic, had joined her on Clementine's side of the bed. Margery had nearly crushed her as she turned over. It was unusual for Clementine to be awake before her, unusual for Clementine to be awake so early at all. Margery got up and wandered downstairs with the cat in her arms.

'Don't listen to her!' Clementine said, glaring at the cat as Margery entered the kitchen with Pumpkin in her arms. 'She's been fed, it was the first thing I did when I got up.'

Margery smiled and plopped Pumpkin down gently on the floor. The cat weaved around her legs as she put a slice of bread into the toaster and turned the kettle on.

'Aw, she is lovely though, isn't she?' Clementine said, as Pumpkin wandered over to her so she could scratch behind her ears. 'Maybe she can just have a very small second breakfast. I'm thinking of making her an Instagram page, Margery. Now I've got the hang of the phone.'

Margery rolled her eyes at the exchange. 'You're up early,' she said, though it came out as more of a question than a statement.

'Yes. Well.' Clementine looked guiltily at the notes she had been writing at the kitchen table. 'I'm just trying to work this all out.'

'You know…' Margery said, as she buttered her breakfast, 'I did have an idea, but it's more trouble than it's worth, Clem. We'll have to be careful if we go ahead with it.'

Clementine picked up the pad and pen she had been using to write suspects for Mrs Large's murder onto from the table. 'What is it, Margery? It's worth a go, isn't it? For Mrs Large. Even if it takes ten years, we'll solve it.'

'Well, I hope it doesn't take ten years,' Margery said, with sudden alarm. She could see all their lovely plans for retirement melting away under the sheer force of Mrs Large's death. She sat down at the table and reached for her yarn bag on the chair next to hers. There was only a week left to finish the crochet robins for Dawn and she had managed a grand total of three.

'Well, I can remember the number plate is all.'

'The number plate?' Clementine asked, drawing away on the notepad, she looked up. 'Oh… the man's number-plate?'

'Yes,' Margery said, peering at the clock which showed the hideous time of nine thirty. She had slept for far longer than she had meant to. Margery told Clementine the numberplate.

'Okay.' Clementine wrote that down. 'Can we search that online do you think?'

'I think we can use the DVLA website?' Margery shrugged. 'Shall we have a go?'

'I'll boot up the PC!' Clementine cried excitedly. Margery and Clementine had a very old and very dusty Windows PC in one corner of their spare room. Clementine had once taken it apart with a screwdriver and then taped it all back together when she had lost the screws because, 'the fan is too noisy, Margery,' and it had never been quite right since. Though Clementine did still use it occasionally to play the copy of The Sims she had accidentally stolen from the library twenty years before.

'No, good Lord, no!' Margery cried back. 'We can use the iPad. It'll take us twenty years to work out if you have to boot that old thing up.' She marched into the living room to fetch it.

'While you're setting that up, I'll do my advent calendars.' Clementine had several chocolate advent calendars lining the wall above the electric fireplace, and one stuffed with gin miniatures that she opened in the evening. Margery was not entirely pleased with the gin calendar, as it coincided quite horrifically most of the time with Clementine's 'Christmas testing' of supermarket own brand Baileys.

'No, don't start doing that, it'll take too long,' Margery sighed, sitting back down at the table. Clementine got up from her seat anyway and opened the kitchen cupboard. She pulled the refill bag of Quality Street they had bought at the supermarket the other day.

'You know what the worst thing about Christmas is now, Margery?' Clementine began, ignoring Margery's plea to sit down as she opened the bag and poured it into the nearly empty Quality Street tin lying on the kitchen table. 'They got rid of the toffee deluxe but not the toffee penny.'

Margery hummed in agreement as she turned the iPad on and waited for the screen to jump to life. 'That's true, Clem.'

'And its replacement is simply awful.' Clementine picked up one of the sweets in its blue wrapper and glared at it. 'Chocolate brownie for crying out loud! Practically inedible. Why couldn't they add another gooey one?'

'Ooh, like a raspberry to go with the strawberry?'

'Yes!' Clementine said. 'Or a softer, more tooth-friendly toffee penny at the very least, really! If I was the head of quality at Nestlé, I'd hang my head in shame. How many more poor souls will lose a filling over this Christmas season? It's a health hazard. We should report them to the council really, at the very least.'

Margery chuckled, logging into the handheld device and finding the right thing to press to load Google. They had both come on leaps and bounds with technology recently; there had been free computer lessons at the library in the summer, so they had both gone along. Clementine dressed in disguise so they wouldn't make her pay her fines. Margery marvelled at how easy it all was now she had been shown how to do things; they even did banking and car insurance online now. She supposed she had been reluctant before because they had never had any involvement with computers in their work life and the longer they went without using technology, the more alien it felt. Once the DVLA website was loaded she tapped the car registration into the search feature.

'Any luck?' Clementine said, through a mouthful of chocolate.

The screen had loaded and was suggesting a vehicle to her, she clicked Yes on its suggestion of a white BMW and it loaded another page.

'Hmmm.' She shook her head. 'I don't think this is going to be much help. It just tells you if the car is taxed and has an MOT. Not who owns it.'

'Huh.' Clementine sat back in her chair and folded her arms. 'Well, would the police know that kind of thing, do you think?'

'I dare say they would.' Margery nodded, handing Clementine the iPad to look at. 'Do you think we should call them?'

'Yes.' Clementine picked the glasses up from the chain around her neck, put them on and glanced at the screen. 'But maybe we shouldn't tell them why we want to know.'

Margery agreed. 'No, they're already being strange, and we don't want them to suspect us more, do we?'

'Maybe we could go and see Gary?' Clementine suggested. 'See what he knows about the records and the locks and that kind of thing? I bet he'd have some answers. He might know who can get in and out of the storeroom.'

Margery hummed at that, taking a Quality Street from the bowl in the middle of the table. 'Not a bad idea.'

'All right, what's Officer doodah's number then?' Clementine grasped for her phone. 'I'll give him a ring.'

Margery took her own phone out and found Officer Thomas's number on speed dial. She put the phone on speaker and lay it in front of them on the table, and they waited in anticipation. The phone rang twice before the policeman's voice answered.

'Thomas,' he said gruffly.

'Hello,' Clementine said. 'It's us, the dinner lady detectives.'

There was a long pause. When he finally answered there was a distinctly defeated tone to his voice. 'Hello Mrs Butcher-Baker, how can I help you?'

'Can you run a numberplate for me?' Clementine continued. 'Is that how you say it? Run a numberplate? Like in the movies.'

'No and no,' he said. 'Unless you have a good reason. Is this to do with our case?'

'A bit,' Clementine murmured. Officer Thomas sighed.

'Why do you want me to check the numberplate?'

'We, well Margery saw a man outside the school and then we saw him again and followed...' Margery shushed her; it would not do for the police to find out the circumstances in which they had seen him again, or that they had followed him. 'Er, we saw him in a car park and we just wondered...'

'Was he inside the school?' Officer Thomas asked.

'Well, no,' Clementine admitted.

'And did anyone other than Margery see him?'

'Also no.'

'Ladies...' Officer Thomas sounded stern now and not a little bit angry. 'I need you to only ring when you have information viable for the case. Please stop wasting my time. I'll speak to you soon.'

The phone call ended suddenly.

'He hung up on us,' Clementine gasped. 'What are we going to do now?'

There was a sudden loud rapping on the front door. They looked at each other. There was another knock, even louder than the first. Margery stood up from her chair slowly and looked from the kitchen, through the living room, at the hallway front door in dread.

There was another, even more insistent knock, the letterbox slamming under the force of it. Clementine gasped, her hands over her mouth and her eyes wide. Margery decided that she would have to be the brave one this time. This problem would not go away on its own and her mother had always said it was better to face the music now, rather than later. Her mother had also once hidden behind the sofa when a neighbour had come over to ask for the money she had borrowed, but Margery supposed it was better to do as she said and not as she did.

She left Clementine wringing her hands in the kitchen and crept to the front door, wishing for the millionth time in her life that they had had a peep hole installed. She took a deep breath and braced herself before opening it gingerly.

'Hello, Margery.'

'Oh.' Margery could not stop her eyes widening in surprise. 'Hello, Dawn.'

She could feel her heart rate returning to normal at the sight of Dawn standing in the porch, with a sour look on her face.

'I thought I'd try and catch you before you went out for the day,' Dawn said, 'because I need all of the robins you've made. Father Brown is very insistent that we begin to decorate the church hall if we're going to have everything done for the play.'

'Oh. Yes,' Margery said, turning back into the living room to grab her crochet bag. She brought it out into the hallway, Dawn peered down her nose at it. 'I... I haven't managed many, if I'm honest.'

She pulled out the three crochet decorations she had finished and handed them over, Dawn stared silently at them for a moment.

'Well,' she said, finally, 'if that's all you've managed.'

'It is,' Margery said.

Dawn shook her head and put them in the shopping bag she held under her arm. 'All right then. I'll be back in a few days I suppose, unless you'd prefer to spend your time fostering a few kittens?'

She gave Margery a hopeful look and Margery could feel her fixed smile becoming even more forced.

Chapter Twelve

'I know you were disappointed you didn't get to buy yourself a Christmas voucher, Seren,' Clementine said as she helped Seren put the frozen food delivery away. 'But at least now you can get Benjamin something nice for Secret Santa instead.'

'Stop trying to get people to tell you their Secret Santa,' Gloria said, rolling her eyes. Clementine glared back. 'Why do you want to know anyway?'

'So, I can get the person who's got me to buy me a new cleaver,' Clementine said, righteously raising herself to full height.

'Why on earth do you need a cleaver?'

'I'm sorry, Gloria, but what if we ever need to butcher a pig?'

'Why in God's name would we ever need to do that? The meat all comes in vacuum sealed.'

'Gloria, please do not swear!' Clementine chastised her and then turned back to Seren. 'What would you like for Secret Santa anyway, Seren?' Margery was sure she saw Sharon look over in interest; Clementine seemed to notice her looking too, taking out her sleuthing notebook to write something down. 'If you could have anything?'

'Probably a train ticket,' Seren said, rubbing her chin with her fingers. 'I tried to get a train once, but it didn't show up. I always said I'd try again but I haven't got around to it since.'

They were all holed up in the kitchen after lunchtime was over. Well, all except Benjamin. Gloria had sent him back into the canteen to finish cleaning the tables as a punishment, after he had handed out his own homemade mince pies which had turned out to have been made with actual mince only an hour before he had asked what ingredients went into a banana and custard. Margery was becoming more worried about him by the day, and Gloria grew more and more annoyed by her lack of discipline with him.

There was half an hour before they had to run off to the next Christmas concert rehearsal Mr Daniels had arranged. He was holding it in the tiny drama studio today so that the new lights could be fitted in the main hall. Margery was dreading it already. She knew everyone else felt as disturbed as she did that the rehearsals were continuing in the wake of Mrs Large's funeral which was being arranged as they spoke.

'I already know who you got for Secret Santa anyway, Gloria.' Clementine smirked at her smugly. 'Just you wait, I'll know them all by the time we do the present giving.'

Margery rolled her eyes. 'I've just got to go and phone through the ordering. Try not to kill Clem before I get back, will you Gloria?'

'I can't promise anything,' Gloria said, glaring at Clementine as she waltzed off, Secret Santa notebook in hand.

Margery chuckled to herself as she made her way into her office in the dry store, pulling out her own phone as she did. It was not a fancy new one like Gloria or Karen had, but she could call the food suppliers with it. And she could message Clementine on the odd days they spent more than half an hour apart. Not that Clementine ever managed to reply in anything but gif form on their kitchen WhatsApp group.

Margery had always found it easiest to work in the tiny dry store cupboard just off the main kitchen. Though three walls were floor-to-ceiling shelving units, there was just enough space to fit a filing cabinet and a miniscule desk big enough to cash up the till at. The windowless room could get a bit hot during the summer months. The only air that could get in was through a largish metal vent just below where the wall met the ceiling and it never seemed to cool the room at all. But to Margery the dry store was a relative haven, especially on days where everything in the main kitchen seemed to be going terribly wrong. She sat down in the wheeled chair at the desk and thought about turning on the ugly desktop computer that rested on it, thinking better of it in the end. She had only ever used it once when Mr Barrow had installed it for her, and she had immediately deleted several years' worth of health and safety paperwork from the school's shared drive by mistake. She had been too terrified to use it since.

Margery picked up the clipboard with the ordering sheets still attached to it from the computer desk. She was becoming much better prepared every day that she did her new job, feeling more competent in herself. She knew when she had taken on the management role, that it was not only the day-to-day activities of the kitchen team and lunch menu she would be responsible for, but there was a big difference in knowing about the work and actually having to do all the work. There were stock takes and costings to keep on top of, and buffets and canapés to arrange for governors' meetings and afterschool events. The job had seemed quite easy when she had been watching Caroline do it, but it was more of a balancing act than she could ever have imagined.

The mediocre kitchen budget was an entire issue in itself. She was expected to be able to fulfil all these things on a shoestring, while keeping up to date with all the daily and weekly food safety paperwork and staff training. There seemed to be new legislation coming in all the time too. The newest calorie labelling ran alongside her usual menu, so it was not difficult to plan, but it was yet more time taken from the day. There were barely enough moments during the workday to fit all of that in, let alone join in with silly Christmas concerts and monthly meetings with the headmaster. It was no wonder that their last manager had had such a bitter sense of humour and served rubbish food. It would be much easier for Margery to go back to using mostly frozen, bought-in goods, but she was determined to stick to her new, healthier and more nutritious menus.

It had been one thing to be Caroline's go-to person when she was the manager, but quite another to be in charge of all the big decisions herself. Her calendar was completely full of her own squiggly writing. She had never thought about the sheer amount of governors' meetings and summer fete bake sales the small catering team actually had to supply food for until now. It was almost overwhelming after decades of simply being a dinner lady. Some days it felt like the only thing that kept her going was Clementine's unwavering belief in her, and bourbon biscuits.

Still, she was doing okay today, she thought, as she double-checked the ordering before placing the phone call, even with the big heaving plate of things to do. The

Christmas lunch planning for the next week was already finished, though it had taken her most of the weekend. She just had to write the ordering list and make sure it was all there in a week's time when they would be serving the entire school. She was getting more and more nervous about it. It was the day before the Christmas concert dress rehearsal and on the last Wednesday of term, before they broke up for Christmas on the Friday. Plenty could go wrong before then.

Hopefully, after that she could relax a bit and get ready for the long two-week Christmas break, free from thoughts of school until they returned on the third of January. Maybe they would crack open the nice bottle of Cava they had been saving since they got married in the summer. She smiled to herself thinking of the presents she had already bought Clementine, who reverted to being a child at Christmas. They were hidden in a place she would never look, in the under stairs cupboard behind the vacuum cleaner.

Margery had given Ittonvale school and their drama department a great deal of thought since Saturday. Mrs Smith, a nightmare in herself, was right, though Margery would never tell her that to her face. There was something spookier going on. Who had entered the school building at the weekend and let another person in? Who was the strange man they had seen outside the school hall?

Clementine had vaguely mentioned that they should go to Mrs Blossom's house in Ittonvale and confront her in person, but Margery had thought that a terrible idea. For one thing, they had no proof, really, that there was anything to suspect her for. For another, they did not know where she lived. There was the small matter of both schools doing the same concert, but both Mrs Smith and Mrs Blossom seemed adamant that they owned that particular music. Rose swore that Mrs Large had given it to her. Had Mrs Large also given her concert to Ittonvale school? Why? It was a conundrum indeed.

Something pricked her ears as she settled back down with her notepad. At first, she thought that maybe Gloria or Clementine might be calling her from the main kitchen, but when she stood and opened the storeroom door and peered out, they were nowhere to be seen. Closing it again she stood as quietly as she could and listened. It was garbled and not distinct at all, but she could still hear the low voice talking quietly from some unknown place.

Margery briefly considered the possibility that someone had left a radio on in the dry store somewhere but shook the thought away almost immediately. The only person who used the room, for anything other than grabbing a tub of dried herbs or some flour, was her, and she did not have a radio. It must have been coming from somewhere else. She looked around, trying to determine the source. Her eyes landed on the only place it could possibly be from. The vent near the ceiling.

Grabbing her chair, she pushed it up against the side of the wall and stepped up on it, forgetting for a moment that it was a wheeled chair and nearly spinning herself right off it again. She looked around, desperate for something else that would support her weight. Her eyes finally landed on the heavy, plastic kick stool in the corner. Clementine would sometimes borrow it to use as a coffee table in the staff room; the rest of the time it lived in the dry store, gathering dust.

Margery grabbed it from the corner and pushed it against the wall, clambering up onto it, then she put her ear against the wall and listened eagerly. Her head reached just below the vent. The low voice sound had stopped, but then there was something higher and less human. It almost sounded as though an animal had become trapped inside. The noise stopped as soon as it had started. She waited patiently for what felt like forever, but it was no good. Stepping back down from the stool she crossed her arms and peered up at the vent thoughtfully, wondering where it could lead. She decided, for safe keeping, to leave the stool against the wall for easy access next time. If there was one.

It was not like anyone else would need it anyway. Gloria did sometimes use it to get up and clean the extractor fans in the kitchen, but since they had started having to do their own maintenance work some of the fiddlier cleaning jobs had fallen to the wayside.

Margery wondered for a moment if the headmaster would ever actually hire a new maintenance person. She had not heard anything on the grapevine about a new member of staff joining. Clementine was usually the first to hear any gossip of the like, though she supposed Clementine had used to find out snippets of information from the old cleaning team. Maybe her supply line had run out.

'Knock, knock Margery!' Clementine said, announcing herself by swinging the door open and lurking in the doorway. 'I need you to come and tell Karen to stop calling the Christmas decorations, *decs*.' She shuddered in horror at the abbreviation.

'Shhh Clem!' Margery said, raising her index finger to her lips. 'Listen!'

There was silence for a moment and Margery wondered if Clementine would think she was mad but then the noise started again even louder than before.

'What's that?' Clementine whispered loudly. She closed the door to the dry store. 'Where's it coming from?'

'No idea,' Margery said, shaking her head. 'I can't work it out.'

'Ooh what if you get in there and crawl up to whatever it is,' Clementine said, very unhelpfully.

'Why is it always me that has to do all the clambering about?' Margery said. 'Anyway, I'm too big to fit in there even if I could get up there.'

'Don't be so down on yourself Margery, a bit of Pilates you'd squash right up in there,' Clementine said, looking up at the vent. 'Hmmm… what about if we pull the cover off it and then shove a piece of string up there?'

Margery stared up at it too. 'Maybe not a piece of string but it's got to have something above it hasn't it? It must go somewhere.'

'Margery!' Gloria bellowed from the main kitchen. Margery poked her head out of the storeroom door to see what she wanted.

'Look what he's done!' Gloria's face was a picture of horror. 'Come and look!'

Margery forgot all about the man's voice in the vent for a second as she followed Gloria back out into the main kitchen. She dragged Margery out into the canteen where Benjamin stood sheepishly, the tips of his ears bright red. Gloria flashed him the look that she usually reserved for students who asked for second helpings of chips.

'What's happened?' Margery asked.

'Touch one of the tables!' Gloria shrieked, stabbing her index finger dramatically towards them. 'Go on!'

Margery did and realised right away why Gloria was upset. 'Ben,' she said calmly. 'You realise you've cleaned all these tables with squash, don't you? They're very sticky.'

'Yeah, I know that now.' He twiddled the bottle he was holding in his hands, which was unmistakably Ribena and not sanitising spray. 'But it was the same colour as the cleaner, I just assumed…'

'I think we'll do another training session tomorrow, okay?' Margery said kindly. 'Why don't you get a proper bottle of spray and then redo these?'

He nodded and scuttled back into the kitchen.

'Is there not enough going on as it is, Margery?' Gloria asked. 'With Mrs Large dying, to keep on certain…' she paused and glanced around to see who was in earshot, '…members of staff. Did you know that Ben calls streaky bacon, *holiday bacon* because he's only ever eaten it in Spain?'

'I did hear him call it that.' Margery sighed. 'He asked me what omelettes are made of the other day too.'

'You've got to do something,' Gloria said. 'Or there will be consequences. If he asks me what's in banana and custard again then I can't be held responsible for my actions.'

'Let's just get Christmas over with first,' Margery said firmly. 'Then we can think about that in the new year. It's not fair to let someone go this close to a holiday. He might be young, but he has family too, I'm sure.' Gloria glared at her, but Margery walked away before she could argue with her again.

'Come on then, ladies.' She sighed. 'Let's get out of here and get ready for the Christmas rehearsal.'

'Do we have to?' Seren asked. 'It doesn't feel right.'

'I agree,' Margery said. 'But the headmaster wants everything to go on as usual.'

Clementine shook her head. 'Fine, we'll go,' she said, 'but if Mr Daniels makes us dance again today then we are definitely leaving.'

'Ooh, I quite like the dancing!' Karen said. 'It means I don't have to go for a run after work.'

'Well, you're the only one,' Clementine said, giving Karen a disparaging up and down look. 'Come on, let's just go and get it over with.'

Chapter Thirteen

Half an hour later they were all standing in the drama studio again for what Margery felt was the millionth time this week. The room was even worse than the school hall and much more cramped, but they had been resigned to the space so that the replacement Christmas lights could be set up. The school was abuzz with gossip surrounding the hall, and where the money for the new lights had come from.

Sharon and Karen were absolutely convinced that Mr Barrow had sold a kidney to buy them in time for the Christmas concert. Margery knew for a fact it was far less sinister than that because she had access to the catering budget and could see exactly where he had cut it again.

It had made planning for the Christmas bake sale a complete nightmare. There was barely enough spare money to buy icing sugar, let alone bake a veritable feast of assorted cakes. It looked like they would manage it in time for tomorrow, though she had had to call in a few favours with the suppliers and the team had all agreed to make their own cakes and biscuits at home to supplement and bring them in the day before. It was going to be the pinnacle of a lot of hard work by the Education Centre Nourishment Consultant team, which would all be worth it if they won the first prize for best staff bakes, and even better if they won the school's coinciding

Father Christmas Costume Contest, which was always held straight after the announcement for best bake. Clementine had been helping Margery sew their costumes for weeks now. There was no real physical prize for either of the contests, just a badly printed certificate and the respect of the rest of the school staff. Though they usually raised a tremendous amount of money for charity by donating the proceeds, which was a reward in itself.

Luckily most of the team still had their Father Christmas outfits from the previous year's competition, but they had needed to cobble Benjamin one out of one of Seren's old red coats, a big black belt, and a beard that they fashioned from cotton wool. It was usually quite an exciting day all in all. This year was particularly exciting as the Christmas raffle that usually went alongside the tombola and party games was finally back on. It had been cancelled a few years before when the main prize of an outdoor ornamental bird feeder and fountain had been won by someone who lived in a third floor flat.

Mr Daniels was still joylessly trying to explain the steps to tiny Mrs Boch the librarian. He had put the rest of them in groups to, 'work on the song lyrics.' Neither Margery nor Clementine knew what that meant and so they were mostly lounging around chatting, much to his dismay. Margery had begun to feel a little bit sorry for the man. He had not asked for this responsibility. With Mrs Large's death and Mrs Smith's banishment from the school the whole weight of the play was resting on his shoulders; it must have been a heavy burden and Mr Daniels looked ill. The only upside was that he had scrapped the only song Mrs Smith had gone through with them entirely and handed them all a completely fresh script, which was more traditional pantomime than musical fiesta.

'Psst Margery!' Clementine hissed loudly, from where she was standing next to her, 'Let's sneak out of the fire escape next time he looks away.'

Margery ignored her, though she wanted to leave too. The intricacies of the Christmas performance still did not match the level of talent among the staff; it all seemed much too much like hard work. The only thing that kept her there was the threat that Mrs Smith might return soon, and she would be livid if they had all quit before she arrived back from suspension.

'Psst Margery!' Clementine hissed again, loud enough that everyone else turned to look too. 'Where's Seren?'

'I don't know, Clem,' Margery murmured back.

'She'd be the perfect person to play the pantomime horse, wouldn't she?' Clementine mused. 'With her clumsy feet and all. So much comedy value without even really having to try.'

'Is there a problem, Mrs Butcher-Baker?' Mr Daniels asked from where he was sitting at the piano directing Miss Macdonald, who was spinning Mrs Boch. She looked both terrified and green with nausea.

'No, sorry,' Clementine mumbled like a child that had been caught out. 'I'm just bored.'

'Well, have another look at your song lyrics then,' Mr Daniels said, his ears had gone bright pink at the confront-ation. He was obviously not a seasoned teacher yet. 'Try and feel the meaning of them all.'

'I will try, but I didn't bring my reading glasses because we'd already learned the old songs,' Clementine said, pointing at the crumpled song sheet he had given them at the beginning of the session. Mr Daniels glared at her. He turned back to the piano and counted Miss Macdonald and Mrs Boch in again. The rest of the staff looked on joylessly as they twirled.

'Come on, Margery,' Clementine hissed at a volume usually only audible to bats. 'I've got some hot chocolate mix in my bag. We can sit in front of the fire.'

'Where did you steal that from?' Margery asked. 'Not the dry store I hope, it's not even hot chocolate mix, it's packet of gluten-free chocolate sponge mix for the bake sale.'

'And delicious all the same.' Clementine nodded seriously.

'Mrs Butcher-Baker, I'm warning you for the last time!' Mr Daniels stood, obviously gearing himself up for another confrontation.

'What will you do, kick me out of the play?' Clementine asked, her eyes lighting up. 'Fantastic idea, see you tomorrow everyone!'

'I'll make you do a solo.' Mr Daniels lay his only weapon out in front of them all with a small smirk. 'In front of everyone.'

Clementine's eyes boggled from her head as though she was made of plasticine and was being squeezed very hard. 'You wouldn't.'

'I would.'

Clementine seemed to consider this new and horrifying piece of blackmail. 'Well, all right then. I was only joking. Obviously. I'll err… have a look at what the song lyrics mean then, shall I?'

Clementine silenced for the moment, the practice continued. Mr Daniels finished with Miss Macdonald and Mrs Boch finally and summoned Karen and Sharon over, who were sitting in the corner happily sharing a bag of prawn cocktail Wotsits.

With no warning the stage lights in the room snapped off, plunging them all into darkness. Sharon screeched like she was being murdered. The uncomfortable murmuring of the staff picked up in volume. Mr Daniels turned on his phone light and waved it around the room.

'What's happened?' Margery asked him, squinting as he inadvertently shined the torch in her face.

'I don't know,' he said. She could only see his silhouette in the light from the phone, but she could imagine the confused look on his face. 'A power cut, maybe?'

They bumbled around in the dark for a moment. Mr Daniels grasped for the light switch, along with other staff members, their arms outstretched as they ran their fingers across the walls. Margery found herself grasping for Clementine's hand, squeezing it when she did so. They waited in the gloom. It felt like it had been hours, but only seconds could have passed and Margery found herself feeling clammy, the hand she held Clementine's in becoming slippery. She did not like the dark, she hadn't since she was a child. At home they slept with the bedroom door ajar and the hallway light on, though that was more for Pumpkin's benefit than Margery's. She would have spent the entire night crying outside a closed door. Margery knew that they were at the school and perfectly safe, but in the dim light she found her mind travelling to the worst conclusions. Perhaps Mrs Large's killer, whoever it was, was back and had decided to be less subtle in their next attack.

Suddenly the lights above the small stage flickered and began to strobe on and off in a frenzy. The curtains squealed as they squeaked open on their runners. They opened, revealing a horrifying figure in white dangling back and forth, blowing in some impossible breeze.

Margery turned to Clementine; her white fringe was blowing back against her head in the draught, her eyes wide in surprise, and then back at the stage. Margery blinked stupidly as all the hairs on her arms rose; it was hard to make out what was happening as the lights strobed all around them and the curtains flapped so hard it nearly forced them from their runners.

'Leave this place!' A booming voice seemed to sound from all around them.

Someone screamed again from behind Margery, and she wheeled around in panic. 'Leave this place and never return!'

Mr Daniels stormed over to the main panel of light switches and flicked the main bulb on. The room filled with the light from the halogen strip bulbs once more.

Under the bright lighting, it was clear to see that the figure on the stand was nothing more than one of the nice, white tablecloths Margery had been saving for the governors' buffet in the summer term. The draught that had seemed so deadly a moment ago, was from the electric fan that usually lived in the school kitchen. It had been set up at the back of the stage, and was blowing air, harmlessly. Margery could see a pair of dirty kitchen shoes poking out from under one of the stage curtains and knew instantly it who the culprit was.

'You can come out, Mrs Smith!' Mr Daniels yelled. 'I know it's you.'

He spent several minutes wandering around looking for her, peering behind the stage and behind the curtains. He even slammed open the door to the drama studio as if he could catch her if he did it quickly enough. When he turned around again, his face was set in a look of determined malice. He stormed over to the tiny maintenance door by the small stage and wrenched it open. Mrs Smith was revealed. She had the fingers of one hand on the lighting board, and a microphone in the other.

'I didn't do anything!' she said, her voice roaring around the room through the microphone speakers to the sides of the tiny stage.

'You know you aren't supposed to be on school property,' Mr Daniels said. He was trying to sound agreeable, Margery thought, but he did not sound sincere in the slightest. 'Don't make me call the headmaster.'

'I'm going, I'm going.' Mrs Smith slammed the microphone back down with a thump. She exited the cupboard as gracefully as a person can leave a small space that they were not supposed to be in. 'Come along, Seren.'

Seren hopped down from the slightly raised stage area and started to shuffle over to Mrs Smith. She had her hand held out to Seren, like she was her overbearing mother picking her up after she had misbehaved at playgroup. Mr Daniels stood between them.

'Seren has to stay,' Mr Daniels said, his tone calm. 'She's got to practise her part if we're going to be ready in two weeks.'

'But I'm her lift home, and I'm not supposed to be on the premises!' Mrs Smith was purple with outrage.

'Then why are you here?' Mr Daniels said, coolly. 'You can't get us to cancel the concert just because you aren't part of it any more.'

'I thought a ghost might... anyway... whatever... I'm leaving!' With that Mrs Smith stormed out. The rest of the staff stood and watched her go, awkwardly. Margery felt a wave of guilt wash over her.

'But I don't want to stay,' Seren piped, quietly. Mr Daniels ignored her.

'Right,' he said, turning back to the rest of the group and sitting down at the electric keyboard. 'Let's go from the top, shall we?'

Chapter Fourteen

Clementine decided that the time had come to see Gary Matthews as soon as they had left rehearsal. Margery had agreed gingerly; she was still nervous about letting anyone else in on their meddling when the headmaster had warned them not to get involved at all. They had waved everyone else off, the other staff so desperate to get home that they did not see Margery and Clementine hanging back.

The security office was a short walk away from the school, just outside the main gates in an ugly concrete building. Margery sometimes felt sorry for the security staff who had to sit in it all day long, rain or shine, rarely anything exciting happening. Today Gary Matthews was there half asleep behind the tiny desk, his jumper even more stretched than usual under the size of his arm muscles. He put down his copy of *The Shawshank Redemption* and gave them both a beaming smile. Margery remembered Seren telling her about their dating and smiled back.

'Hello, ladies,' he said, the short hairs on his head blowing in the artificial breeze from the space heater he was sitting next to. 'You're late, everything okay?'

'Yes, all fine, thank you, Mr Matthews.' Margery smiled back. It was hard not to like Gary. Even if he always did seem a bit confused about how security actually worked. 'We stayed behind for the Christmas concert practice.'

'Oh right! Well, what can I do for you?' he asked. 'Just don't ask me for another door pass! You know I can't give you one without ID.'

'Oh no, it's nothing like that,' Margery said. 'We just wanted to know what you knew about the keys here.'

'Keys?' he said, his brow furrowing in puzzlement. He cocked his head as though he were a springer spaniel she had hidden a ball from. 'Like the pass cards, yeah?'

'No, like actual keys,' Clementine said. 'Like the ones people have for the storeroom in the school.'

'Oh, yeah I know a bit about that.' He scratched his blond head. 'The caretaker used to sort it all.'

'But we don't have a caretaker any more,' Clementine said. Margery nodded.

'I just know I have to take the master key and lock up after I do my last round at six.' Gary shrugged. 'The headmaster has all the records for stuff like that, I bet loads of teachers have got them, though. I don't think we've ever changed the locks or anything like that. Costs money, see?'

'Oh really? They've never changed them?' Clementine asked. 'Whereabouts does he keep the records?'

'No idea.' Gary shook his head. 'He keeps it all written down though, he told me a few months ago that he likes to have a hard copy in case the computer system ever gets deleted. Can't think why he would think that.' Margery swallowed; that confirmed everything Mrs Smith had told them at the Bell and Hope. If the headmaster had kept records like she said he had, they would surely be in his office.

'Well. Thanks anyway, Mr Matthews,' Margery said. 'Sorry to bother you.'

'No worries, ladies, anytime.' Gary smiled again. 'Anything else I can help you with?'

'No, not really, Gary,' Margery said, but Clementine had other things to ask him.

'Are you still taking Seren to McDonald's, Gary?' she asked, leaning her arm on the security desk as though she had forgotten they were in a rush. 'You be nice to her.'

Gary's face blushed a deep crimson. 'Er... yeah, I do sometimes. Not as much since she moved in with Mrs Smith, you know? Because obviously she left the head-master and that, and Seren has been helping her through her grief,' he said the last word with a smirk.

'She left him, did she?' Clementine asked. 'Why?'

Gary suddenly seemed to realise that he had said much too much, his eyes widening. 'Oh, you know... I don't really know much about it.'

'Come on, Gary!' Clementine chastised him. 'You can't say that and then not tell us what you know!'

'Honestly, mate, I don't know much at all.' Gary sighed, as if realising that they were not going to go away unless he gave them some sliver of gossip. He lowered his voice to just above a whisper. 'All I know is that he asked her to marry him, and she said no.'

'What!' Clementine exclaimed what Margery was thinking. 'Why?'

'Dunno.' Gary shrugged. 'Seren wouldn't tell me. I don't know if she even knows.'

'Gosh,' Margery said, thinking it over. Why would Mrs Smith have turned down a proposal? Maybe it was too soon after her separation from her husband? Though she had seen her flipping through bridal magazines in the staff room, on the occasions they had delivered a tea trolley there. She was also sure it was Mrs Smith they had seen briefly, as they drove through Dewstow town centre a few weeks ago, looking wistfully through the window of the wedding dress shop.

'Margery.' Clementine interrupted her thoughts. 'We'd better get home, it's getting late.' Margery looked at the plastic clock above the desk and saw with a start that it was already half past five.

'Good luck on the rest of your search, ladies.' Gary smiled at them, picking up his book again.

Margery and Clementine walked together across the staff car park to the little white Nissan. Margery rooted through her bag for the keys, glad to be going home and enjoying an evening of rest. Well, she hoped it would be restful. She was so glad they had already finished the Christmas concert practice tonight; that would have been the last straw for her if it had gone on any longer. It was bad enough that Mr Daniels had booked double sessions all next week. Apparently, they were not prepared enough, and the teachers had been working on the students' play for ages longer now, he said he did not want them to outshine the staff's play. Margery didn't see how they could catch up.

'Hey.' Clementine nudged her with her elbow. 'That's the headmaster.'

Margery looked up just in time to see the headmaster's smart, silver saloon car leaving through the main school gates and disappearing onto the main road.

'So, it is.' She shrugged. 'And?'

'Well, this is a perfect opportunity,' Clementine said. Margery looked at her in puzzlement.

'Perfect opportunity for what exactly?'

'To find out who has the storeroom key of course,' Clementine said, as though Margery was a very stupid person she was trying to explain something very simple to.

'I don't think that's a good idea.' Margery shook her head. 'Every time we go to the school after hours something bad happens and the police and the headmaster have warned us not to do exactly that. We've pushed our luck enough by talking to Gary.'

'Well technically it's not even after hours yet.' Clementine smiled. 'It's only just evening, there's been later governors' meetings, and how helpful have the police been really?'

Margery thought about it. She did want to know who had a key to the storeroom. It would probably solve half the mystery in itself. But another part of her wondered whether they should just ask the headmaster who had a copy and be done with it. Not that he would tell them anything, and then she supposed he would know that they were investigating, and he would not be pleased at all. Maybe this was the best way to find out, now that Gary Matthews had not proved particularly helpful.

'Come on then.' She sighed, putting her car keys back in her bag. 'Let's go. Quick, before I change my mind.'

They scuttled back across the car park, to the school's main entrance. The wind was picking up, and it was going to be a particularly unpleasant evening if the gloom descending in the sky over the playground had anything to do with it. Margery pulled the collar of her coat closer to her neck to try and defend against the chill, though it was useless without the warm woollen scarf she usually wore. They were almost at the staff door when Clementine grabbed Margery's wrist suddenly.

'We can't go in this way,' Clementine said. 'They'll see it on the security system, won't they?'

'Could we not just say we forgot something?' Margery asked, already wishing she had not given in and that they were already on their way home, listening to the *Muppets Christmas Carol* soundtrack she had bought in a charity shop.

'Ooh, good thinking Margery.' Clementine beamed at her and swiped herself into the building. Margery followed, breathing a sigh of relief that Clementine had reneged on whatever terrible idea she had to break into the building.

The school hallways were spooky after it had shut for the day, too shadowed and much, much colder. Margery thought for a second that she could see her own breath in the cool air, but it was just a figment of her imagination. There was the odd teacher milling about still, but everyone else had already left, leaving the classroom doorways looming in the silence. The decorative Christmas tree bulbs had all been turned off already, and the strip light running along the halls were dim and artificial, the hazy gloom making Margery squint.

The headmaster's office seemed to take forever to get to, but they finally made it. They stood outside for a moment, considering the heavy wooden door with the chunky gold name plate prominently displayed in the middle.

'Right then,' Clementine whispered, gesturing to the door, 'after you, Margery.'

Margery shook her head and hissed back at her. 'This was your terrible idea, Clem!'

'Well, how else are we going to get in?' Clementine breathed, tapping her fingertips gently against the heavy door. 'It's probably locked, just give the door a little tap and we'll break it down.'

'What?' Margery said. 'How are we going to break it down? It's solid wood. Do you want to break an arm as well?'

The door hinges creaked suddenly, and they both nearly jumped out of their skins as it squeaked open. The head of the cleaning team, Louise, exited the headmaster's office. She was huffing and puffing as she dragged the vacuum cleaner from the room, its lead trailing behind it.

'Hi ladies. You all right?' Louise smiled at them both, though she looked exhausted 'You're here late, aren't you? Been taking us ages to do all these rooms with the Christmas concert practice, Mr Daniels turned out to be a bit of a Christmas monster, hasn't he?'

'Hello Louise, yes all good thank you.' Margery nodded at her, hoping her smile did not look too forced, and that Louise would forgive her for the lie. 'Just seeing if the headmaster is still here.'

'Oh no, you just missed him,' Louise said, plopping the vacuum cleaner down on the floor and putting her hands on her hips.

'Oh no,' Clementine said. 'Well, I suppose we could leave him a note, couldn't we Margery?'

'Yes, I suppose we could,' Margery said, her voice feeling forced and weak to her own ears. 'Do you think you could lock the office in a minute instead, Louise?'

'Oh, I don't lock it anyway,' Louise said brightly. 'Gary comes by on his rounds and does that, they wouldn't let me have any keys after last year! The old cleaners used to have a master key apparently. It's a bit annoying really, teachers are always asking me to tidy stuff or empty their bins and then when I get there, I can't get in. They all seem to have their own office keys though, it's a joke.'

'That does sound annoying,' Margery agreed, sincerely thinking of all the times she had been glad to have her own full set of keys. 'Do you want a hand with anything? We don't mind.'

'No, of course not!' Louise chuckled to herself. 'I've just got to get up to the science block and then we're done for the day too.'

'Well, we'll let you get on then.'

'No worries,' Louise said, hefting the vacuum cleaner back under her arm. 'Have a nice evening, ladies.'

She headed back down the corridor and Margery and Clementine watched her leave. Once they heard the sound of hoovering begin again from a distant room, Clementine grabbed Margery's hand and dragged her inside the office.

'Right, quick,' she said, slamming the door behind them. It thumped closed. 'Let's find that list and get the hell out of here.'

'Agreed.' Margery nodded. She had always liked the headmaster's study, but she had never dared touch anything inside, in case she broke one of his fancy paper-weights or the selection of pens he exclusively used. He swore the one he used to sign documents was a Montblanc John F. Kennedy special edition, but Margery knew the exact stall he had bought the knock-off from at Dewstow Saturday Market. It was the same one Ceri-Ann had bought her fake Rolex from.

Clementine went straight to the headmaster's desk and began to rifle through the drawers; Margery scanned the room. There were numerous places where a list could be. Mrs Smith had only said what the notepad looked like, not where it was. She sighed and joined Clementine behind the desk, making a beeline for the bookcase behind it. It held only educational teaching books, and the Roald Dahl novels Mr Barrow liked to read from during assemblies.

Clementine was already done with the desk. It had contained nothing but the usual stationery and a small, square box designed to look like a Christmas present. Clementine popped it open and held it up to the light. They looked at each other, and then back at the ginormous engagement ring Clementine had revealed. Gary must have his information correct, and there was an enormous diamond to prove it. Margery briefly wondered if the headmaster still felt a flame for Mrs Smith, and why she had spurned him in the end; she certainly did not seem happier now. Her thoughts were interrupted by Clementine closing the lid with a clack and shoving the box back into the drawer.

'Careful, Clem, we need to leave everything as we found it.'

'Yes, I know,' Clementine said haughtily. 'But I can't remember where I got it from.' Margery chuckled. 'Come on, Margery, we haven't looked in the cupboard.'

Margery began to rearrange all the objects on the desk Clementine had moved in her search, while Clementine herself marched over to the walk-in cupboard in the corner. She flung the door open and pulled the string light switch, the bulb pinged on with a click and she whooped.

'There's some records in here, Margery! Er well actually… there's a few.'

Margery left the desk and wandered over to the cupboard to see. Inside there were three floor-to-ceiling shelving units. Along with all the headmaster's other junk he had obviously collected over the years, each of the shelves had a row of red notepads neatly lined up along it. They were numbered and Margery was sure the headmaster had them organised in a way that made perfect sense to him, but that was no help to them at all.

'Christ,' Clementine said under her breath. 'Well, I suppose we'd better start going through. Keep a look out, will you?'

She began to take the books off the shelf one at a time to check them individually. Margery sighed to herself. They could be here a very long time at this rate. She squeezed into the cupboard and began checking the books on the other side. Luckily for them, the headmaster had written exactly what each one contained on the inside cover. They just had to find the right one.

Margery joined Clementine in pulling each book down in turn. She opened one to the first page. There was information here that went back for years, did the headmaster really need all these hard copy records? All this kind of information could have been backed up on a computer with the original documents by now. Wasn't that the point of USB sticks and external hard drives? Surprisingly, it did not take that long to find what they were looking for. Clementine tapped her on the shoulder when she found it and smiled, showing her the first page.

'Excellent, Clem.' Margery's smile faded when she looked down and saw the mess Clementine had made in their quest, the books were strewn all over the floor. 'You can't leave it like that! Pick them up!'

Clementine rolled her eyes but bent to pick the notebooks up regardless. Margery heard a noise and poked her head out of the door; the doorknob to the room was turning slowly. Racing into action she closed the cupboard door quietly and turned to Clementine with her finger over her lips. Clementine stared back wide-eyed and then reached up and pulled the light switch, they were plunged into semi-darkness. Margery had not been able to shut the door completely in the seconds she had, and they could see through the thin strip of light out into the office.

She peered through at the person that had disturbed them and to her surprise she found that she knew who they were. He looked very strange out of his work clothes, with his blond hair on show. He had come around the desk and was looking intently at the headmaster's computer. Margery heard Clementine gasp from where she was crouched next to her. She wished she had her glasses on, so she could see properly what he was doing.

Benjamin tapped away at the keyboard lightly, though they could not see the screen. Whatever he was there for, it did not take him long and she heard the computer chime at him as he shut it down again. He looked around and over his shoulder. Margery wondered if he might take anything from the room, but he snuck back around the desk and left as quickly as he came, the door shutting behind him with a soft click.

'What was Ben doing here?' Clementine asked. Margery shook her head. Her guess was as good as anyone's. 'And after hours?'

'I thought you said this didn't count as after hours?' Margery raised an eyebrow at her; Clementine grinned in return. 'But I don't know. It seems very strange.'

'You don't think the headmaster would have asked him to do something on the computer?' Clementine asked, standing up with her arms full of notebooks.

'I can't see what he would have asked.' Margery shook her head, as she helped her put the books back on the shelf. Unlike herself and Clementine, the headmaster was quite computer literate. Even if he did have a problem with his computer, she was sure he would have called for the IT department to come and solve it. She could not imagine him trusting his important files and documents to a young kitchen assistant, especially when he was not even in the office. She felt like they were in a bit of a bind though. She could not openly ask him about Benjamin, and she could not openly ask Benjamin what he had been doing without revealing that they had also been snooping around in the office.

She was interrupted by the flash of Clementine's phone camera, nearly blinding them both in the darkness of the cupboard they were still standing in. She blinked rapidly as squares of light bounced around her vision.

'Sorry, Margery!' Clementine said. 'Just taking a photo of this key book thing. I'll put it back.'

Margery sighed, hopefully there would be something more useful to them written on the pages of the notepad, but somehow, she doubted it.

Chapter Fifteen

The rest of the week flew by for Margery and Clementine in a whirlwind of concert practices and crocheting. Mr Daniels had them stay for an hour every day after school, to make up for lost time, he said. He was even more of a slave driver than Mrs Smith had ever been, in Clementine's opinion anyway. Margery had heard little else from her all week once the key records had not revealed anything particularly useful. Gary had been right, a lot of staff had keys to the storeroom from when they were given out originally and Margery suspected that older staff had simply passed their keys on to newer staff when they retired. If they went by the record book, they would be adding dozens of suspects to the list. It was hopeless.

Margery could not believe that by this time next Friday they would already be on their way home to enjoy the Christmas break, though it felt like an absolute age away. Especially as they still had the bake sale to get through on Saturday. The planning for it had been a lot more than Margery was expecting and they had only just managed to finish the cakes in time. Luckily, Margery had caught Ben before he managed to pour the entire bottle of brandy over the Christmas cakes in one go. Benjamin's meddling in the headmaster's office was still a major concern, but they had not seen him near the area again, even though

Margery had sent Clementine to hang around outside the office door every afternoon at home time.

Clementine, for some inexplicable reason, had offered to help her with the Christmas dinner ordering. Margery knew she should probably do it all, but there was so much else to worry about and Clementine had looked so pleased with herself for trying to be helpful that she had not been able to tell her no. Gloria assured Margery that she would help, winking as she did so. They had pottered off to ring the butcher together; Clementine's excitement at being able to be helpful had made Margery smile at the time. She knew all she really had to do to have a successful Christmas lunch was stick to the classics and make sure that they had enough potatoes peeled, but she felt obligated to make this year's the best Christmas lunch ever. It felt like her reputation as the new kitchen manager was all resting on that moment.

The usual excitement of the Christmas break, however, was completely tarnished by the arrival of Mrs Large's funeral. The day came cold and crisp, the frost still on the ground as Margery stared up at the church steeple in her best funeral outfit. She pulled her black wool coat tightly around her neck, trying to stop the chill getting in. At any other time, the cold snap would have been beautiful to behold, but the view of the icy graveyard around the church was putting a dampener on Margery's mood.

The headmaster had cancelled all lessons for the day and Mrs Large's family had invited anyone who was free to attend. Margery felt terrible that they had not been to visit her husband yet, or even sent a card on behalf of the dinner lady team, but it had felt too awkward to. Neither Margery nor Clementine had known her particularly well, which was unusual because they knew most people at the school after being there so long. Margery supposed they had just not run into her very often.

Clementine reached over with the arm not holding the bunch of flowers and took Margery by the hand, giving it a gentle squeeze.

They had had to make a special trip to the supermarket in the morning because Dawn Simmonds had finally started to notice that Clementine had been stealing flowers from her garden. It would not do to rock the boat any further with her for fear that they would accidentally give her more blackmail material and practically be forced to join the Women's Institute. Luckily, Margery had very nearly finished the next lot of Dawn's crochet robins so their troubles should soon be over, though it meant that she had to take her crochet bag nearly everywhere they went. She hoped that they were up to Dawn's standards, which if her immaculate garden was anything to go by, were very high indeed.

'Come on, Margery,' Clementine said gently. 'It'll be all right.'

Margery knew that it would be perfectly all right for them, but she was looking over at the family car that had just arrived. The car door had opened, and Mrs Large's husband and sons had clambered out. Margery could not stop looking at the children's pale, drawn faces. Those poor boys, she thought, how cruel and unfair the world was. The hearse carrying Mrs Large pulled up behind the family car and Margery and Clementine finally made their way inside the small stone church.

Clementine put the flowers with the rest of the collection as they entered, and they joined the rest of the dinner ladies who were already sitting together in one of the long pews. Karen was handing out tissues down the row, her face drawn into a grim line. Even Ceri-Ann had put her phone away for once, out of respect for the solemnity of the event. The only dinner lady missing was Seren. Margery scanned the church for her and found her sitting next to Mrs Smith on the other side of the room.

Dawn Simmonds was playing the organ at the front, to the best of her abilities. It obviously was not a good enough performance for Mrs Smith, who kept glaring at her from her seat at the back of the church. Margery was amazed she felt brave enough to show her face. She knew that if she were the main suspect of a manslaughter investigation then she would never leave the house again, let alone go to the deceased's funeral. Rose had obviously thought about it for a second at least, because she was wearing a black headscarf that covered most of her face. Mr Barrow was nearer to the front with a few other members of staff. Maybe that was who Rose was really hiding from. Margery stared sadly for a moment at the row across from the one reserved for Mrs Large's immediate family, where the school recorder choir, composed mostly of first and second years, sat. They were all clutching their recorders and most looked close to tears already.

Clementine was fiddling with the rings on her fingers as more school staff and parents arrived. 'It seems like we only get invited to funerals nowadays, it's so depressing. It used to be all weddings, didn't it?'

'A sign of our age I think,' Margery whispered back, looking down at the order of service that Mrs Mugglethwaite had given her as they entered the church. Mrs Large's smiling face peered back at her. Margery recognised the photograph, as it had been used in last year's Christmas concert programme. How different everything had seemed last year, so much more hopeful. For the hundredth time since the accident Margery tried to think who could have wanted to hurt Mrs Large, and came up short, as she had each time.

'I've only got one cardigan,' Clementine continued sadly, pulling at the threads of the black cardigan she was wearing. 'It'll wear out before I go at this rate, you've washed it so much that the sleeves have gone bobbly.'

'Don't worry, I'll knit you another.' Margery patted her on the shoulder. Gloria turned to give them a stern glance from the pew in front and they fell silent again. Clementine was right. There had been a notable uptick in funerals as time had gone on, some much worse than others.

Clementine's mother had died a few years ago and the arrangements had proved impossible. They had to have the service at the church in Ittonvale because she had fallen out with the priest at Dewstow church the year before she had died. Margery could see the very same priest watching at the front of the church patiently, his head bowed respectfully. The reason for old Mrs Butcher's apocalyptic fallout with the mild-mannered man had been because he had asked her to stop bringing multipacks of crisps to eat during the Sunday service. A request Margery had not dared to say she thought was reasonable in front of a grieving Clementine. If that wasn't bad enough, when they had arrived at Ittonvale church on the day of the funeral, they discovered that Mrs Butcher had also fallen out with the organist. Out of pure spite she had proceeded to play all the hymns in a key too high for anyone in attendance to sing. The whole experience had been very awkward, but in a way, it had also been a fitting tribute to the only woman Margery had ever met who was more abrasive than Clementine, whose mother had once changed her GP's surgery because she did not like a woman who had started working at her usual one. Clementine had been adopted as a baby, and though she had not been related to her mother by blood, you could not have found two women so similar in temperament. It was also revealed, when the occurrences stopped after her death, that Clementine's mother had been the person sending envelopes stuffed full of glitter to neighbours she didn't like. It had been a real epidemic before; the police had even put up wanted posters in their search for 'The Glitterer'.

'Good Lord,' Gloria said, her eye caught by something behind Margery. 'Who on earth is that?'

Margery swung her head to see who Gloria was exclaiming about and felt her jaw drop. Through the entrance to the church sauntered a glamorous-looking woman in a tight red dress and a much too large matching hat. The dog under her arm was wearing the same.

'Mrs Blossom!' Clementine gasped from next to her. 'What's she doing here?'

What was she doing here? Margery wondered how on earth Mrs Large knew Mrs Blossom so well that she would come to her funeral. Mrs Smith seemed to be wondering the same thing. She had turned almost completely around to glare at Mrs Blossom, who eyed her wryly and then took a seat on the other side of the church. Margery could no longer see her without appearing to be rudely staring at the people behind her, so she turned around and was confronted by Gloria's curious face.

'Mrs who?' Gloria hissed. 'How do you know her?'

'We don't. We don't know why she's here either,' Margery said. Clementine continued to try and stare at Mrs Blossom, craning her neck to look at her. Gloria did not look at all appeased, but Dawn Simmonds had stopped playing the organ and the church fell into hushed whispers.

Dawn moved to the small CD player by the side of the organ, pressed play and then sat back down gently. The warbling tones of Eva Cassidy filled the air and they all stood, turning to the back of the church. Margery found herself looking up at the light pouring in through the stained-glass windows above them instead of the arrival of the coffin, and Mrs Large's two young sons walking slowly behind it. She could not stand to look. The coffin was brought up to the front of the church and carefully placed onto stands, the music faded, and Dawn got up to turn it off. Margery looked down at the photograph of Mrs Large again.

Mr Large gently ushered his boys into the pew and then sat down next to them when the priest requested that they sit. The priest began his sermon, but Margery found she could not take her eyes off Mr Large. He had always been thin, the few times she had met him while she was catering parents' evenings, but Margery could see that he was practically gaunt now. His cheekbones were hollow and the circles under his eyes were dark and pronounced. A lot of terrible things had happened recently, and she could see them all written on his face; she felt an awful stab of pity for the man.

The priest finished his initial sermon and welcomed Mr Large up to speak. He almost staggered to the pulpit, taking a fold of paper from his pocket with thin, shaking fingers.

He stumbled over the words as he began his eulogy, and they came out as a sob. 'I-I-I've lost my best friend.'

Soon there was not a dry eye left in the room.

'Hello, George. How are you getting on?' Margery asked Mr Large awkwardly at the Bell and Hope a little while later. They were standing in the queue for the buffet table. Mr Large turned and gave her a small sad smile, his hand still on his youngest son's shoulder.

'Okay, all considering, Margery,' he said with a sigh. 'I thought the worst would be over, but it feels like it's just beginning.'

Margery nodded in sympathy. When her mother died, the funeral had seemed the very beginning of the grieving process. The cost alone had been astronomical, and that had been without the family disagreements. Her brother had talked her into paying for the bereavement letter flowers for the hearse, but they had been so expensive she had only been able to have 'MA' spelt, instead of the long simpering message he had wanted.

'I just wish we knew a bit more about what happened.' He whispered so that his son would not hear. 'The police are still going over everything. Saying it's all inconclusive.'

'Are they really?' Margery whispered back, forgetting they were not supposed to be meddling. 'What do they think—'

She was interrupted by the buffet line lurching forward suddenly. Mr Large helped himself to a paper plate and offered one to Margery too. She took it as George began helping his son help himself to the sandwiches. Mrs Blossom had not appeared at the wake, though both Margery and Clementine were keeping an eye out to confront her if she did. Mrs Smith was not in attendance either; it seemed she did not have the gall to gatecrash the wake as well as the funeral.

'It all just seems like a lot of work at the moment,' George said. 'With the boys and the dog, we'll get through though.'

'Is there anything Clem and I can do?' Margery asked, looking at his exhausted face. 'We can drop off some food or…?'

'Thank you for the offer,' George said, 'But we're doing all right. The only thing I'm really struggling with is keeping up with the housework and that can wait.'

'We'll help,' Margery smiled at him gently. 'We can go over later and do some bits for you if you'd like?'

'You really don't have to.' He sighed again, even more heavily than the last time, 'I don't want you to see me as a charity case.'

'Really, it's not a bother,' Margery said. 'We could pop over before our Christmas concert rehearsal next week too, if that's all right with you?'

'Well.' He thought about it. 'The boys are at their grandmother's this week and next so I can sort everything. Liz didn't really have a will, so I've had to sort all of the financial side of it.' Margery winced at the depth to his ordeal. 'I wanted to stay a while longer, there's so many more people arrived than I thought would, but I have to go back and feed Percy.' He looked over at his son, his face falling. 'Oh, Percy's the dog,' he said, noticing the puzzlement in Margery's face.

'Well, why don't we just pop in and feed the dog every night, so you don't have to worry?' Margery asked, 'It's really no bother. We'll can stop in on our way home today too.'

'That would actually be very helpful.' He smiled a feeble smile at her again, his lips barely twitching upwards. 'You've convinced me.'

The queue moved onwards again. Margery helped herself to a cheese sandwich. She did not feel up to eating much more than that.

–

The drive to the Large household was very quiet. Margery thought that his despair had been quite catching at the funeral and the wake; it had felt for a moment as though they were all processing his grief with him. Rose had made herself quite scarce after the funeral, not appearing at the wake. Margery supposed that maybe Rose had felt she needed to pay her respects but had no desire to deal with the stares and discussions that would come with showing her face elsewhere. They arrived outside George and Elizabeth Large's house, which was ironically quite small. It was not in a part of Dewstow that they visited often, and Margery was glad that he had written down his address so she could type the postcode into the satnav. Margery parked on the roadside and wandered up the driveway, ringing the doorbell out of habit, though she knew no one was home. George and his children were still at the wake saying goodbye to relatives. The house was the only one on the road without Christmas lights. It looked stark and bare in comparison and all the lights internally were off too. There was not even the slightest glimmer of a decoration inside the house.

She stepped forward and opened the door with the key George had given her, wrestling with the big bag of leftovers she was carrying as she did so. Clementine followed behind her with a similar bag. They had stopped by their house and grabbed as much from the freezer as they could carry; the least they could do was make sure that the Large family's children were well fed in their mother's absence and give George one less thing to worry about. She put the bag down on the kitchen table and flicked on the light switch. The house looked neat enough, George could not be struggling that much. But the carpet did look as though it could do with a hoover and she could see as she entered the kitchen doorway that this morning's washing up had not been done; the cereal bowls were still piled up in the sink.

'All right then,' Clementine said, as Margery put the food into the fridge, 'where shall we start?'

'Shall we feed this Percy first and then I'll try and find the freezer?' Margery said, wishing she had asked Mr Large where the dog would be. She had half expected it to bound out at them as soon as they had entered the door. She could hear scratching from a room just off the kitchen, the skittering of nails on tile and then a dog's nose appeared at the bottom of the gap between the door and the floor.

'Speak of the devil.' She chuckled. 'Let's get you fed then, Percy.'

She opened the door for the dog, who bounced out excitedly. The yellow Labrador retriever jumped up at her, batting at her with his big paws, his claws scratching the material of her woollen skirt.

'He's here!' she called to Clementine, as she batted him away. 'Hello, Percy.'

'Speaking of dogs,' Clementine said as she joined them both in the kitchen and patted Percy's head when he lunged towards her, eager to meet them both. 'Why was Mrs Blossom at the funeral?'

'I have no idea.' Margery opened the tin for Percy, putting it in the bowl and then watched the dog wolf down the food like he had never eaten before. 'I've been thinking about the play Mrs Large gave Mrs Smith.'

'Me too!' Clementine said enthusiastically. 'Hear me out, what if Mrs Large has something to do with Mrs Blossom's play?'

'Why would she?' Margery asked.

'No idea,' Clementine said watching the dog eat. 'But if she did, surely she'd have spoken to Mrs Blossom in some way?'

'How does anyone talk to anyone now?' Margery shrugged. 'Email maybe?'

Percy finished eating and leapt back up at Margery excitedly. Margery stroked the dog's ears and tried to think of how to find out that information.

'Maybe she'd have something on her computer at school?' Clementine leaned back against the counter. 'And who do we know who can break into a computer?'

'No,' Margery said. 'This is getting too stupid, Clem, even for us. We can't bring other staff members into it as well, especially ones who don't know we know they know how to break into other people's computers.'

'I know,' Clementine sighed. 'Forget I said anything.'

Margery went to the sink and turned on the hot water tap, filling the washing up bowl with soap and water. She put the bowls in to soak, to wait for the dried-on cereal to soften in the hot water.

'Margery!' Clementine called from another room. 'You need to see this!'

Margery followed the shout and soon found herself in the hall and facing the open door that led to a small home office. Clementine beckoned her over.

'Look at all this!'

Margery looked. On the walls of the office hung several large posters in frames and there were several smaller photographs hanging around and above the door frame. Each poster was from a different school concert and each photograph was of Mrs Large with a set of students on one of their recorder club tours.

'Lovely, Clem.' Margery scratched her head in bafflement as she looked up at them all. 'Now, let's get back to tidying up, this room looks fine to me.'

'Look closer, Margery.' Clementine stabbed a finger at the nearest poster. 'Look what school all these are from!'

'Oh.' Margery stared at the poster she was pointing at. 'These are all Ittonvale school posters.'

'Yes!' Clementine tapped the poster. 'This one's the summer play they did about the inventor of self-raising flour a few years ago, *Banishment to Bicarb!*'

'And there's last year's about the Battle of Hastings,' Margery said, looking at the poster next to it. 'I remember reading about that one in the paper.'

'*Harold the Hasty!*' Clementine said. 'They said the sets were magnificent.'

'Why on earth did Mrs Large have all of these?' Margery gestured to the walls. 'There isn't a single Summerview school one here.'

'I don't know, Margery.' Clementine shook her head. 'But it's very strange.'

Chapter Sixteen

The next morning was a damp, wet December Saturday. Clementine's dream of a white Christmas seemed unlikely as the rain hammered down on the car roof while they rolled into the school car park. Margery's driving had become even more nervous since she had given much of the reins over to Clem for her to practise, and it was especially difficult to do the gears when the sleeves of her costume kept getting in the way. She wished she hadn't put the white faux beard on before they left that morning, it had made visibility while driving much worse than usual. She was surprised today that she had managed to get them there in one piece at all, let alone the cherry Bakewells in the tin on the back seat. Clementine turned and smiled at her, the pom-pom on the end of her Santa hat swinging around with her.

'Don't worry, Margery,' she said, reaching over from the passenger side to pat her knee in comfort. 'We've just got to get today over with, raise a bit of money for the school and then it's basically Christmas.'

Margery smiled back at Clementine's rare optimism. 'You're rushing ahead a little bit there aren't you? We've got a Christmas concert and a lunch to do first.'

'Yes, but then it's all Christmas all the time.' Clementine grinned. 'First thing we'll do is open the Christmas gin I bought from Tesco.'

'Christmas gin?' Margery scoffed. 'What makes it Christmassy?'

Clementine pondered, tapping her chin with her fingers. 'Well… erm… well you know it's more about the occasion than the product, Margery. Anyway, we'll drink it with a sprinkling of cinnamon on top, or something.'

'That just sounds less like a Christmas tradition and more like a reason for you to drink all day, Clem.' Margery chuckled, trying to roll up the sleeves of her Father Christmas outfit and failing. 'Oh, come on then, let's go. It can't possibly get any worse, can it?'

They exited the car and made their way into the school, wandering the halls in the direction of the canteen kitchen. The automatic hallway strip lights flickered on ominously as they made their way down the corridor and Margery wished for the hundredth time that morning that they were still tucked up in bed. Though the day would not be too strenuous: all the cakes they had made were on the trolley in the walk-in fridge ready for them to wheel around to the leisure centre, where the bake sale was taking place. Margery carried her cakes very carefully in the tin; dropping them would be a disaster.

'Do you know who might know about that number-plate if the police won't help?' Clementine said suddenly as they continued down the hallway and through the double doors to the canteen. 'Mr Fitzgerald.'

'Really? Do you think so?' Margery asked quizzically. 'His shop's full of junk, how would that help us find a numberplate?'

'He's the volunteer car parking monitor for Dewstow town centre events, isn't he?' Clementine shrugged. 'Always wandering around writing things down on his little clipboard, surely he might have seen that car before.'

Margery hummed. 'It's not the worst idea. At least we'd be trying something.'

The canteen looked exactly as it had when they had left the afternoon before. Margery wandered over to the kitchen door and went to unlock it. It was already unlocked, and the door swung open easily. They stared at it, bewildered.

'I could have sworn I locked it Thursday night, Clem,' Margery said, turning to Clementine in disbelief, the keys still in her hand.

'You did.' Clementine whispered back. 'I saw you do it.'

They crept into the kitchen and Margery nearly slipped on the floor. Stepping back, she flipped the light switch on, nearly barrelling into Clementine as she did so. Looking down at where she had slid, she saw the clear imprint of her boot's sole in the white substance coating the floor. For a moment her brain told her it had finally snowed before it caught up and she realised that it was icing. She stepped over it and walked around into the prep section of the kitchen, her mouth dropping open in horror as she did so.

The cake trolley, which had been safely away in the walk-in fridge, was now out on its side in the middle of the kitchen and all the cakes were on the floor. The individual fruit cakes Seren and Sharon had spent months feeding brandy and hours decorating were all destroyed. Margery heard Clementine draw in a sharp intake of breath from next to her. All their hard work was ruined.

The worst part was that it did not look at all accidental. Royal icing was smeared all over the gas hobs and fridges. There was even sponge cake smashed all over the ventilation extraction that ran above the length of the stoves.

The big main prep table to the side held the remains of the tiny marzipan snowmen and women that Karen had spent so much time making and decorating for each individual fruit cake. They were all piled up into a ball like a heap of bodies after a massacre.

'Ladies. Do you think this hat is too ridiculous?' Gloria stepped up behind them, in an elf outfit with a pointy eared hat, her arms laden with cakes. It took her a moment to process the state of the room she had just walked in to. 'Oh my God, Margery, what the hell?'

'I don't know,' Margery said, shaking her head in despair. 'I just don't know.'

Gloria stared at the ruined desserts, open-mouthed for a moment before snapping back to reality and turning to Margery. 'How the hell did this happen?'

'The door was open when we got here,' Margery gestured at the mess with the keys, 'and well… this.'

'Good Lord.' Gloria stared wide-eyed. 'But no one else has a copy of the key, do they?'

Margery stared down at the cakes again. 'No, you know they don't. Gosh, it's just like the storeroom key again. The only people who are supposed to have a kitchen key are me, the headmaster and security.'

'Well, I can't see either of those two being options for this,' Gloria said, shaking her head. 'The headmaster wouldn't have and Gary Matthews in security would have been more likely to just eat them all.'

'Yes.' Margery lifted her foot and scraped the icing from her shoe with a piece of blue kitchen roll. 'This seems malicious.'

'Well,' Gloria said quietly, 'I think we all know someone who plays tricks to get her way, don't we?'

Margery considered Gloria's face carefully. She could only be talking about Mrs Smith, but there was something about Gloria's expression that was off. Margery had known Gloria long enough to know when she was hiding something.

Clementine shook her head dismissively. 'Rose is a bit off, and I must admit that that stuff in the drama studio the other day was strange at the very least, but can you really see her doing this?'

'She managed to get into the school easily enough then, didn't she?' Gloria said. She waved her hands in dismay at the mess.

'I just can't see her doing anything like this,' Margery said, looking around at the mess again. 'Seren wouldn't have gone along with it. She did so much of the work for the bake sale.'

'And they're joined at the hip now,' Clementine said, completely ignoring how hypocritical she sounded as she stood in Margery's personal space, their hands so close they were almost touching.

'How would anyone else have got in?' Gloria asked. 'If they didn't have a key? You said only managers have one.'

Margery thought about it. There were very few ways into the kitchen, especially as it was on the first floor. But there were ways and means if you knew what you were doing.

'The window by the fire escape is still broken, isn't it?' Gloria asked.

They all looked over to it, where the latch sat limp against the bottom of the window frame. You'd only need to give it a little push from the outside to force it open. Margery sighed; she had been meaning to have the window fixed since she had taken charge, but without a maintenance person it had proved too big a task. She had let it slide and then forgot about it in the chaos of her first few terms of management. This was all her fault.

She strode over to it and saw that it was indeed open, not by much, but a sliver. Someone had been here, they must have clambered through from the fire escape, destroyed all their cakes, and then left through the kitchen door, which opened from the inside by the latch. But why?

'It's okay, Margery,' Clementine said, patting her shoulder kindly. 'We'll figure it out later.' Gloria glared at them both as she poked at the pile of icing on the floor with the toe of her kitchen clog.

'Okay,' Margery said, turning away from the window and taking a deep breath. 'What do we have left for the bake sale? Let's do an inventory quick before anyone else gets here and—'

She was cut off by a blood-curdling shriek coming from the kitchen doorway; she spun around to confront it. Sharon had collapsed against the nearest prep table wailing in grief at the sight of the ruined cakes. Karen was trying to console her delicately, but she looked just as upset as Sharon did.

'What happened to our cakes!' Sharon screeched, taking off her Santa hat to dab her eyes dry. 'What are we going to sell now? How will we win the competition?'

'We'll still get best costumes,' Karen said. Sharon shook her head sadly.

'No, we won't, look, there's icing sugar all over your trousers.'

'We'll say it's snow!'

'Can we use that emergency money, Margery?' Clementine asked. Margery nodded. They had been collecting any spare change they found in the canteen for the last several years. It had been slowly dwindling due to the canteen almost being completely contactless now, but they would still find the odd ten pence that had rolled under a table.

'Yes, you go and get it.' Margery said, as Clementine rushed off to the secret hiding spot. 'We'll stay here and set up the tables in the hall. Sharon, Karen, get down to the shops now and grab whatever cake they have!'

Gloria shrugged as Karen and Sharon jumped to attention as though Margery were a particularly fierce corporal and not a mild-mannered kitchen manager wearing a false beard.

'Get the ones on the bottom of the pile, they'll be the most squashed, so it'll look more like we made them,' Margery said.

Karen hopped up from the floor tapping her smart watch, Sharon fell backward as she did so. 'Fantastic, come on Sharon, this is a great chance to get our steps in.'

'What if they don't have any cakes?' Sharon said as Karen dragged her up onto her feet, her baggy Father Christmas trousers tripping her as she tried to stand.

'Then just get a couple of Twixes and a packet of Kit-Kats,' Margery said seriously. 'We'll put them in the blender and shove some cream cheese on top, call it a cheesecake.'

Clementine arrived back with the old mustard tub full of money. Margery knew that it only contained eleven pounds after the time she had forgotten to order washing up liquid, but she was sure Sharon and Karen would be able to get something they could pass off as their own. Watching them both waddle from the room in their ridiculous costumes, she hoped they would not get stopped by any children wanting to give them Christmas present lists at the shops.

'Right,' Margery said, ignoring the way Gloria was still staring at her dumbfounded. 'Let's have a tidy and then go and see what trouble Ben and Seren have made with the tables in the sports hall.'

'What about this mess?' Gloria asked, her face was a picture of concern. 'I don't think a tidy will be enough.'

'We'll send Ben to clean it up,' Clementine said, pulling off her fake beard in frustration. 'He'll be useless at sales anyway.'

'We'll all come back and have a proper clean later,' Margery said to Gloria. 'We'll just put the food in the bin now so that we don't get ants. What else can we do?'

Gloria did not look convinced.

–

Forty minutes later and Clementine was straightening the meagre selection of supermarket cakes on the Father Christmas themed tablecloth, just in time for Mr Barrow to throw open the double doors in the hall to the public, the students and their parents. It seemed as though he had completely forgotten about the costume contest; he was still wearing one of his day-to-day suits with a tatty-looking Santa hat perched carefully on his head as to not ruin his hair.

Mrs Boch and the rest of the librarians kept waving at them excitedly from their spot opposite. Clementine glared at the array of Alice in Wonderland themed cupcakes they had for sale, muttering under her breath that they had obviously had them made professionally. In comparison, the PE teachers had only bought a singular batch of battered-looking Rice Krispie cakes. They all seemed terribly bored and only one of them had bothered to dress as Father Christmas at all. Margery did not think they would even get a mark on the score sheet for their attempt at the costume contest. Mr Daniels walked around with a clipboard doing the scoring in Mrs Smith's absence, looking everyone in attendance up and down in a judgemental manner.

The bake sale usually worked much better in the smaller school hall, Margery thought. The lighting was not as harsh, and you couldn't see how bad everyone's bakes were quite as clearly. The sports hall was much too big a venue for such a small event, and they had only managed to fill half of the room, though it was claustrophobic enough with everyone's much too large Father Christmas outfits. Margery was struggling to see from behind her hat and beard.

She put on a very large false smile as she saw Mrs Mugglethwaite, who worked at the post office, waltz through the double doors into the hall. She had arrived with the rest of her gang in tow. They all got the bus to and from the town centre together and were the main source of gossip in Dewstow, as well as all being as thick as thieves. Today Martha Mugglethwaite was wearing a ginormous faux fur coat, matching hat, and a festive brooch in the shape of a holly leaf. It looked as spiky as her tongue.

Margery felt Seren, who was standing beside her, stiffen at the sight of her. There was some historical nastiness between them. Margery felt obliged to support her co-worker who was upset enough at the news that her cakes had been destroyed.

'Why don't you go and have a wander, Seren?' she suggested. Seren nodded in relief, her Santa hat bobbing as she did so. 'We don't all need to be watching the stall at the same time. Go and buy a, well... whatever that is.' She gestured with her hand as she looked in alarm at the English teachers' table and their *Animal Farm* themed sugar cookies and the towering, true to scale *An Inspector Calls* themed gingerbread house. Miss Macdonald gave her a smug smile and waved over at them. Margery waved back timidly.

'Hello Margery, fantastic costumes.' Mrs Mugglethwaite had come straight over. Seren slipped away and out of sight into the crowd entering the hall. 'Lovely to see you both, how are you getting on? We never see you on the bus anymore.'

Clementine sighed deeply as though she was about to announce she had a terrible illness. 'All good thank you, Martha. Though we had a small issue with our bakes today.'

'I can see that,' Mrs Mugglethwaite said, staring down at the sad plate of squashed cakes they had been able to salvage and the obviously supermarket-bought ones on the plate next to it. 'I'll have one of your famous cherry Bakewells and a coffee anyway.'

'Lovely!' Clementine sprang into action and bagged up the cake, while Gloria hurriedly poured hot water from the water dispensing jug into a plastic cup, ignoring the way it melted partially under the heat. 'Fifty pence please.'

Mrs Mugglethwaite rummaged in her bag for her purse, finally finding it and bringing it out. She stopped and stared for a moment at Benjamin who was making himself useful by organising the plastic teaspoons and single-serve sachets of Kenco.

'Have we met?' she asked. He looked up, startled.

'I don't think so,' he said. He looked like a rabbit caught in bus headlights.

'This is Benjamin,' Margery said, to break the tension between them. 'He's our newest dinner person.'

'Newest Education Centre Nourishment Consultant you mean, Margery.' Clementine scoffed.

Mrs Mugglethwaite opened her mouth as though to ask something else, but she was interrupted by a commotion on the other side of the hall. Seren, Mr Barrow and Mrs Smith all seemed to be involved in an altercation. Mrs Smith had obviously spared no expense on her outfit, she had gone full Mrs Claus in a much too tight red dress with white trim, and matching cape. She was shouting and waving her arms around, the cape flinging side to side as she did so, while Mr Barrow tried to placate her. Seren stood behind them wringing her hands together and looking between them nervously. Margery left her post at the stall and rushed over.

'I'm a customer!' Mrs Smith spat. 'I'm allowed to be here!'

'The terms of your suspension were very clear.' The headmaster's face was purple with indignation. 'You're not to come anywhere near school property, you know that. Don't make me call the police.'

'Police!' Mrs Smith sneered, stepping towards him. 'What are they going to do? Arrest me?'

'Well, if you carry on…'

'Don't be such an idiot, James, you know I didn't come here that weekend for Christ's sake. I don't understand why you're still punishing me—'

'It's nothing to do with that,' he interrupted her.

'Of course it is.' Mrs Smith stabbed him in the chest with a well-manicured finger. He stepped back with his hands raised in defence.

'You!' The scream silenced all of them. The entire populace of the sports hall had already been quietly murmuring at the altercation between the headmaster and his deputy, but now their voices dropped to complete silence as everyone listened.

Mrs Blossom stood in the doorway. The index finger of her right hand raised and pointed directly at Mrs Smith's face. Mrs Smith stepped back wide-eyed, as Mrs Blossom stepped forward. Ittonvale's tall music teacher, Tilly, stood awkwardly behind her, holding Mrs Blossom's sheet music bag. Margery's eyes were drawn to the mole on her nose; she felt cruel for staring and looked away immediately.

'How could you?' Mrs Blossom hissed at her so violently that Mrs Smith would have found herself covered in spit if she had not moved. Even the headmaster was stunned into silence as he looked between them both, his mouth falling open.

'What are you talking about?' Mrs Smith asked, she sounded menacing, but Margery knew her well enough now to hear the fear underneath it. 'What have I done?'

Mrs Blossom began to laugh, a nasty, unsettling laugh, devoid of any happiness. 'What haven't you done! Was it not enough to take my play?' She wailed as though she was in dreadful pain; Margery felt Clementine grasp for her hand in surprise.

'What does that even mean?' Mrs Smith cried back. 'I haven't done anything of the sort!'

'Where is she?' Mrs Blossom demanded. Her eyes wet with tears.

'Who?' Mrs Smith asked, though the answer seemed to wash over her as she did so. Margery saw the realisation flicker behind her eyes as she noticed that Mrs Blossom was missing her usual companion.

'Ada of course, you stupid witch!' The staff in the hall gasped as Mrs Blossom sneered at Mrs Smith. 'What have you done with my dog?'

'I-I-,' Mrs Smith stammered. 'I haven't done anything with her, what's happened?'

'Just you wait till the police have checked all the evidence.' Mrs Blossom turned to leave, then spun back around to glare at Mrs Smith again, bumping into Tilly as she did so. The woman was so tall that Mrs Blossom's head bounced off her stomach before she jumped back. 'You'll get yours, Rose, I'll see that you do. And you two!'

She pointed at Margery and then at Clementine. They looked at each other in shock.

'I don't know who you are...' Mrs Blossom shrieked at them. Tilly held her back again. 'But don't think I don't know you're helping her! I saw you at my school!'

The headmaster turned to consider Margery and Clementine carefully. Margery felt herself withering under his gaze like a lettuce leaf that had accidentally been left under the kitchen's heat lamps. Mrs Blossom stormed from the hall as quickly as she had arrived. Tilly followed. Mrs Smith was red in the face and looked as though she might start to cry at any moment; the knuckles of both her hands were clenched tightly together in fists.

'Okay. Come on, I'll walk you to your car,' Mr Barrow said, gently touching Mrs Smith's elbow. She flinched away from him as though she had been burned by his fingertips, glaring at him as she turned on her heel and left. Seren rushed after her. Mr Barrow watched them leave, his face falling as she went, the fingers of his arm still outstretched as though he was trying to reach for her. Margery and Clementine looked at each other, eyebrows raised.

Chapter Seventeen

'Do you think Gloria could be right about Mrs Smith?' Clementine asked, as Margery locked the front door and stepped off their front doorstep. 'Why was she at the school again anyway? And that whole thing with the Mrs Blossom's dog going missing! Does she want to get arrested?'

Margery did not know what to think if she was being honest with herself. She had been pondering it all night long, tossing and turning in their bed while Clementine snored next to her. She could not see why Mrs Smith would want to destroy all their hard work and yet she had created several scenes at the school since she had been suspended. She was not an easy person to get on with either, there had always been a bit of animosity between them, but Margery had thought that they had finally struck up a sort of friendship with her. A truce at the very least.

What she was even more unsure about, was why Mrs Smith would do anything of the sort to their kitchen. If it had been her, it was a real step into something more like chaos than anything else. She just could not see it. She couldn't see her stealing Mrs Blossom's dog. Rose was nasty, abrasive, sometimes flippantly rude, but she wasn't as cruel as she made out she was. The whole situation with

Seren living in her house for free proved that unequivocally. And no matter how much she hated Mrs Blossom, Margery could not see her harming a living creature.

'I think we should go and see Gary on Monday morning. Whatever Mr Barrow says. Whatever the police say. As if they'd help us anyway!' Margery finally said, slipping the front door keys into her bag as she followed Clementine down the garden path. 'Find out a bit more about the two people on the CCTV, see if we can see who went into the kitchen yesterday morning. They've got to have got in through that fire escape window and then opened the kitchen door from the inside. There's no other way.'

They had called Officer Thomas again yesterday afternoon to report the damages to their cakes. Officer Thomas had been polite enough on the phone, but he hadn't been able to keep the laughter out of his voice. He had eventually told Clementine in no uncertain terms that it was a matter for the school to sort out and not the authorities, though Clementine argued with him for much, much longer than was appropriate. The headmaster had brushed them off when they had approached him after the incident; he had stormed after Rose as she left, and they had not seen him again. Mr Daniels had eventually announced that the English department had won both the bake sale and the Santa costume contest, much to the dinner lady team's despair. Then they had all gone home empty handed, Miss Macdonald waving two freshly printed certificates spitefully at them as she left.

'I wish Rose would tell us her alibi,' Clementine huffed. 'She'd have been off the hook by now and we might be one step closer to finding the real culprit. The pliers being in Mrs Large's office seems to mean she did it.'

She stopped walking and turned to grab Margery's hand. 'You don't think Mrs Large would have put it up?'

Margery thought about it for a long moment. 'But, why? What reason could she have had? And with who?'

'With Rose?' Clementine suggested. 'The two of them put it up wrong and then Mrs Large dies, and Rose pretends she doesn't know anything about it.'

'Seren swears she has an alibi too.' Margery sighed.

'Well, I wish she'd spit it out.' Clementine took her by the arm, and they began down the road again. 'And I wish Officer Thomas had never given us his number.'

'It hasn't been very helpful, has it?' Margery said. 'Oh God, quick Clem, hide!'

They were too slow to duck behind the nearest bush and worse, Dawn saw them try. She rushed over to them from where she had been trimming her hedge, still holding the garden shears in her hand, puffing heavily in her big winter coat.

'Hello!' she called loudly. 'I can see you!'

Margery and Clementine stood up from where they had been crouched down, smiling guiltily. Margery had been avoiding Dawn for days, it seemed their luck had finally run out.

'Oh, hello Dawn!' Clementine cried in faux jubilation. 'We didn't see you there!'

'Of course you didn't,' Dawn said sarcastically, glaring between them both. 'How's the crochet coming along, Margery?'

'Okay...' Margery squeaked. 'I've managed nearly ten more now...'

'Ten!' Dawn raised her eyebrows. 'Well, remember I said I'd forgive that if you both join my choir. We're so short on numbers still and we're supposed to be performing in town later. You just have to say.'

'Oh, you know we can't, Dawn.' Margery shook her head. 'We've got the school concert still.'

Dawn tutted and shook her head at them both. 'Well, think about it, will you? The WI need all the help we can get with the church carol performance. This year's sign-up has been very, very disappointing indeed.'

She gave them one last glare and then went back to pruning her hedge. They continued their journey to the town centre, Clementine hissing about how gardening in mid-winter was almost psychotic and they ought to report it to Officer Thomas in case Dawn turned out to be a mad axe murderer.

They continued their slow journey into Dewstow town centre. Margery had thought they might take the car, but Clementine would not hear of it, insisting it was a December tradition that they walk the short distance to the town centre on a weekend and go to all the shops for their Christmas shopping. Then they would wander around the market, get a hot chocolate each, look at all the bits and bobs on the stalls and buy a new ornament for the tree. Then they would finally get the bus home late afternoon, laden with the gifts they had bought.

The high street had been closed to traffic for the day and was finely dressed in turned off Christmas lights, ready for the big light switch on at five thirty. The stalls running down it for the weekend market were wonderfully festive and there was a long queue of children and parents waiting to enter the library, where Father Christmas was meeting families in his grotto. Helpers dressed as elves entertained the gathering crowd, as a band on the small stage at the bottom of the street blasted through one rock cover of a

Christmas song after the other. Dawn's choir was gathering behind the stage, ready to go on after. Margery had no idea how Dawn had beat them into town, though Clementine suggested that she had probably teleported there. Clementine took her hand, and Margery looked at her gleeful face as they walked. There was an enormous real fir tree at the top of the high street by the Bell and Hope, beautifully decked out with all the trimmings. The weather was crisp and although it was not Clementine's dream wonderland of snow, Margery felt privately that this was the next best thing.

'Hello ladies!' Mr Fitzgerald who ran the oddities shop called over to them from one of the stalls on the high street. Today he was wearing a very thick purple cape over a thick winter coat and shivering slightly, the ends of his long grey beard tucked underneath his scarf. The soup kettle behind him blasted steam up into the cold air. He waved at them so frantically that Margery thought his leather gloves might fly off. 'Fancy a mulled wine?'

'What are you doing here?' Margery asked as he spooned out a big ladle of wine from the kettle into a paper cup, she thought they might have to walk all the way down to his shop to see him. 'Who's watching the shop?'

'Jason's there.' Mr Fitzgerald smiled. 'I'm just having a little Christmas break running this stall.' Margery briefly wondered how Jason would serve customers or use the till, being a Jack Russell terrier, but she pushed the thought down and took a sip from the steaming paper cup he handed her.

'Have you been busy?' Clementine asked, sipping from her own cup. 'We've got a huge list of things to get.' She pulled an Argos catalogue from her bag. 'Ooh, while we're here, will you keep an eye out for any other dinner ladies for us? I think I've very nearly worked out the complete who's-got-who for Secret Santa, but I can't be certain. If you see anyone buying a something for five pounds, you'll let me know?'

'My dear,' Mr Fitzgerald began gently, as though Clementine were a coiled spring that was about to ping off into his eye, 'I hate to be the bearer of bad news, but I don't think that's how Secret Santa is supposed to work.'

'I've been telling her that.' Margery shook her head; he smiled at her.

'Nonsense,' Clementine said, flipping through the catalogue, where she had circled several items. 'The whole point of it is to know exactly what everyone's got, so that you know who to ask to swap with you later.'

'Also…' Mr Fitzgerald said, peering at the catalogue in Clementine's hands. 'I don't think they do the Argos catalogue any more do they? Isn't the whole debacle done online?'

'This is from 2013.' Margery pointed to the date on the front of the catalogue. 'At least your collection of them in the shed might be worth something now.'

'I know but I just like having a hard copy to choose from. And what are you talking about, Margery? They've always been worth their weight in gold. Gosh, I could have sworn it was less time ago than that.' Clementine shook her head. 'It's my age, the older I get the longer ago the other day was.'

Margery nodded, she too was a victim of Clementine's 'the other day', which could range from a few weeks to several decades ago.

'You wouldn't happen to have seen a car, would you?' she asked Mr Fitzgerald as she handed him a five-pound note to pay for the wine. 'Sorry, that sounds really silly now I've said it out loud! I mean a particular car when you've been on duty.'

'I have definitely seen a few cars there.' Mr Fitzgerald chuckled. 'Do you know what your specific car looks like?'

'Yes.' Clementine smashed the ancient catalogue back into her bag. 'Margery knows the numberplate.'

'Well, I must be honest and tell you that I do not possess a photographic memory.' He shook his head sadly. 'In fact, if anything I have the opposite. My brain's like lots of old Scrabble tiles all stuck together sometimes. Have you asked the Dewstow Facebook community page?'

'No, because we don't want the person to know that we want to know who they are,' Clementine said, a little too honestly. Margery hoped they could rely on her ignoring of Mr Fitzgerald's past indiscretions to keep his silence.

'Well,' he said finally, 'I might be able to help another way.'

'How?' Margery asked, shifting the cup to her other hand as it burned her palm.

'Let me have a think,' he said, needlessly mysteriously. Margery took a sip of the wine, which was still boiling hot. She regretted taking such a large gulp instantly as it burned her tongue.

The rest of the day had been much the same after that. Margery tried to concentrate on smaller matters, like helping Clementine find the perfect new ornament for the Christmas tree, but horrible thoughts kept simmering up to the forefront of her mind. Mrs Large's accident, the funeral, Ben in the headmaster's office. It all seemed a bit hopeless. They eventually settled on a bauble with seven swans a-swimming painted delicately onto it. It would go very well with the rest of the set they had already collected.

The number five bus finally arrived, they paid the driver and made their way towards the back, where they always sat when they needed to get the bus anywhere, with much more difficulty than usual laden under the weight of all their shopping bags.

'Hello Margery, Clementine,' Mrs Mugglethwaite called cheerily from where she was sitting holding court at the front of the bus. 'Nice to see you again so soon. Did a bit of shopping did you?'

'We did.' Clementine smiled back at her, waving the bags excitedly as they sat down in their usual seat.

'Oh Margery,' Mrs Mugglethwaite said, 'I've worked out how I know your new boy!'

'Really?' Margery asked quizzically; if she was being honest with herself, she had completely forgotten all about that. 'How?'

'He works at the hospital.' Mrs Mugglethwaite smiled widely. 'Always so lovely and polite he is, I saw him quite a bit when I kept getting tennis elbow.'

'The hospital?' Clementine said, the shopping bags all but forgotten. 'Are you sure?'

'Yes of course.' Mrs Mugglethwaite smiled again. 'I saw him there on Thursday when I went for treatment for my housemaid's knee. Terrible joints run in the family you see, I'm back and forth like a yoyo. Last year I had tennis elbow, I've never so much as played a game of ping pong.'

'Gosh,' Margery said sullenly. 'Are you sure? He never said he had another job.'

'I am amazed looking back that you would give him time off during the day.' Mrs Mugglethwaite took a sweet from her bag and unwrapped it. 'Surely you need him at lunchtimes.'

'He was working with us on Thursday lunchtime.' Margery shook her head. 'It can't possibly have been him.'

'It certainly looked like him.' Mrs Mugglethwaite popped the sweet in her mouth. 'Are you entirely sure he didn't sneak off to his second job?'

'No… I don't think so,' Margery said, too surprised to form a convincing argument.

'You can't be paying him enough, Margery.' Mrs Mugglethwaite smirked smugly. 'He'll be down at the post office asking me for a job if this carries on!'

She turned around in her seat, with her back to them again.

'Well,' Clementine mused quietly, 'I always knew there was something strange about Ben. He didn't know how to turn the washing machine on at work the other day and then when he did manage it, all the tea towels came out pink because he decided to wash his socks in there too. Don't get me started on him putting his kitchen shoes in the dishwasher, it boggles the mind.'

'It doesn't mean anything. He's only bad at kitchen related things, he seems quite handy with a tool kit…' Margery whispered to Clementine, suddenly realising what she was saying. 'He's handy with a tool kit… oh my… Clem you don't think Ben put the stage up, do you?'

Clementine's eyes widened. 'He does love fixing things, doesn't he? You're right, he seems quite good at most things except the job you actually employed him for! Gosh, Margery, are you sure he didn't lie on his CV?'

'I rang all his references, and they gave him top marks.' Margery slumped back in defeat as the bus lurched up a particularly steep hill. 'And he was definitely there last Thursday. I'm sure of it.'

'Was he?' Clementine muttered, 'Wasn't that the day he said he had the dentist?'

'Well… maybe… but…' Margery began to say but then realised she could not remember.

'Bit strange,' Clementine said. 'If he did do it though, he must have been told to do it. Can you see him thinking of putting the stage together himself?'

Margery could only nod in agreement. 'No, you're right, someone would have put him up to it.'

'Officer Thomas said there were two people on the CCTV, didn't he?' Clementine asked.

'He did.'

Margery stared out of the window as the bus whipped around the edge of town. A brightly coloured building caught her eye through the darkness of the afternoon, and she instinctively reached up to press the stop bell. Clementine watched her curiously. The bus rolled to a halt and Margery stood to get off. Clementine followed a moment later, pulling all their shopping bags up with them.

'Goodbye, Mrs Mugglethwaite!' Margery said, in the best faux cheer she could manage. Mrs Mugglethwaite and Mrs Redburn waved them both off as they clambered down the bus steps and back out into the cold. Clementine looked around at the bus leaving them behind, and then back at her in confusion.

'Where are we going, Margery?' she asked as she scuttled along behind her.

'I'm just so sick of being worried all the time, Clem. I know it's awful about Mrs Large and I feel terrible that the police haven't worked out what happened, and even worse that we haven't either!' Margery could feel the panic rising in her chest, she felt almost hysterical. 'And if Ben was the person who put the stage together then that means I employed one of the people who killed Mrs Large!'

'It's all right, Margery.' Clementine reached for her and pulled her into a hug. 'It's okay, it's not your fault, is it? Even if Ben did do it, it's not your fault. Yes, it's terrible, but it's nothing to do with you. You can't control what other people do.'

Margery accepted Clementine's comfort, and they stood at the side of the road for a while as the traffic drove past and the day grew darker, Clementine whispering soothing nonsense to her. Eventually Margery pulled away and wiped her eyes.

'It's just been a lot, hasn't it?' she said, waving her arms to try and explain how much of a lot it had been.

'It has,' Clementine agreed. She looked around at the empty bus stop. 'So, why are we here at the Dewstow community page's most complained about eyesore?'

Margery chuckled as Clementine gestured around at the ugly industrial estate. 'Oh, it's so silly. I just saw the building and thought it would be something to do to take our mind off things for a bit, let's just wait for the next bus and go home.'

'You can't be serious, Margery!' Clementine cried. 'We can't leave now! We haven't been here for ages! I'm glad we stopped. Come on.'

Margery smiled and took her hand. Clementine chuckled gleefully as they approached the glowing façade of the bowling alley. 'This is going to be fantastic. Remember when we had a team-building day here in 2009 and Caroline replaced one of the balls with a melon she'd painted?'

They made their way inside the brightly lit building. The Christmas music blaring from the speakers was drowned out only by the clattering of bowling balls against pins; the only decoration was the sad wilting tinsel that had been draped over every surface. They walked through the lobby, past the busy arcade full of children and to the reception desk where to Margery's great surprise, Mrs Smith was sitting, looking absolutely miserable and shining a ball with a microfibre cloth and polish. They stopped dead and stared at her.

She was wearing a colourful Hawaiian shirt and a Christmas Santa hat and Margery found she could not look at her directly, because of how unsettling it was to see her in such casual dress. Especially with the addition of the tinsel she had draped around her neck, like a very itchy scarf. Shelves of bowling shoes were piled up behind her on racks.

'What are you doing here?' Mrs Smith hissed as she noticed them watching her, slamming the ball down on the counter in front of her so hard it left an indent in the surface. 'Get out!'

'You… you…' Clementine seemed completely lost for words. Margery could not seem to find any either. 'What are you doing?'

'What do you think I'm doing?' Mrs Smith growled through gritted teeth.

'I don't know,' Clementine said, her eyes like saucers as Mrs Smith continued to glare at them both.

'Well, are you happy?' Mrs Smith rolled her eyes at them and picked up the ball again. 'Now you know my secret? You'd better leave before my supervisor comes over and asks why you haven't bought anything.'

'Is this… is this where you were?' Margery asked her. Mrs Smith froze. 'The weekend the stage was put up?'

'Yes,' Mrs Smith whispered, she would not look either of them in the eye, her jaw clenched tightly.

'You're working here?' Clementine asked. 'Why?'

'Divorce is very expensive, Mrs Butcher-Baker,' Mrs Smith said, without an ounce of humour. 'You may remember my now ex-husband finding out about my affair with James not long ago?'

'Of course, we all remember your affair with the head-master.' Margery nodded grimly. She did not think she would ever be able to forget about it; unfortunately for her the upsetting details were burnt into her memory forever.

'Well, he got a solicitor, and he took me to the cleaners.' Mrs Smith looked like she might cry. 'All I've got left is the house, our holiday home in St Martin's-on-the-water and the chateau in Dormond. I'm stuck paying off the legal bills now. He even took the dog!'

Margery gasped, that must have been the worst of the betrayal. She couldn't imagine Clementine taking Pumpkin with her if she left. For one thing, Margery was Pumpkin's favourite and Clementine would probably drop her back home by the end of the day.

'Could you not just sell one of the holiday homes to raise the money?' Clementine asked, her brow furrowed. Mrs Smith glared at her as if it were out of the question.

'So, you see why I asked you to help me?' Mrs Smith asked, changing the subject. Margery nodded. She briefly thought about reaching out and patting the distraught woman's hand resting on the bowling ball but thought better of it.

'Is it fun working at the bowling alley?' Clementine asked, stroking her chin in thought. 'I suppose it must be. Ooh, do you get to use the slushy machine?'

Mrs Smith ignored her and began to polish the bowling ball again. 'Anyway, fat bit of help you two have been. I'm still not allowed to work on the play, I'm still not allowed to go to the school, and I still can't tell anyone where I was that weekend because then everyone will know I'm struggling! It's a mess.'

'Not even the headmaster?' Margery asked gently. 'I'm sure you can tell him, can't you? Wouldn't he understand? He loves you.'

'He can't know. Not if I'm ever going to win him back... I mean...' She stopped talking suddenly, as though she realised that she had said too much.

'We're still trying,' Margery said. 'Against the wishes of the headmaster and the police.' Mrs Smith nodded.

'Right, we'll stay and play a round then,' Clementine grinned, 'and then we'll get one of those blue drinks.' Mrs Smith shook her head at her in exasperation, the iced slushy machine behind her whirring.

'I don't have any shoes small enough for your tiny feet.' She smirked at Clementine. 'Why won't you just leave. Is it not embarrassing enough for me without you staying and gawping?'

'I'll have you know that my feet are a size four!' Clementine piped up. 'A perfectly reasonable size and much cheaper overall, because I can wear children's shoes.'

'I don't think it's embarrassing,' Margery said quickly. 'I think it's admirable that you didn't just steal your ex-husband's money.'

Mrs Smith sat back in her chair and regarded her carefully.

'Well,' she said, seemingly unable to find any words, 'thank you, I suppose.'

'How are you?' Clementine asked, suddenly serious. 'What happened with Mrs Blossom in the end? Yesterday, I mean.'

'Nothing more than you saw.' Mrs Smith shrugged, her stance nonchalant, but the hurt written on her face. 'She thinks we stole her dog because it went missing that morning, which obviously we did not.'

'You don't think that the strange man we followed the other day wasn't supposed to take her?' Margery asked.

'He and the dog seemed pretty chummy to me.' Mrs Smith turned to search for a pair of shoes small enough for Clementine.

'They did.' Margery tapped her fingers to her mouth and tried to remember the exact events of that day.

'So, after that I had the police over last night asking stupid questions again.' Mrs Smith handed Clementine her shoes and then turned to Margery from her seat behind the counter. 'Size?'

'Six. Really?' Margery asked. 'Whatever for now?'

'Lots of weird questions about Mrs Large,' Mrs Smith said, turning back to the shoes again. 'And about the dog. Really, it's you two who should be worried about being accused next if this is how they're going to play it.'

'What!' Clementine said. 'But we didn't take her!'

'Well, I know that, she would have eaten your cat,' Mrs Smith said, passing Margery her shoes and then picking the bowling ball and polishing cloth back up. 'But Rhonda's obviously got it into her head that we took her. They're looking at the CCTV from the school and her house now though, so that will probably exonerate all of us.'

'Can you really not just show the police your payslip from here or something?' Margery asked. 'Get yourself off the hook?'

'I don't know anymore, Margery,' Mrs Smith said wearily. She looked as tired as Margery felt and Margery felt a sudden stab of pity for her.

'Come on, Clem,' Margery said, grabbing Clementine by the arm and turning to go. 'Let's leave Rose to work in peace. Sorry to bother you, Rose.'

'You know…' Mrs Smith said thoughtfully from the counter, 'I do get fifty per cent discount for friends and family, so if you did stay…'

Clementine whipped around again, already beaming. 'Which are we? Friends or family?'

Rose looked like had never considered it in her life.

'Co-workers,' she said, after a long pause.

'Good enough for me!' Clementine grinned ecstatically, pulling Margery towards the counter. Mrs Smith looked on in horror, as though she was regretting what she said. 'Come on, Margery, let's have a game. A Christmas treat!'

Chapter Eighteen

A few hours later and they were back in the safety and warmth of their own living room feeling freer than they had in days. Margery had not been convinced that the Christmas tree could take another bauble, but miraculously Clementine had managed to get every single one from the box in the attic onto it. Though it did seem to sag dangerously under its own weight. The new decoration they had bought from the market sat at the very edge of a branch so precariously that it probably would have blown over if they breathed too close to it.

She sat next to Clementine under a blanket on the old worn sofa and sipped at the hot chocolate from the mug in her hands. The CD player under the television set hummed carols pleasantly and they basked in the glow from the electric imitation gas fireplace, which Pumpkin was balled up in front of. The light reflected off the decorations and glimmered prettily around the room. Even their brand-new Wi-Fi router box was decorated with tinsel. Margery closed her eyes and let her head rest back against the seat in relaxation.

'I rang Ceri-Ann to ask her where on earth our Christmas cards are,' Clementine said abruptly; Margery opened her eyes again with a start. Ceri-Ann had come over to do a photoshoot with them in early November at Clementine's behest for their Christmas card this year. She had assured them it was going to be classic and tasteful but having seen her other works, Margery was not so sure.

'What did she say?' Margery asked, leaning forward to put her mug down on the coffee table in front of them.

Clementine beamed and put her mug down next to hers, careful to use the coaster with a picture of them on their wedding day on it.

'She said she's going to drop them over tomorrow.' Clementine smiled even wider. 'It's so exciting, isn't it! Personalised Christmas cards, just like the celebs have!'

There was a knock on the door, they both looked up sharply.

'Do you think that might be Mr Fitzgerald?' Margery whispered.

'I'll get it,' Clementine said, throwing her half of the blanket off her lap and getting up. 'You stay there, but make sure you keep one of those needles handy in case it's a burglar.'

Margery looked down at the plastic crochet hook on the coffee table in front of her. She would probably end up giving herself a splinter if she tried to stab anyone with it. She could hear Clementine talking to someone through the closed living room door, though she could not pick out any words. It was all very muffled with the draft excluder still resting against the bottom of the door. Margery picked up the crochet hook, just in case. A few minutes later Clementine arrived back in the living room with an A4 ring binder.

'Was it Mr Fitzgerald?' Margery asked.

'It was!' Clementine sat back down next to her, forgetting all about the blanket in her haste to open the ring binder. 'Look at these mad records he's kept. He wanted to give me all of them from every year since 1986, but

I managed to convince him that the last five should do.' She flipped the folder open. Inside were pages and pages of paper, all headed with different town events from Dewstow and Ittonvale, and then with the name of the car's owner, the car numberplate, the time they arrived and then left all written in neat columns. 'Gosh, well this isn't normal, is it? How many laws do you think these break?'

'Not normal at all.' Margery shook her head. 'This is why Mr Fitzgerald isn't welcome at town meetings any more probably.'

'And he kept trying to bring his cat.' Clementine pulled on her glasses from the chain round her neck and began to run a finger down the numberplates in search. 'Remember Mr Tiddles? Before he had Jason?'

'How could I forget?' Margery sighed as she looked at the amount of paper in the folder and wondered if they would ever find the man. They were relying on him being in there somewhere when he may well not be.

–

Clementine shook her awake at three o clock in the morning, and they had a brief and very subdued celebration because she had found the stranger's numberplate among all the others. Margery had fallen asleep in the armchair, surrounded by pieces of paper, her crochet thing in the bag by the chair, still unfinished. She had crawled upstairs after Clementine and slept until the alarm went off at six thirty. The sun was still not in the sky outside the window, as she drew the curtains back and peered out into the gloom.

The man's name was Michael Leith. At least, they were hoping it was. There was still a chance that a different owner had taken the car to the Ittonvale town summer fete or Dewstow's harvest festival. Now they just had to work out how to find out who he was, from just his name. Margery was very worried they wouldn't be able to pull it off. Nevertheless, it was a lead, which was a small win in her book. She pottered into the bathroom in her shabby dressing gown and looked at her tired face in the mirror; the circles under her eyes seemed to grow larger by the day. Clementine followed behind her, her brow scrunched with worry.

'You're trying to do too much,' she said as Margery splashed her face with freezing cold water from the tap, the boiler not quite kicking into life. 'You need to learn to delegate a bit more, that's the whole point of being a manager. Making other people do stuff for you.'

'I'm sure that's not the point, Clem,' Margery said. 'The point is that you're the person to blame when it all goes wrong.' She sighed, moving aside so Clementine could brush her teeth.

'Stop doing the crochet,' Clementine said, eyeing her seriously. 'Tell Dawn to do one.'

'I can't.' Margery shook her head. 'It's penance for the pond and the hedge that we destroyed, or we'll have join her choir.'

Clementine rolled her eyes so hard that Margery was worried she had caused them permanent damage.

'Well, let's just join the choir then, she'll soon kick us out when she realises we sound like banshees when we sing. And that hedge was a monstrosity, Margery. We should have called the council and had them remove it years ago. Anyway, it's fine now, isn't it! She goes out there to trim it every day with a tiny pair of scissors. Has she nothing better to do? It's the middle of winter for crying out loud, let it grow free!'

'You're only saying that because you hate mowing the lawn,' Margery said, smiling at Clementine's rant. 'You can barely walk down our garden path the grass is so long.'

'That's neither here nor there, Margery,' Clementine said through a mouthful of toothpaste. 'Our lawn looks much more interesting than her hideous topiary contraption, she acts like it's the royal botanical garden. We should ship her off to live inside one of those ugly old jam jars at the Eden Project, that would solve all our problems.'

'They're biomes, Clem,' Margery said, as Clementine rinsed, 'and you said they were lovely when we visited.' She sighed. 'I can't work out what's going on at the school. It all seems connected, but I can't piece it together. It's driving me mad. The sooner we find this Michael, the better.'

'I agree.' Clementine wiped her face on the hand towel next to the sink and turned to her, serious for once. 'What do we do when we find him, though?'

'I don't know,' Margery said sadly. 'Everything we find out just seems to cause more questions.'

'We still don't know who put the stage lights up or took the tools, or put them in Mrs Large's office,' Clementine said. 'It's all a mess. I think we should just stop caring and enjoy the lead-up to Christmas. You've certainly got enough to do as it is. Let the police do their work, they don't want us doing anything anyway.'

'Yes,' Margery admitted, she did have a lot left to do. Crochet notwithstanding. 'Maybe you're right.'

'I'm always right,' Clementine said, leaving the bathroom, Margery rolled her eyes and followed her down the stairs. 'The first thing we stop doing should be helping

Rose out, it's been nothing but trouble and it's not really getting us anywhere, is it? She obviously doesn't really want any help, or she'd just tell them she was at her other job on the weekend the stage was put up.'

Margery had to agree. 'Okay.'

'But we do need to think what we're going to do about Benjamin.'

Margery sighed. 'What about him? We can't prove he's done anything and I certainly can't tell him to leave his other job. If he even has one. Martha Mugglethwaite isn't always right with her astute observations.'

'Forget about that, remember he was doing something to the headmaster's computer? That's strange.' They reached the kitchen and Margery flipped on the kettle. In her tired haze of the last few days, she had entirely forgotten about the incident with Ben and the computer.

'Well,' Margery said, feeling like she was grasping at straws, 'maybe there's an innocent reason?'

Clementine did not look convinced as she rooted through the kitchen cupboard. 'I suppose. But also, does it not seem weird to you that he can't cook at all, and he's supposed to have loads of experience?'

'Yes, of course it does. But it doesn't prove anything else, and we have no evidence.' Margery thought about it. 'At least we can discount Rose as having a part in any of it. For now, anyway.'

Clementine put the mugs down on the counter by the kettle and turned to eye her carefully. 'What's the plan then, Margery?'

Margery sat down at the table and thought. Finally, she picked up her phone. 'What was the man's name again?'

'Michael Leith.'

Margery tapped the name into the Google search bar on her phone; if nothing else it was worth a try. The screen filled with search results instantly and she scrolled through them.

'I think I've worked out why he seemed so friendly with Mrs Blossom's dog, Clem,' Margery said, showing her the phone screen.

'He owns a dog day care!' Clementine exclaimed. 'What on earth will they come up with next? Let's go down there after school and sort this all out.'

–

When they arrived at the school an hour later, they bumped into Mrs Smith in the corridor. It was impossible to miss her with her ginormous sunglasses and a huge faux fur coat draped over her shoulders as though she were the star of a music video. Seren pottered along behind her like a chicken following a peacock.

'You're here?' Margery asked her. 'Are you supposed to be here?'

'I'm reinstated.' Mrs Smith smiled smugly.

'You told the headmaster your alibi?' Clementine suggested. Mrs Smith shook her head.

'I did. I sucked up all my pride and told him.' She scoffed, dramatically flipping her bob back behind her ears. Margery thought she must have been boiling in her huge coat with the heating on full blast all over the school. 'But it was all for naught, no thanks to you. The police worked out who put the stage together anyway apparently, I'm off the hook.'

'Really?' Margery heard Clementine gasp from next to her.

'This means you never figured the case out.' Mrs Smith smiled again. 'Which means I'll be seeing you next year for the Christmas concert auditions!'

Clementine groaned. 'No!'

'Yes!' Mrs Smith cried gleefully.

'Wait, who did the police say did it?' Margery asked. She was baffled at what conclusion they must have come to.

'They didn't.' Mrs Smith shrugged again. They swept up the corridor together; Margery's brain felt like it was working in overdrive as she tried to piece it all together.

Chapter Nineteen

Margery's usual haven in the dry store was not so peaceful for the rest of the day. The revelation that Mrs Smith was back, and the repercussions that was going to have on the Christmas concert planning, was all the staff could talk about. Mrs Smith had already spun into the kitchen and demanded that the rehearsals double in number. Even more horrifyingly, she had also announced that they would be having extra singing practice at her house after work hours. Mr Daniels had traipsed in behind her, pale-faced and miserable in her presence.

To make matters even worse, Clementine kept popping into the dry store to talk about which order she felt was best to watch the *Friends* Christmas specials in. Gloria kept arriving to moan at her about either Sharon, Karen or Seren, who were all apparently 'terrible people who have no concept of food safety'. The only person safe from Gloria's wrath was young Benjamin, but only because he had changed all the lightbulbs in the staff changing room and was currently hero of the day, even with Margery and Clementine's suspicions.

As a compromise between her sanity and her availability as a kitchen manager she had closed the storeroom door, though she had not locked it, feeling that that was a step too far. Anyway, the headmaster might come by and summon her and Clementine for the talking-to he had obviously planned for them after he found out they were investigating again. They had been so late for work that they had been able to slip away earlier, but she was now terrified of when the conversation would eventually happen. It would not do to seem unavailable.

Margery thought about just packing everything up and leaving her paperwork for another day. She was sure if she went back into the main kitchen, she could easily find something else to do. Something a bit more mind numbing and relaxing, a bit of washing up or checking the date labels in the fridge. Instead, she went through her check list again; she had to get it done before the next disturbance. At least, Margery thought, Mrs Smith being suspended had meant she was not constantly popping in and ruining every conversation they were having. They had been in the middle of a fantastic debate earlier about what was whose favourite squash, Margery and Clementine held a torch for Tesco's own Cherries and Berries, when Mrs Smith had suddenly arrived and announced loudly that she only drank elderflower cordial.

She froze suddenly, dropping the pen she had been holding. There was a noise again, as strange and disembodied as the other day. She listened as hard as she could, till she could only hear the ringing of her own blood in her head. Margery put the clipboard back down and clambered up on the stool where she had left it. She pulled herself up to the vent again and listened.

Someone was talking. It sounded like a woman's voice though she could not be entirely sure, it was so muffled. She made an executive decision and popped the cover from the vent, dropping it onto the top of the chest freezer next to the stool. She steeled herself, took a deep breath, leaned forward, and stuck as much of her head inside as possible.

It was very dark and dusty inside the vent, and she had to fight the instant surge of claustrophobia that swelled inside her. Margery concentrated, listening to the voice, which was much clearer as it boomed around the metal inside of the vent though still not entirely perfect.

'…If anyone finds out…' A woman's voice said. From the little Margery could hear they sounded very upset.

'Calm down, Matilda, it's not that bad…'

'Not that bad!' the woman cried out interrupting. 'How could this possibly get any worse?'

Margery felt like she knew that voice, both of those voices, and that name. But she could not place either of them without sight. It was hard to hear much else as they reduced their voices to murmurs. She heard what sounded like a door slamming somewhere and then there was nothing again, but a very faint scratching noise.

'Who the devil could that have been?' Margery whispered to herself, removing her head from the vent, and stepping back down onto the floor. She sat down on the stool and wondered what to do now. How could she find out where the people had been and who they were? Her train of thought was interrupted by Clementine. She slammed the door open so hard Margery could hear the dent it must have made in the plastic cladding on the wall.

'Margery, quick!' She panted as she rushed into the room. 'We've got to get out of here!'

'What's going on?' she asked, looking at Clementine's wide, frantic eyes.

'The headmaster's coming, and he doesn't look happy.'

'For us?' Margery got up from her chair.

'For us! Come on, let's go out the fire escape.' Clementine grabbed her by the hand, and they left the dry store, running straight into Mr Barrow, who was walking down the narrow corridor towards them.

-

The headmaster considered them from across his desk. His mouth was drawn in a thin, angry line. Margery did not see how they were going to get out of this one. She wished that he had never found out about their visit to Ittonvale school, in fact, she wished they had never gone at all. It seemed futile now that Mrs Smith had been reinstated without their help.

'Okay then,' Mr Barrow said, at last. 'Let's start at the beginning.'

They both nodded; Margery flinched under his cold gaze.

'So, tell me,' he said, bringing his fingers to his face to stroke his own chin. 'Have you found out who put the stage up?'

'No. We thought the police had?' Margery said shaking her head. Clementine did the same. To her amazement the headmaster did not look angry any more, just worried. His brow was creased, and his red hair was not slicked back as it usually was. He looked tired, very tired. It was the face of a person who has a lot weighing on their mind. Mr Barrow sighed and leaned back in the chair, considering them.

'I just... look.' He paused as if he wasn't sure what he should say to them, or how much he should admit. 'Usually, all that rigging is very safe. I used to help the caretaker put it together you see,' he said in way of explanation. 'And the person they think put it up... well, I just can't help but think they're wrong, and now a dognapping too.' He shook his head at the thought of it. Then lowered his voice. 'Between you and me…' Mr Barrow looked past them to the closed office door to check it was still firmly shut. Margery and Clementine waited in anticipation. 'Ittonvale school's headmaster rang me in tears. Apparently, there was a near case of arson in the school hall. It was lucky the sprinkler system went off or there would be nothing left of it.'

'What?' Margery asked, when she finally found her voice again. 'Do they know what happened?'

'Something to do with the tree lights, the fire brigade said.'

'Were they as old as ours?' Clementine said. 'If so then it's not much of a surprise, is it? That tree in our hall is basically a disaster waiting to happen.' Margery grimaced thinking of the ancient Christmas tree lights that Summerview still decorated with.

Mr Barrow shook his head. 'Well, this is the thing, Ittonvale had those new LED ones, the battery-powered ones. They're supposed to be incredibly safe, or they would have been if they'd been on the tree. Mr Drake told me that they'd been swapped out for old ones and they set the tree on fire. They're looking for the new ones still. It was just lucky that no one was in the hall, and they managed to put it out before it caused any major damage. Luckily their drama teacher changed the rehearsal time last minute.'

Margery gasped remembering how lovely Ittonvale school hall had looked when they had been hiding on its balcony. All those pretty paperchains made by the students would have been destroyed if the fire hadn't been put out.

'To me, it's all just very odd.' Mr Barrow continued. 'A near miss like that at Ittonvale after our own accident, and your cakes being ruined.' He shook his head in concern, seeming to notice Margery raising her eyebrows in surprise. She was amazed that he cared so much about their cakes, she would have thought he would find their upset silly. Mr Barrow cleared his throat, clearly battling with something internally. 'I have something to show you.'

He tapped away at his computer keyboard. Margery turned to look at Clementine who was fiddling with the rings on her fingers. Mr Barrow turned the screen around so they could see the video player he had opened on it.

'Seren told me that she and Rose hadn't been the ones to break in through the kitchen window, and please forgive me for not trusting a member of your staff, Margery, but I decided to see whether she was telling the truth.'

'And?' Margery heard Clementine say next to her as the headmaster pressed the play button on screen.

'She was. I've watched them coming in through the main entrance on the other camera and Seren used her card to enter the building.' Onscreen, CCTV footage of the kitchen fire escape whizzed by until the headmaster reached the part he had been looking for. 'But look.'

'Who's that?' Clementine asked. Margery shook her head, watching intently as the person rushed up the stairs and clambered up and into the school through the kitchen window.

'No idea.' Mr Barrow said. He threw his hands up in confusion and leaned back in his chair again, folding his arms as he did so. 'Could be anyone with that outfit.'

He rewound the footage and they watched it again. Whoever it was, they were indeed as incognito as if they had been invisible in the Father Christmas outfit. It was like they knew that they would be on camera and where the cameras were. Who would know such an intimate detail, Margery thought, unless they had access to the CCTV footage in the first place and knew where the cameras pointed? As it was, all Margery could gather from the grainy video footage the headmaster had presented them with, was that the person had taken part in the costume contest. They could have been anyone.

'I know I told you not to investigate, but you proved the police wrong last time something strange like this happened,' Mr Barrow said. 'I was hoping you might have an explanation for some of it.'

'Not yet,' Clementine said. 'We have lots of leads but nothing substantial. Any other information will cost you five pounds.'

'Clementine,' Margery chastised her.

'Come on Margery, we're running a detective business!'

'We are not!' Margery eyed the headmaster, who looked amused. 'We really aren't!'

He held his hands up in surrender. 'There's another thing… the police have decided who put the stage up. I don't agree with them of course, but that's another thing I'm hoping we can solve. There's too much strangeness going on if who they think did it, truly did it.'

'Who do they think did it?' Margery asked, intrigued.

The headmaster put both hands flat on his desk and sighed. 'They think Mrs Large did. I'm supposed to be telling the governors tonight, but I can't, I just can't. It can't be true!'

Margery heard Clementine gasp next to her. 'How on earth do they think Mrs Large did that? On her own!'

'I've honestly no idea what they're thinking.' Mr Barrow snorted in disgust. 'They seem convinced that her husband somehow helped her and that he came into the hall through the blind spot on the CCTV and then let her into the building.'

'What?' Margery exclaimed, just as Clementine cried, 'Really! Why?'

'I know, I know.' The headmaster rubbed his eyes and sighed before continuing. 'I watched the CCTV of the school entrance with the police when the first accident happened. We all just assumed it was Rosemary because she said she lost her card and the person looked like her, but now I know it can't have been.'

'What are you saying?' Margery asked. 'Who do you think it was?'

'Well, I know that it couldn't have been Edward because he told me his alibi and anyway, the person on the CCTV from that day is definitely a woman, and you can clearly see someone letting them into the building. The police are convinced that it was Mr Large. They are absolutely fixated on it. And of course, they had decided that one of the drama department must have done it because they'd be the only people who would care enough. But surely if she just came to the school to put the stage up there wouldn't be all this secrecy.' The headmaster shook his head and leaned back in his chair. 'Rosemary was working, the police already confirmed it with her manager and Mr Daniels was at his sister's hen party, apparently. I didn't ask to see any more after the first few photos he showed me of them drinking unnaturally coloured drinks together.' Mr Barrow grimaced. 'So, out of the three of the teachers involved in the play, only Mrs Large is left, but I just can't imagine her doing something like that no matter what they say, can you?'

Mr Barrow closed his eyes and shook his head. Margery couldn't imagine it, yet it made a certain amount of sense. No one else would have been at all interested in putting the stage up for the drama team, and Mrs Smith had sworn on her own mother's grave repeatedly that Mrs Large had given her Mrs Blossom's play.

Mr Barrow continued, 'But it obviously wasn't Mrs Large on that video I showed you of last Saturday for… obvious reasons…'

Margery nodded grimly. It did put Mrs Large very much out of the running as suspects went for the cake debacle.

'I know you helped Rosemary, which I am a little embarrassed about, I should have believed her. I… I, well I understand why she didn't tell me where she was on the day, a shame she didn't feel she could disclose that to me before.' His face crumpled for a moment before he pulled himself together. 'Anyway, now I'm wondering if I can help you. What do you need to figure this out?'

Margery thought about it. Having the headmaster on their side could be very useful indeed.

'We need access to the rest of the CCTV,' Margery squeaked. 'And the data from the card scanner at the entrance from the week before the accident.'

He considered them both carefully; Margery could almost see the cogs turning in his head as he weighed up the pros and cons of giving two members of his catering staff access to the most private parts of the school.

'I will need your upmost discretion.'

'Of course,' Margery said.

'I'm very serious, Mrs Butcher-Baker. No one must know.'

Margery turned to look at Clementine and she nodded back.

'Fine,' he said, sitting back in his plush office chair. 'Give me till tomorrow to sort it out with Mr Matthews. The police are bringing the footage back in the early afternoon so that would be a good time, after school finishes and the students have left.'

They nodded again. Margery felt their luck beginning to change. Mr Barrow stood and stretched his hand out to her. Margery rose from her seat and took it.

'Good luck both of you,' he said, shaking her hand hard. 'I think we're all going to need it.'

Chapter Twenty

After they left the headmaster's office, they drove straight to Michael Leith's dog day care. Well, they tried to. The weather that afternoon was even more atrocious than it had been on the day they had lost him at the traffic lights. Even though they had his address this time, it took a long, long time to find the right street and even then, they trundled along at five miles per hour, desperately peering at each house looking for the right number.

'Is it not that one, Margery?' Clementine said from the driver's side of the car as they crawled along, in a way that anyone looking out of one of the neat, living room bay windows they passed would find extremely suspicious. 'This is a weird place to have a dog hotel.'

'Dog day care, and I don't think so.' Margery was beginning to think they would never find it as she peered through the condensation on her own window into the night. The light from the streetlamps flickered in the darkness, the rain creating a static effect.

'Oh, it's definitely this one!' Clementine squealed, taking her hand off the steering wheel to point at one of the estate's identical houses; the car veered dangerously before she grabbed it again to steady them.

'How can you tell?' Margery asked; her voice petered out as she realised the reason why. Not only was the white car on the driveway, but Mrs Blossom was also standing on the drive too, Tilly the music teacher from Ittonvale school standing behind her. They were both holding an umbrella with 'Singing in the Rain!' written underneath the Ittonvale school logo and both had an armful of laminated papers. Clementine stopped the car on the side of the road closest to the pavement.

'What shall we do, Clem?' Margery said, twisting her hands together with nerves. 'Should we just go?'

Mrs Blossom was already striding over to them. Clementine panicked and tried to drive away, but she stalled the car quite spectacularly. They both stared at Mrs Blossom wide-eyed in fear as she arrived at the driver's side window and rapped her knuckles against it sharply. Clementine rolled it down, her mouth pulled into a strained smile.

'Hello,' Clementine said. Margery could hear the nerves in her voice. 'How are you?'

Mrs Blossom looked slightly taken aback as she peered at them both inside the car; the umbrella above her head haloed her face. It rested against the car door as she examined them through the window. Margery could see that the papers in her arms were missing posters. 'My dog is still missing, so not well, you could say. Are you getting out of the car?'

'No,' they both said in unison.

'Well maybe we can talk like this then.' Mrs Blossom did not seem as menacing as she had the other day in the school hall. In fact, today she seemed almost unnervingly calm. Margery wondered where this was going.

'You were at my school, were you not? You work with Rose Smith?' Mrs Blossom stared at them both with her eyebrows raised. Clementine tried to cover her work pass with her hand, but it was too late.

'So, tell me,' Mrs Blossom said. 'Where's Ada Bones? And what the hell is going on?'

'We don't know,' Margery said. Clementine nodded in agreement, her fringe bouncing wildly against her forehead as she did so. Mrs Blossom stared at her carefully, as though she did not believe a word she had said. Margery looked across the road to the house where Tilly was still standing under the porch bundled up in her big winter coat, the phone in her hand pressed against her ear. She waved over to Mrs Blossom.

'Coming, Tilly!' Mrs Blossom called back, barely looking away from Margery and Clementine for a moment. 'If you aren't going to tell me where Ada is, you could do the decent thing and tell me your names.'

'Well, I'm Sharon and this is my best friend Karen,' Clementine said, brightly.

Mrs Blossom gave them such a stern look that Margery flinched.

'I can see your name on your work pass,' she said coolly. 'Clementine.'

'I'm Margery,' Margery said. 'We're both Mrs Butcher-Baker.'

Mrs Blossom raised her eyebrows but did not comment.

'There really is no need to be angry, Mrs Blossom, we didn't take Ada Bones, honestly.' Clementine pleaded.

'Then why are you both here?' Mrs Blossom demanded to know. 'Did Rose send you to gloat, does she have Ada?'

'No, I don't think so.' Margery shook her head. 'She's got no time for a dog now. Er… well… we're here to find out why Mr Leith was at our concert rehearsal.'

'Oh.' Mrs Blossom looked sheepish suddenly. As if what Margery had said was embarrassing. 'Well... he was there on my orders.'

'Why?' Clementine asked.

'Because I wanted to see if it was true.'

'If what was true?' Margery scratched her head. Mrs Blossom looked away for a moment as if deciding whether to tell them or not. The rain poured heavily from her umbrella, the mist of water entering the car window.

'If Elizabeth had given Rose the same play as she gave me,' Mrs Blossom finally said. 'Which she had.'

Margery thought back to the look on Mrs Smith's face when they had overheard Mrs Blossom talking to Tilly when they were hiding at Ittonvale school. A sudden clarity flooded her brain.

'Has Mrs Large always written your school plays, Mrs Blossom?' she asked. Clementine gasped from the car seat next to hers. Mrs Blossom drew herself up to full height, as though she knew she was cornered.

'For a long time.' She sighed and looked down at the missing dog posters in her hand. 'I've never been much of a writer, I'm much better as a director.'

'Why would she write plays for you?' Clementine demanded. 'What on earth could possibly be in it for her?'

'I fund the recorder club trips away. Well, I did before... before she died. I don't suppose there will be many more now they have no teacher.' Mrs Blossom smiled at them both gently. 'I was sorry to hear about Elizabeth, and not just because of the plays. It may have started as a business relationship, but we became quite good friends by the end.'

That explained the photograph in the Large house, Margery thought.

'We always thought she did charity fundraisers to get the money for those,' Clementine said in a hushed whisper. Mrs Blossom's hearing must have been fantastic because she leaned in again.

'They probably covered the entry fee.' She smiled kindly. 'But not the three nights in Florida for the American championship last year, for a team of twelve and two chaperones.'

'Gosh,' Margery said.

'Indeed.' Mrs Blossom nodded, turning as though to leave, her umbrella scraping against the car window. 'Actually...' She spun back to them again; Margery flinched. Clementine put her finger on the car's controls as though she might just roll the window back up anyway but thought better of it at the last moment.

'Look, I'm sorry about my outburst the other day. I just got a bit carried away in the heat of the moment, you know? I just want my dog back, that's all.'

'Thank you,' Margery squeaked. 'But we don't know who took your dog.'

Mrs Blossom sighed. 'Don't lie to me.'

'We really don't!' Clementine cried from next to Margery in the driver's seat.

'You tell Rose that she can drop her over any time she wants,' Mrs Blossom said. 'No questions asked.'

'She doesn't have her either,' Margery said, shaking her head. 'Really.'

'There's too much animosity between us for me not to suspect her.' Mrs Blossom shrugged.

'She really doesn't,' Margery said again.

Mrs Blossom hummed quietly, drumming her nails on the car's open window.

'Wait, hang on a minute,' Margery said, shaking her head. 'Why were you worried Mrs Large had given you the same plays? You said to Tilly that Mrs Smith had stolen it.'

'You heard that, did you?' Mrs Blossom asked, her forehead wrinkling.

'Yes, when we came to your school. We thought you meant that Mrs Smith had stolen the play from you.'

'Ahh.' Mrs Blossom's smile faded for a moment but then appeared again. 'Elizabeth had told me that she couldn't do the play for me this year, because she needed to give it to Rose. Apparently, Rose had been having some writing trouble after a silly fling she had ended.' Margery and Clementine looked at each other. Mrs Blossom continued. 'But I convinced her to send it anyway. She owed me because I'd already paid for the accommodation and bus for next year's European recorder *Wettbewerb* in Berlin. Then I sent Michael to check that Elizabeth hadn't given it to Rose to use, which she had. So, Rose did steal it, just not in the way you thought I meant probably.'

'Mrs Smith couldn't have taken Ada Bones,' Clementine piped up, much braver now that Mrs Blossom was on her way to leave, 'because she was probably working at the bowling alley, I mean... doing something else.'

Mrs Blossom looked amused at that. 'Yes, the police said she had an excuse. I was very upset that day, I shouldn't have come to Summerview school. To be honest, I didn't know she'd been suspended.'

'So, you don't know anything about the fire at Ittonvale?' Margery asked, 'The police haven't found anything?'

'How do you know about that?' Mrs Blossom asked curiously. 'No, they haven't found a thing, what a mess. While we're all answering questions, why are you so sure that Rose didn't take my dog?'

'Well, where were you when she went missing—' Margery started to say.

Mrs Blossom cut her off. 'At home.' She looked close to tears. 'I put Ada down for her nap and then later when I went to wake her up for dinner I couldn't find her anywhere. I called and called for her, but she didn't come. The police are looking for her as we speak.' She held up the missing posters she was still holding in one hand. 'As am I. How did you find Michael anyway?'

She looked at them curiously, the rain still bouncing from her umbrella.

'He dropped this.' Margery pulled Ada Bones' treat bag from her handbag and held it up to show her. 'It took us a little longer than expected to trace him, though.'

Mrs Blossom raised her eyebrows; she looked impressed. 'Would you mind if I take the bag back, please? I can't tell you how annoying it is to carry treats in their original packaging, and that one is properly lined.'

'Of course,' Margery said, Mrs Blossom reached into the car and took the bag from her fingers. 'Mrs Blossom?'

'Yes?'

'Who is Michael, exactly?' Margery asked, Mrs Blossom looking at her curiously. The water continued to pour from her umbrella and run down the car windows. 'To you I mean.'

'I'm assuming that if you are outside his dog day care then you already know.' Mrs Blossom shrugged. 'He looks after Ada Bones when I'm busy, well most of the time. Tilly always has her all-day every Saturday so I can have a break. Anyway, Michael's helping us put up missing posters.'

'So, there was no other motive?' Margery asked. 'Sneaking around outside the school at night?'

'It does sound bad when you put it like that!' Mrs Blossom cringed. 'No really, that's the only reason. Because if she was using all of it then I wouldn't be able to perform it would I? What would the press say?'

'I'm sure the local paper wouldn't even care.' Clementine rolled her eyes. 'They never report on our plays anyway.'

Mrs Blossom scoffed. 'Well, that's because Rose is always writing to them and complaining that they don't focus on your school enough, it's enough to put anyone off. And her plays simply weren't as good as Elizabeth's, it's a shame she never gave her the chance to shine when she was alive. Anyway, it's not my fault we're a superior school and I'm better at implementing the scripts, is it? It's just a shame Elizabeth isn't here to finish a new play for me.'

Margery wished that she was too. It seemed Mrs Large being alive would solve a lot of problems, not least that she was the only person who had ever seemed to be able to rein Mrs Smith in. Now Rose was an unhinged drama magnet, sucking them all down into the Christmas concert black hole along with her.

'Why are you putting up missing posters if you're so sure Rose has Ada Bones?' Margery asked; the question had been floating at the forefront of her mind for a while.

'So she feels guilty and brings her back of course,' Mrs Blossom said, as though Margery was a very dim light bulb that should have been replaced a long time ago.

'I have more questions,' Clementine said, looking at the dog treat bag again. Margery nodded back. It would be good to find out from Mrs Blossom who she suspected of starting the fire at Ittonvale school.

'Why is your dog called Mrs Ada Bones? And where did you get her dress?'

Mrs Blossom smile was almost luminant with the joy of being asked. 'Well Ada Bones isn't as stupid a name as Sunflower or Banana, is it? I just like my dogs to have a nice, normal name…'

Margery let the conversation fade out as they bickered about good names for dogs. Clementine's ability to strike up a new friendship with a stranger could sometimes wear quite thin. Through the windscreen she could see Tilly the music teacher, still waiting impatiently by the house as the rain poured down. Her face twisted into a glower as she stared over at them, probably sick of having to stand in the rain.

Chapter Twenty-One

Mrs Smith's large living room was a claustrophobic nightmare by the time they arrived that evening, there were so many staff stuffed into it. They had nearly fallen over the big pile of shoes and coats on the way in, and Seren was desperately trying to tidy them as best she could. Every time she had got it all sorted into a neat pile, someone's shiny winter raincoat would slide off and she would be back to square one. Margery dreaded to think how long it would take for them to all get the correct coat and leave the house later and it was already six thirty.

Once Mrs Blossom had left on her mission to put up her missing dog posters, of which she had flung a pile of into the backseat of their car with the promise they would put some up at their school. Every surface of Mrs Smith's silver living room had someone sitting on it and Margery didn't think she had seen anyone but Rose smile since they had arrived the hour before. She would certainly be saving on the heating this evening; the warmth of all their bodies crammed in the house was horrific. Margery regretted wearing her extra thick socks and cardigan. Margery and Clementine had managed to get the last tiny space, sharing the edge of the arm of the sofa nearest the open double doorway into the hall. She was glad that the doors were open, she did not think she could bear to be in the room if they were not. The only person who was not red in the face was Karen, and that was only because she had managed to jimmy open the bay window behind her from where she was sitting on the windowsill. She looked like she was contemplating leaping from it and escaping but her plans had been scuppered by the vast Christmas tree with its ridiculous number of silver baubles blocking most of the window.

Still, it wasn't all bad. They were starting to sound like less than a group of people who had been thrust together and forced to sing, and more like a half-decent amateur choir. Margery thought it possible that Mr Daniels had managed to convince Mrs Smith to do the songs in a key they could all sing in and not just her vocal range. Although she did not feel like any of them should give up their day jobs anytime soon, they might well be passable for the end of week concert. It was all coming together now. Mr Daniels and Mrs Smith had mashed both their concert ideas together and it was a strange jumble of the two, now Mrs Smith had finally got rid of the songs she had inadvertently stolen from Ittonvale school. Mr Daniels' absence was notable this evening, Margery wondered what Mrs Smith had told him to stop him from coming.

Mrs Smith had said that Mrs Large had given her the sheet music and lyrics for the concert; Margery kept thinking about Mrs Blossom's revelation. It whirled around her head now. She wanted to tell Mrs Smith about it; maybe she would after the practice session was over, but she didn't know how to bring it up. Margery had not known Elizabeth Large to have anything to do with Ittonvale before, it had all been a very well-kept secret and she had not seen it coming. Especially as even the police were now convinced Mr and Mrs Large had entered the building to put the stage together that fateful weekend and were probably moving to arrest Mr Large as they sat at the rehearsal. Margery suddenly wondered if they should have warned him, but she did not have his phone number.

Margery was sure there must be a perfectly feasible reason for Ittonvale's near miss fire, although the head-master had said that the police were still investigating. Anyway, even if the police were right and George and Elizabeth Large had put up the stage, Elizabeth at least couldn't have had anything to do with that, she had been dead for weeks now. As alibis went it was rock solid. It left at least one criminal still out there somewhere though, unless George did not have a good reason to be let off the hook. The doorbell rang, silencing those in attendance as they listened to the first few notes of *Greensleeves*.

'Who the devil could that be?' Mrs Smith glared around the room as she held court at the keyboard in front of her. 'Seren, get the door, will you?'

Margery could see Seren stuffed behind one of the grey sofas trying to pour squash and hand out custard creams from the silver tea trolley. Mrs Smith had promised refreshments and had then demanded Seren hand them out. With that and the coat mountain, Seren was almost purple in the face with stress. Margery felt incredibly sorry for her.

'I'll get it.' She squeezed out of the space before Mrs Smith could stop her and went out into the hallway. Clementine, who had never been any good at being told to stay put, followed behind her. Mrs Smith began the song again and the voices of the poor staff still trapped in the room wailed out. Margery could see a silhouette through the stained glass of the front door but could not quite make out who the person was. She was wondering if she could view them through the peephole without them seeing her when Clementine strode forward and thrust the door open.

'Oh.'

The three of them looked at each other in shock.

'Mrs Blossom.' Margery breathed out. 'What are you doing here?'

'Hello again Karen, I mean Margery.' Mrs Blossom smirked, peering closely at Margery's face. 'I wasn't expecting to see you here.'

'We're doing our Christmas concert practice,' Clementine said in explanation.

'Is Rose here?' Mrs Blossom peered behind them. 'I'm assuming she is if that wailing from the other room is anything to go by.'

'She is,' Margery said, gently.

'Margery, Clementine, we need you for the final song.' Mrs Smith's voice interrupted from behind them, changing from warm to cold when she saw who her visitor was. 'Oh… it's you.'

Margery turned to see Mrs Smith glaring at her from the living room doorway. Margery could not fathom how she had dragged herself through the amount of people to leave the room, it must have been an extraordinary feat.

'It's me,' Mrs Blossom said as Mrs Smith stared daggers at her from across the hall. 'How are you, Rose?'

'Much worse for seeing you.' Mrs Smith sniffed. 'Here to accuse me of stealing another play, are you? Or setting fire to your car or house or whatever?'

'Well…' Mrs Blossom said. 'If the shoe fits.'

They glowered at each other. The hallway fell into an uncomfortable silence only punctuated by the murmuring of the staff in the living room.

'Where's my dog, Rose?'

'I honestly don't know.' Mrs Smith shrugged. Mrs Blossom's face fell.

'Is it really true?' she said sadly, looking from Margery and Clementine to Mrs Smith and back. 'You didn't take her.'

'No.' Mrs Smith shook her head as Mrs Blossoms face fell. 'But I'll help you look for her… if you want.'

'Gosh.' Mrs Blossom sighed. 'I think I knew that really. We don't exactly get on, but I can't imagine you hurting my dog.'

'No,' Mrs Smith said curtly, her lips pursed like she was chewing on a piece of lemon peel. 'Though the police were more accusatory when they visited to ask me about it. Luckily I had proof I was elsewhere.'

Mrs Blossom looked up at the ceiling briefly and sighed. 'Yes, quite. I heard about your other… ah… role… Rose. Sorry about that, I hope it all works out for you.'

The awkward silence in the small hallway would have been almost suffocating if it was not being punctuated by stifled coughs and muttering from the nearby sitting room.

'Yes. Well,' Mrs Smith said, coolly.

There was another, much more awkward pause.

'Yes. Quite,' Mrs Blossom said. 'Listen, hear me out, will you? See the thing is, I thought it might be nice to combine our plays, a super play if you will. Both schools together. Forget all this silliness. As I don't currently have a school hall to perform in due to the open investigation.'

'No,' Mrs Smith said, immediately turning around to go back into the living room.

'Give it a think!' Mrs Blossom cried desperately from the doorstep. 'You don't have to decide yet. Well, I mean the end of term is on Friday, so you have to decide pretty soon…'

Mrs Smith turned around to glare at her again. 'No.'

'Just sleep on it,' Mrs Blossom pleaded again. 'We've done so much work, not including the rewriting we had to do when you stole the play…'

'I didn't steal the play.' Mrs Smith was purple with anger.

'Yes, yes… fine.' Mrs Blossom rolled her eyes. 'I know, I know. Will you think about it?'

'Fine,' Mrs Smith said, Mrs Blossom smiled widely, but she raised her finger in warning. 'I'll think about it. For old times' sake. But you can't do our play.'

'What if you both do an older play and take it in turns?' Margery suggested.

'Are you kidding, Margery? We can't do a new play now.' Mrs Smith scoffed. 'We'll both do the same play and then the public can decide whose was better. You can go first of course, Rhonda.'

'If you think your version is good enough to follow ours…' Mrs Blossom began. Margery raised her eyebrows at her; she looked away and began to scrabble through her bag. 'I mean, sounds fantastic. Thank you all.' She finally pulled a pile of Ada Bones' missing posters from her handbag and held them out to Mrs Smith.

'I'm still thinking about it,' Mrs Smith said, taking the posters gingerly.

'Yes, of course,' Mrs Blossom said, putting the shopping bag she was holding down on the inside of the doorway with a clunk. 'Anyway, I'll be off then. See you on Thursday, Rosemary.'

'I said I'm still thinking about it!' Mrs Smith said, but Mrs Blossom was already halfway down the drive. Mrs

Smith brought her fingertips to her temples and closed her eyes. 'Infuriating, that woman.'

'You secretly still want to be best friends with her, don't you? You miss her.' Clementine smirked at her as she leaned against the banister of the stairs. 'Being friends with Seren has melted your cold exterior. You're like a crème egg.'

'Crème eggs aren't hard,' Mrs Smith snapped, opening her eyes to glare at Clementine.

'They are if you have weak teeth,' Clementine said, taking her notepad from her pocket and checking something written on it. Mrs Smith scowled at her. 'Remember when I cut my gum on one, Margery? Or was that a mini egg? I can never remember. It was Easter, I know that because I can remember that we forgot to pre-order our hot cross buns from the bakery, and we had to buy brioche burger buns instead...'

'What's that?' Mrs Smith demanded, trying to snatch the notepad away from Clementine. Clementine moved away in a rare display of speed.

'It's my special Secret Santa working out book.' She grinned. 'I've nearly got it all figured out...'

'Get back into the living room before I fire you both from the Christmas concert,' Mrs Smith snapped, shooing them both.

'You know we don't even want to be in the play!' Clementine said, but they went back into the living room regardless.

Chapter Twenty-Two

'Please don't tell me this is the whole order?' Margery stared down at the tray of vacuum-packed meat that the butcher had brought in. He had rushed back to his van almost as soon as he had arrived; Margery wished he had stayed long enough to explain the delivery to her. She had been distracted by helping Seren with the jacket potato prep. 'Where's the rest of them? They're the smallest birds I've ever seen.'

Clementine's eyes bulged as though they might pop out of her head as they both looked down at the tiny birds in the tray. Margery slid her reading glasses on and looked at the invoice properly. 'I can't believe this.'

'Oh,' Clementine whispered. 'Oh no. Why are they so tiny, Margery? I asked for the biggest ones they had on the phone!'

'Because partridges are very small, Clem,' Gloria said, from where she had appeared behind them. She took the invoice that had far too many noughts on, eyebrows raised. Margery noted that she did not seem surprised at all, in fact she would go as far as to say the opposite. 'Very small and very expensive.'

'Oh God. Margery, I'm so sorry!' Clementine stared at the tiny birds in horror. 'I just thought they'd be lovely and Christmassy. Sounded much more festive than turkey!'

'You need to ring him and get him to come back and pick them up,' Margery said, trying to keep her tone even and not let her dismay show. 'We can't serve five tiny partridges to the whole school, and besides, they cost most of the Christmas budget put together! Oh God, what are we going to do?'

'Margery, please do not...' Clementine started to say and then thought better of it. 'We could just put a lot of extra roast potatoes and gravy on the plates, drown out how small they are, you know?' Margery glared at her. 'I mean, let me sort it, I'll fix it don't worry.'

'I am worried,' Margery said.

'Yes, well perfectly natural to be worried. But don't worry.'

'What are we worrying about now?' The headmaster said, carrying the bowl of hot porridge they prepared for him every morning. Margery flinched at the sight of him. Clementine tried to drape the delivery document over the top of the teeny birds to hide them, but it was too late.

'Gosh, those turkeys are a bit odd aren't they, Mrs Butcher-Baker? Shouldn't they be a bit fatter this time of year?'

Margery closed her eyes and let Clementine blab away as she produced an excuse for the man. The big end of term Christmas dinner was tomorrow. Everything was prepared and ready to cook, except the meat and the enormous logs of premade Christmas pudding which remained in the freezer. All the potatoes were peeled and being held in buckets of water in the fridge with the other vegetables ready to parboil, Seren's special stuffing recipe just needed balling and Margery had already bought an enormous amount of powdered custard and gravy granules from the dry stock supplier. Even the ready-made brandy sauce was ready to go in cartons in the dry store. She hoped that they could fix this somehow. She should never have let Clementine oversee anything so important.

'Margery?' She opened her eyes. Benjamin was standing before her, his cheeks pink, his eyes watery. 'Can I talk to you?'

'Yes, of course. let's go to my office.' Margery took a deep breath. 'Clementine, please sort this out, call the butcher back. Tell him we'll take anything he's got left! God help us that there'll be something left. Come on then, young man.'

They walked down the passageway together and into the dry store. She motioned for him to take a seat on the fryer oil tub. He sat down gingerly, taking off his hairnet as he did so.

'What's going on, Benjamin?' Margery asked gently, though she was still on edge from the wrong ordering. She wondered if he was going to confess to what he had been doing in the headmaster's office, and what she should be doing about it as a manager.

The headmaster had not mentioned anything about his computer having something wrong with it, so she had let it slide for now, but so many things were troubling her about Benjamin. For one, he really could not cook, she didn't know how he had even managed to pass his course at catering college. For another, as Mrs Mugglethwaite had told them, he was already working at the hospital. Even stranger than she found both of those things was his uncanny ability to fix anything he was asked to. She looked over at him, his head drooped down on his chest as feisty as a lettuce leaf that had been left behind in the bottom of the salad crisper. Benjamin took a deep breath.

'You know that lady who's been looking for her dog?'

'Yes.' Margery nodded; she knew Mrs Blossom far too well at the moment.

'I was fixing the chair in Mr Daniels' office and I found something.' He said the words in a rush; they all tumbled out as though his mouth was trying to work faster than his brain. He pulled the thing he wanted to show her from the big pocket on the front of his tabard and held it up.

'This is her dress.' Margery gasped as she took it from him. 'Ada Bones' dress. Where was it?'

'Mr Daniels' office.'

'Mr Daniels doesn't have an office.'

'He does now.' Benjamin nodded. 'He has Mrs Large's old office.'

A quick jump into a figurative grave, Margery thought to herself. The woman had barely been dead a few weeks and Mr Daniels had already taken her office.

'It was just on the floor as I went in,' Benjamin said, gesturing with his hands as if that explained it.

'You're going to have to go back a bit, Ben,' Margery said, still staring at the tiny blue dog dress that had been mentioned on Mrs Blossom's missing posters. 'The dog wasn't in the office?'

'No.' Ben shook his head. 'Not that I could see, I just finished fixing the chair and then I came straight over to show you.'

'Why were you fixing the chair?' Margery asked.

Benjamin smiled. 'Mr Daniels asked me to.'

Margery sat in surprise for a moment, still clutching the dress in her hands. 'You haven't been taking the tools from the storeroom, Ben?'

'No,' he said. 'I have my own. I used to before... but not any more, I swear.'

Margery shook her head in disbelief. 'How did you used to get in the storeroom before, without me knowing?'

'Sometimes I borrow Gloria's key,' he said in explanation.

Margery raised her eyebrows at this interesting new piece of information. 'Gloria's key? What do you mean by Gloria's key? Why does Gloria have a key?'

Benjamin shrugged again. 'I dunno. She's always had a key.'

That was news to Margery. Gloria's name had not been on the headmaster's list of storeroom key-holders. She wondered where she had got it from and why she had kept it. Margery's own key had been the former kitchen manager's. 'Okay, carry on, tell me more about the dress. Where in the office was it?'

'It was behind the desk. I saw it stuffed behind there and thought it might have fallen down,' Benjamin explained.

So, it had been hidden, and in the same place that Margery and Clementine had found the pair of pliers that had been taken from the storeroom.

'I was going to ask Mr Daniels about it, but another teacher came along and asked me to leave.'

'What teacher?' Margery asked.

'Um, I dunno her name, but she was very tall, had blonde hair and uh, well I don't want to sound rude, but she had a mole on her face, on her nose.'

Margery flipped through all the teachers of Summerview school in her head. She could not place a single person with a mole on their nose that would be prominent enough for Benjamin to comment on. The only person of that description she could think of did not even work for Summerview. They worked for Ittonvale. She thought about it for a moment in surprise. Tilly, the music teacher. What on earth could she possibly be doing at Summerview?

'Benjamin,' Margery said quietly, 'I need to ask you something and you can't lie to me, please?'

He nodded, his eyes like saucers.

'Why were you in the headmaster's office on his computer last Monday?'

He opened his mouth and then closed it again. He breathed out deeply. 'I've been going to his office in the morning and afternoon and deleting any responses he's had for the caretaker position,' he said the sentence in a rush, the tips of his ears turning bright red as he did so.

Margery had not been expecting that answer at all. 'What? Why on earth would you do that?'

'I just don't want anyone else to do it, I'd be really good at it! Everyone knows I would,' Benjamin said, his face crumpling as tears welled in his eyes. 'But I don't have the qualifications he wants. I thought if I fixed enough things then I could prove to him that I deserve it.'

'That's really not how things work.' Margery shook her head, trying to get the surprise to leave her voice. 'You can't do things like that. It's not good practice, is it?'

'No, I know.' Ben put his head in his hands; he looked as though he might cry. 'But once I started, I just couldn't stop. I even went to the post office and changed the phone number on the advert to my mobile number in the window when Mrs Mugglethwaite wasn't looking.'

'But how did you get into his computer?' Margery was baffled by the entire revelation.

'His password is Mrs Smith's birthday.' He fiddled with the sleeve of the polo shirt he wore under the tabard and looked at her again. 'There's something else too, something even worse…'

'What?' Margery asked. 'What could be worse than that? You weren't the one who put the stage together, were you?'

'Oh no, nothing that bad!'

'But you've been borrowing the tools from the storeroom?' Margery asked. 'To fix things around the school? Why wouldn't you have put the stage up, why should I believe you?'

'No, no, I swear I didn't! I've got my own tools. I keep them in my locker, I'll show you!' he said putting his hands up in his defence. 'But the thing is…' Before he could tell her anything the dry store door burst open and Seren rushed in, the invoice from the butcher in her hand.

'Margery, the butcher won't take the partridges back, they don't have any turkey, they told us to try Tesco!' she said, her voice rising in a panic. 'And Gloria and Clementine are fighting!'

'Oh God.' Margery put the tiny dress down on the chest freezer and massaged her own temples. 'Come on, Ben, let's get back. We'll talk about this more later. Thank you for telling me.'

Benjamin nodded and rushed back into the kitchen after Seren. Margery followed. In the centre of the main kitchen Gloria and Clementine stood opposite each other, both wearing a matching glare.

'What's going on?' Margery finally asked.

'Tell her, Gloria,' Clementine said. She was acting as though she were full of bravado, but Margery knew her well enough to tell when she was terribly upset.

'Tell her what?' Gloria glowered back at Clementine. Sharon and Karen watched from between them nervously, still pretending to prepare the soup of the day.

'Tell her what you did!' Clementine hissed again, more urgently this time. 'Tell her what you've been doing!'

'She should know what I'm doing, she should know what everyone's doing as the manager!' Gloria spat. 'But she hasn't been doing her job very well has she? Always letting you mess around, or Ben get away with things.'

'I don't mess around!' Clementine wailed. 'Not much, anyway! Just a normal and perfectly acceptable amount.' Gloria scoffed and rolled her eyes; she turned away with her arms folded.

'What's going on?' Margery said. 'Gloria? I thought you were happy with the way things are going?'

'You can't be serious, Margery?' Gloria wouldn't look her in the eye. 'We've spent less time caring about kitchen stuff at the moment and more time doing that stupid play.'

'Well…' Margery began to say, but Gloria cut her off again.

'And you know what? Maybe I would have liked to be asked to be manager. I'm doing all your second in command stuff without even a pay rise.'

'All you had to do was say, Gloria.' Margery pleaded. 'I had no idea you felt like this.'

'Tell her, Gloria,' Clementine said again, much quieter than before.

'Fine.' Gloria pulled herself up to full height. 'I ruined all the cakes.'

There was a loud and unanimous gasp from the entire kitchen team. Even Clementine's jaw dropped in surprise.

'That isn't what I meant!' Clementine said, her eyes wide. 'I was talking about how you said partridges would be fine when I was ordering them.'

'Well, it's all out now, isn't it!' Gloria's face was red with anger, but she looked away uncomfortably as though she could not bear to look any of them in the eye. 'And I didn't think you were stupid enough to actually order them.'

'Why did you do that?' Margery asked. 'You helped make those cakes too.'

'I didn't mean to.' Gloria sighed. 'I knocked the trolley over when I was getting it out of the fridge. They all fell on the floor and went everywhere.'

'So, you're the one who climbed through the fire escape window. But why?' Margery asked. Gloria shook her head. Margery couldn't believe what she was hearing. She had always trusted Gloria implicitly. Maybe she was not a good manager as Gloria had said, she had been trying her best, but maybe it wasn't enough. She looked over at the clock, they were running out of time to get lunch ready.

'No, I would have used my kitchen key obviously, but the door was already open.'

'So, you aren't the person we saw on the CCTV?' Margery shook her head. 'In the Santa outfit?'

Gloria stared at her as though she had gone mad. 'No of course not, I assumed you had just forgotten to lock the door, like you've forgotten to call the ordering in or forgotten to put the cleaning rota up these last few months.'

'Why should I believe you?' Margery demanded, glaring at her second in command. Gloria scowled back at her. 'I've just been told that you have a key to the storeroom, why Gloria?'

'Caroline gave it to me.' She shrugged. 'Years ago. She used to make me fetch things from there, obviously because she was too lazy to fetch things herself.'

'And you just kept it?'

'Yes. Why not? What are you insinuating?' Gloria said, waving her arms in anger. 'Oh, for crying out loud, Margery, you can't be stupid enough to think I had anything to do with the stage, do you?'

'Well… no but… what about the fire escape…' Margery tried to say, but Gloria cut her off.

'Well, if you remember back to that day, I was dressed as an elf!'

–

'Hello, Mrs Butcher-Bakers!' Gary Matthews smiled as they entered his security office. 'How are you? Oh, and hello, sir.'

'Hello, Gary.' Mr Barrow smiled at him as he arrived in the small security office behind Margery and Clementine.

'Hello, Gary, yes all fine.' Margery panted. They had had to rush to keep up with the headmaster and his long legs once they had summoned him from his office. 'Anyway listen… you've got to show us the CCTV footage from the weekend the stage was put up, please and then we need to find out how someone got in today.'

'I don't think…'

'Show them please, Gary,' the headmaster said. 'Mrs Butcher-Baker said there is new evidence. Show them the footage from Saturday morning, the same one the police have seen.'

'No worries,' Gary said, wringing his hands together. 'Give me a minute.'

'No problem,' Margery said, wiping the sweat from her brow.

'Right.' He nodded at her and tapped away on the keyboard of the computer in front of him for what felt like an age. Margery stood with her hands resting on the desk. Clementine rapped her fingers on the counter restlessly. 'Let me bring the footage up. It's all kind of condensed from where I put it together for the police. Don't get your hopes up though, whatever you want to see it for. It's not great footage. For some reason the school can buy five hundred copies of *Macbeth*, but they can't afford cameras that don't make everything look like it was filmed with a spoon. Oh, sorry Mr Barrow, I mean...'

The headmaster narrowed his eyes but gestured for him to continue.

Gary brought the video up and ushered them over, around the counter. Margery sat down in the uncomfortably warm chair he had just left, and Mr Barrow and Clementine stood around her. Gary stood and loitered awkwardly behind them.

'So, the only thing we really got was this bit of them coming in the entrance Saturday morning.' Gary sighed, reaching over and pressing play on the video, 'And as you can see, it's not great.'

Gary was right, it was not great footage at all. All that money on the new security system and the headmaster had obviously not spent any of it on cameras. Not that she knew much about them but even to her untrained eye it was poor quality. The camcorder that Clementine had filmed everything on back in the early nineties had provided better material.

'The other thing is that we didn't get any footage of them leaving, at all.' Gary shrugged.

'That's why the police think what they think,' Mr Barrow told Margery and Clementine. 'About the blind spot.'

The video played, the blob on screen waited and waited, until finally someone opened the door from the inside and then they entered the main entrance doors. Margery stared at the screen as the doors closed behind them; the person on the inside must have used the emergency open button to let them in. The figure was wearing a dark coat and winter hat and scarf; it was almost impossible to tell who it was from their shape on the screen. Except for one thing that Margery noticed. She squinted closer.

'Can you play it again?'

Gary obliged obediently and she watched. The person was holding something under their arm.

'Pause it please, Gary.' He stopped the video. They both stared.

'Oh my,' Clementine said. Under the person's arm was a bag. But not just any bag. 'Well, it's definitely not Mrs Smith, is it? But are we sure that's Mrs Large? I know Officer whatsit and his protégée are, but I'm still not convinced.'

'I don't think it's either of them either,' Margery said, thinking back to what Benjamin had told her in the dry store.

'You what? Who do you think it is?' Gary peered closer at the screen, 'How can you tell? And what do you mean, not Mrs Large? Do you think it was Mrs Large, Mr Barrow?'

'I do not.' Mr Barrow sighed angrily. 'I've been able to keep from announcing it so far, but I don't know how long I'll be able to hold out. Officer Thomas took Mr Large in for questioning yesterday.' Margery felt a stab of worry for the Large family's children, who had been through enough without their father disappearing as well.

Margery pointed to the book bag under the person's arm. 'Look at the bag.'

'Okay, and?' He turned to stare at her with raised eyebrows.

'Well,' Margery waved her hands trying to explain, 'is it Mrs Large's recorder bag? That's what she'd have had with her. Can you zoom in on it?'

'Oh right,' Gary said. 'Bit of a fancy carrier for a recorder. Look it's got embroidery on it and everything.'

It did have embroidery, Margery thought. The very same kind of embroidery that she had seen at Ittonvale on Mrs Blossom's chair. There were far, far too many questions and so few answers. 'I'm sure that Mrs Large's bag wasn't embroidered, was it?'

'No.' Mr Barrow shook his head. 'Hers was from the recorder club trip to Dormond, it was purple.'

Margery supposed Mrs Large could have upgraded at some point, maybe Mrs Blossom had bought her a new one with her hush money. Even if Mrs Large had put the stage together, that didn't mean there was any malicious malpractice to it, and she certainly couldn't have started the fire at Ittonvale or been the one to climb through the kitchen window and enter the school through the kitchen door. But still, it niggled her. There was a malicious intent there; if you were planning to innocently put a stage up then why the effort to conceal your identity? Why have your partner in crime let you into the building after they had entered it through a known CCTV blind spot? Worse still, how did they know about the blind spot? She put her head in her hands and groaned. Gary smiled at her uneasily.

The woman on the video spun around and looked directly at the camera. The quality was poor enough that they could have been assumed to be Mrs Smith, they had the same kind of bob after all, and their face was too blurry to have any discernible features. But it was not Mrs Smith. After all, Margery thought to herself, blonde and silver could probably look very similar in black and white and the bottom of their face was covered by their scarf.

'This is from the weekend the stage was put up?' Margery asked. 'You're absolutely sure?'

'Yeah,' Gary said.

Mr Barrow nodded. 'Four o'clock on that Saturday.'

'Well, that's not Mrs Smith.' Margery said definitely. She had never been surer of anything.

'What? Really?' Gary said. 'The police assumed it was Mrs Smith, it looks just like her.'

'It can't have been her,' Clementine said. 'We can prove it. But it's not Mrs Large either. Who do you think it is, Margery?'

Mr Barrow gave her a surprised look. 'Yes Margery, who do you think it is? Have you worked it out?'

'Look, do me a favour and show me something from yesterday, us all going in in the morning please. We got to work at about eight,' Margery asked Gary. He nodded.

He worked his magic on the computer screen and a few minutes later the footage of them entering the building played. Margery watched herself and Clementine swipe their cards on the door and enter the building.

'Definitely not Mrs Large,' Clementine said. 'Look how tiny Margery and I are going into the building. The person who went in on the day the stage was put up is much, much taller on that video.'

Gary switched back to the video of the woman with the bag. 'Oh yeah. Look, their head is much closer to the top of the door, isn't it? How does that prove anything though?'

'Well Mrs Large was much shorter than me or Clementine,' Margery said, 'which is really saying something!' Clementine chuckled beside her.

'I didn't like to say, but yeah.' Gary smiled at her. 'But you know what? I reckon I've seen that haircut before.'

'You know,' Mr Barrow said, 'I think I have too.'

'That lady from Ittonvale school, she has that haircut and she's quite tall. Do you know her?'

'I do.' Margery nodded, turning on the office chair to look at him. 'Well, not personally. Tilly…'

'Matilda,' Mr Barrow said.

'Pardon?' Clementine asked.

'Her full name is Matilda Jackson. Her nickname's Tilly.'

Margery suddenly had an epiphany about where she had heard the name before. Matilda. That was what the person had called her when Margery had been eavesdropping through the vent in her dry store. She cursed herself for never figuring out where the vent led; if she had been able to work that out then she would know who Matilda had been talking to that day and some more of this would have made sense.

'Has she been here today, Gary?' Clementine asked.

'No,' Gary said. 'I've been watching the cameras all day. There's been nothing unusual.'

Margery supposed that she could have come into the building through the exit to the school hall, but even if that were Matilda on the CCTV from the day the stage had been put up, who had helped her? How had she got into the building today? And there was still the matter of the tiny dog dress that Ben had found on his adventures.

'Well,' Margery said, finally feeling defeated enough to leave. 'Thank you, Gary, that was very helpful.'

'Yeah of course, no problem.' He smiled at her. 'Glad I could be of service. Anyway, gets a bit boring in here sometimes. Well apart from the police coming the other week and that.'

Mr Barrow looked down at Ada Bones' dress again; Clementine had got it out of her handbag and laid it on the desk.

'I think I'm going to have to call the police again,' he said gingerly. 'They ought to be on the lookout for Matilda, have her explain herself. Why was she trespassing here? At least we should probably be able to rule out Mrs Large now. Get poor Mr Large out of custody.'

Margery nodded, at least they had managed to clear poor Mrs Large's name, even if it was too late. But the tiny dress on school property meant that Ada Bones had been taken here after her dognapping. Where was she now? Had Matilda brought her here and why? Margery hoped that they could find her, for Mrs Blossom's sake if nothing else.

'You don't think that whoever broke in on the bake sale morning had Mrs Blossom's dog in their bag, do you?' she asked, but it was clear from the expressions of those in the room with her, that they did.

Chapter Twenty-Three

They managed to leave Mr Barrow on the phone to Officer Thomas and join the kitchen team as they had stomped into the school hall just after three. It was the earliest they had ever been summoned for a rehearsal and Margery could see the annoyance on the dinner lady team's faces. She herself, wanted nothing more than to go home and do a nice winter jigsaw puzzle but it looked as though they would be in the hall for a long time. Mr Daniels was over in the corner of the stage, screwing together the last of the concert stage décor which was all gaudy snowmen and angels. Margery briefly wondered how he was getting on with Rose since her return; he had not seemed particularly thrilled to see her back.

Mrs Smith entered the room, back to her usual self again as though she had never been suspended at all, in a smart tailored suit once again. She broke into song at the sight of the piano and for a moment the hall was filled with overdramatic wailing. Before Mrs Smith could finish her melodramatic rendition, Mrs Blossom was entering with her staff wailing back and it became half a duet, half singing competition. Mrs Smith ended on a high note, eyes closed as though she were auditioning to be in the cast of *Cats* as the rest of the Summerview Secondary staff stood and watched awkwardly.

'Fantastic.' Mrs Blossom clapped as the Ittonvale staff cheered. This sort of thing was obviously a regular occurrence at Ittonvale Secondary. Mrs Smith stood from the keyboard and took a deep bow. Margery saw Seren raise her hands together as though she were going to clap also, and then put them back down at the sight of the rest of the Summerview staff's confused faces. Mr Daniels grimaced, finishing screwing in the last screw of the big faux Christmas tree, dropping the tool he had been using on the floor and jumping from the stage. He made sure to flip the power switch back on before he marched out of the room; Margery heard Karen oohing about the 'beautiful decs' behind her. The door slammed behind him.

'Now…' Mrs Blossom said, 'should we get my ladies on the stage first? I'm assuming that would be easiest because you already know all my songs, don't you?'

Mrs Smith glared at her, but Mrs Blossom just smiled. 'I'm joking, we'll go and sit over here while you all warm up and then we'll go on after.'

'Come on then ladies, up on the stage!' Mrs Smith smiled, the first genuine smile Margery thought she had ever seen her do. 'For the final time before the big show tomorrow.'

'This is terrible,' Clementine hissed to Margery as they clambered up the little staircase onto the fold-out stage. Margery eyed the brand-new light fittings nervously as they dangled from the rod above them. As they climbed, she tried not to let too much of herself brush against the Christmas tree resting against the stairs. She heard Karen warn Sharon against knocking over the lovely decs and Clementine turned to give her a withering look.

'I know, I know.' Margery smiled at her expression, as they made their way to the other side of the stage. 'Thank

God we don't have long left till Christmas, I can't wait to have a break from all this.'

'Yes definitely.' Clementine nodded. 'They're decorations for God's sake. Much too important to be abbreviating all over the place.'

Margery nodded and opened her mouth to reply, but Clementine had turned away from her and stared at the side of the stage they had been clambering up only moments ago.

Something was wrong in the room. Margery could not put her finger on it, but the air did not feel right. A wave of confusion ran up her spine. Margery spun around to see where Clementine was staring, just in time to see the real Christmas tree in the corner catch alight. Not just alight, she thought in horror, it went up like a beacon. The flames zoomed up it and in seconds they were licking the ceiling as the room filled fast with thick, black smoke.

The plastic decorations and lights they had scoffed at so many times during the Christmas period were melting; toxic goo was dripping from the branches of the tree. What was left of the tree anyway, it was more a skeleton now. The branches slicked away in the fireball. The stairs they had climbed up less than a minute ago at the side of the stage had begun to catch light too, the carpet on top of them beginning to burn. The air was heavy with chemicals. Flames rushed up and along the metal fittings for the lights and the long curtains that draped the floor-to-ceiling windows along the hall wall were suddenly on fire too. The blaze rose until it consumed even the fire exit door.

'Oh God, Margery!' Clementine grabbed her hand. They jumped down the short distance from the front of the stage and ran towards the main hall double doors along with everyone else in the room.

'It's locked!' Gloria pounded the handle of the main door, sweat dripping down her face. The door did not budge an inch. Mrs Smith pushed her out of the way and she and Seren began a tug of war with it as Sharon smashed the glass of the fire alarm next to the door. The alarm blared out in the room as the air began to smoulder. Margery could barely see them through the heaviness of the smoke as it burned her eyes. She dragged Clementine down to the floor where the air was cleaner, desperately trying to remember their fire safety training. The Ittonvale staff were frozen in place in horror.

'Clem!' Margery cried over the wailing fire alarm; her voice felt unnaturally high. 'What should we do?'

'We need to get over to the window, Margery!' Clementine shrieked back, her hands firmly over her ears to block out the noise. 'Come on, we can crawl over!'

Margery tried not to breathe too deeply; every breath contained less oxygen and more smoke. She was beginning to feel as though she was choking, dark spots rising in her vision as she struggled to draw breath. More worrying to her was Clementine's asthma which was always in the back of her mind anyway. If she felt dizzy with lack of air it must have been a million times worse for Clementine, who was already crawling her way through the hall, as the smoke rose, and staff ran around in panic.

She peered through the smoke and followed Clementine blindly as they crawled. It seemed like madness to be going back towards the source of the fire and she fought her own instincts to get up and run back the way they had come. Clementine reached the only window without a burning curtain above it and tried to open the latch.

'It's painted shut, Margery!' Clementine's eyes were wide, she grabbed Margery's wrist and held it much too tight. 'We're trapped!'

Clementine began to cough. A wheezing, gasping cough that was almost a choke in its viciousness. Margery stared at the closed window as fear washed over her. She looked around, trying to find something, anything to help them. The rest of the staff were still trying to desperately pry the main doors open. Her eyes fell to the wheeled piano in the centre of the room.

'Seren, Gloria, Karen!' she screamed through the darkness as she rushed over to it. 'Help me!'

Sharon was the first over, she kicked the brake on the piano's wheels off with her foot and they began to push. Gloria and Seren were not far behind, and they joined them. Margery could see Karen rushing over from where Mrs Smith was still pounding on the main doors. With difficultly they wheeled the cumbersome instrument into position in front of the windows.

'Okay, ready? One, two...' Margery shouted, her throat feeling as sore as if she had tonsillitis, '...three!'

It was not easy going, it would not have been in normal circumstances, let alone when everything was on fire, but somehow, they managed it. Clementine waved to them madly as they approached, as though she was directing traffic at an airport. As they neared the large floor-to-ceiling windows they let go and the piano careened forward. Margery closed her eyes praying it would go through on impact. There was a tremendous crash and the sound of breaking glass; she squeezed her eyes shut tighter and prayed and prayed that it would be enough.

She felt someone grab her arm and opened her eyes again. There was a big hole where the glass in the window had been, the smoke billowing out of it already. The dinner lady team were already making their way out of it into the playground where the piano sat, looking not much worse for wear.

'Come on, Margery,' Gloria said, dragging her forward, 'watch the glass!'

Margery followed her outside and they all collapsed on the floor of the playground, at a safe distance in the icy cold air. Margery looked around at the assembled staff, who looked as shocked as she felt. Benjamin still had his hands over his ears at the blaring of the alarm. Mr Barrow rounded the corner wearing his hi-vis fire marshal jacket carrying a handheld radio walkie-talkie.

'Everyone okay?' he asked as he sprinted over, his long legs making short work of the distance and his eyes wide. 'The fire brigade is on its way.'

Margery nodded and turned back to look at the hall again. You could barely see inside, the smoke being so thick. The tree must have been long gone by now. The smoke hit the frigid air and rose like steam into the dark afternoon sky. She looked around desperately for Clementine and found her propped up against one of the brick benches on the playground, Mrs Smith saying something to her. Mrs Blossom sat slumped across from them blinking rapidly. Margery rushed over to Clementine, joining Mrs Smith in kneeling down in front of her. Clementine reached for her hand immediately.

'Are you okay, Clem?' Margery managed to ask, though her voice felt weak and feeble. Clementine was sitting on the poured concrete gasping and wheezing for air. 'Let me run and get your spare inhaler from the kitchen.'

'I'm fine!' Clementine croaked out. 'Just leave me here, I'll be all right.'

'Oh yes, so sorry, I forgot you were a doctor. Tell me again where you got your medical degree?' Mrs Smith said, kneeling next to Clementine, her eyebrows joined together as she looked at her. She gave Margery a small, forced smile. 'Don't worry, Seren is calling for an ambulance.' Margery could see Seren on the phone, pacing back and forth behind them.

'Called me an ambulance so I don't die!' Clementine wheezed out dramatically. 'You *do* want to be friends with us!'

Mrs Smith rolled her eyes, but quickly went back to looking concerned. Clementine's breathing was getting worse, her face was ashen. Even through the stupid remark, Margery could see the panic in her eyes. She cursed herself for leaving both their bags in their staff room. She could picture exactly where the second spare inhaler was in her locked locker. Clementine continued to struggle to draw breath, her grip on Margery's hand tightening.

Chapter Twenty-Four

Margery sat with her hands folded in her lap, mainly so the nurses would not be able to tell how much they were shaking if one of them wandered over. She looked around the small room, with its dowdy curtains and plain cladded walls. Clementine was lucky to have her own room at all, and not to have been shoved into one of the Nightingale wards with their multiple day bedrooms. Not that Clementine would get to take any great enjoyment of the facilities, being as she was currently fast asleep with an IV drip in her arm and an oxygen mask over her face. The plastic clock on the wall read that it had just gone six thirty in the morning.

The nurse on shift had suggested to Margery that she could go home and come back after she had had a rest, but Margery could not bring herself to leave. She would never have slept at home without Clementine anyway. Gloria had offered to stop in and feed Pumpkin and then had returned with a set of clean clothes for them both, putting their fight aside for the time being in Margery and Clementine's moment of need. The relief Margery had felt at getting changed out of her smoky cardigan had been immense.

The ambulance had arrived just before the fire engine, and the paramedics had put Clementine straight on a nebuliser. It had been much too serious an attack to sort out on the floor of the playground and she had been blue-lighted all the way to Ittonvale Hospital. Margery felt it strange to think that Mrs Large had died in this very hospital on a different floor. Clementine would probably like telling the story when she recovered. The medical staff said she would be fine, and that they could go home as soon as Clementine had been checked over in the morning. Margery hoped with all her might that they were right. She could not bear it if they were not.

When her mother had died Margery had felt as though a piece of her world had disappeared and it had never really returned. Other people's sympathy had not helped; eighty-nine had indeed been a great age, but Margery suspected that she herself could have been eighty-nine years old when her mother had died, and it would not have hurt any less. The feeling of loss had faded with time but never really went away entirely.

She had felt the same when the cat they had owned before Pumpkin had taken to hiding under the bed crying in pain and refused to come out again. Clementine had taken a photograph of her holding the cat the week before with their old film camera. It was the last picture she had of her and the cat together before Marbles had taken the sad trip to the vet to begin her final journey. When they had finally got around to having the film developed, Margery had framed the photo and hung it up in their tiny spare room, though she didn't know why. Maybe to try and take some of the power out of the image of her and the skeletal creature in her arms that had once been a beloved family member, now buried under a lavender bush in the back garden. To try and do away with the sadness, she had told herself at the time. It had not worked, and she still could not look at the photo in the frame fully when she hoovered and dusted in the room, always keeping it slightly out of eyesight.

Maybe she was just not good at dealing with those sorts of things, but Margery could not imagine living without Clementine. She had always secretly hoped that she would die before her, had even told her so before. Clementine had scoffed with her mouthful of Quality Street toffee pennies and said that Margery would be so lucky, and that she had better start eating more butter if she was going to catch up with her.

Margery watched Clementine's slow breathing as she lay in the bed with the thin blanket over her. Stared at the canula sticking out of her wrinkled hand. Usually between them they made sure that Clementine's asthma was very well controlled; Margery always carried a spare Ventolin inhaler in her handbag. It was usually so little of a problem that she would forget how dangerous it could be. Hopefully they could go home later in the day, now there were no outside stimulus aggravating her lungs. It had brought home to her how old they were getting.

She yawned, stretched, and decided that as Clementine was not going anywhere anytime soon, she would go out into the corridor and see if she could get a cup of coffee and ring the headmaster to update him on the situation. She gave Clementine one last look as she left the room; she looked so peaceful, and calm compared to the panic the night before.

Margery wandered out into the hall. It was still quiet, though she knew the ward would soon be bustling with the breakfast trolley and medical staff doing their rounds. As it was, there was only a singular nurse at the station on the far end of the ward. He smiled at her as she closed the door to Clementine's room with a soft click. She walked over to the vending machine and peered at the note stuck to its front, *out of order.*

'That machine's broken,' the nurse said cheerily from his seat. 'But the cafe's opening in a minute just downstairs, one floor down. You can't miss it.'

'Oh okay, thank you.' Margery could not imagine the day being any less hellish, but a coffee would definitely take the edge off.

She pottered down the stairs, feeling too wobbly and nervous to brave the lift, and out into the vestibule where they had stood waiting the other day. Sure enough, the cafe staff were just raising the shutters of the canteen. She stood in front of the display counter wondering whether she should also get a piece of cake, though she did not feel up to eating much and six thirty was possibly too early for dessert, even for her. She decided eventually to just get a coffee and hurry back upstairs, squinting at the blackboard behind the counter, the wide array of hot drinks baffling to her with the lack of sleep.

'Flat white please,' Margery said, hoping that her voice was sure enough that the staff member with his back to her would not realise that she was not entirely sure what that was.

'No problem, love.' The young man turned and acknowledged her, busily getting the milk out of the fridge, and turning again to the coffee machine. He began to froth the milk in great swathes of steam. Margery frowned at his turned back; she shook her head.

'I can't believe you're here, after what just happened,' she said, amazed. He paused at the sudden change of tone in her voice, the milk almost frothing over the top of the jug before he turned the machine off.

'I…' The young man turned, the coffee forgotten for a moment, and stared back, his eyebrows raised. 'I work here?'

'Yes,' Margery said, leaning forward to get a better look at him. 'This is your part-time job, isn't it? You know, when Martha told me you worked here too, I wondered what you were doing, but it never crossed my mind to ask.'

'No, I definitely work here, only here.' He shook his head, pointing to his hospital name badge.

Margery peered even closer at him. The man in front of her was not Benjamin. She had been so convinced that it was, he was the spit of him. It was hard to tell because of the uniform he wore but she could have sworn it was, the name badge certainly indicated so, but he did not seem to know her at all. He passed her the coffee and gave her a frayed, awkward smile, while he moved to the till. She tapped her card on the card reader obediently, turning to question him again as it beeped.

Someone yelled something from the back of the cafe and the young man disappeared. Margery felt rooted to the spot, almost not noticing the coffee burning through the cardboard takeaway cup to the skin of her palm. Did Ben have a brother? He had never said anything of the sort. But surely even if he did have a sibling, they wouldn't both be called Ben, that seemed ridiculous. The young man came back to the counter and saw her still standing there.

'Are you all right? Can I help with anything?' he asked, seeming genuinely concerned. 'You seem a bit lost, did I give you the wrong drink?'

'No, no,' Margery said, she gave a small bark of laughter, shaking her head. 'It's… well it's silly really but you look just like a member of my staff.'

'Oh.' He smiled at her. 'Well, I am a twin.'

'You're a twin?'

'Yeah. So, my brother Pete works for you then, does he?'

'Pete?' Margery said, bemused. 'No… Ben works for me.'

The penny dropped and they both stared at each other for a moment. Margery shook her head.

'You're Ben, aren't you?' she asked. 'He used your CV to apply for the job?'

The real Ben nodded. 'Yeah. I can't believe he's done that again.'

'Wow,' Margery said, she felt like she might need to have a lie down after all this drama. She leaned against the counter. 'Again?'

'Yeah,' Ben said. 'He got me fired from the bakers in town for pretending to be me on my days off. God, this explains why I'm paying so much tax. I kept asking my manager to ring HMRC for me.'

Margery sighed. This was a conundrum indeed and a difficult conversation she was going to have to have, although it also explained so many things.

'Why would he do that?'

'He's watched too many TV shows, thinks he's a chef.' The real Ben laughed, joining her in leaning back against the counter. 'Nah I mean, he's probably just trying to help. We live in a flat in the town centre together and we're always struggling with rent, and I couldn't get him a job here because he's terrible at cooking and that. Never thought to ask him where he was getting the money from. Maybe I should've.'

'Are you going to struggle if he gets fired from this job?' Margery did not want to sack him, but he had violated several laws, not to mention her trust. There was also the small matter of the million different safeguarding issues involved in holding a DBS check that was not really his while working around a few hundred teenagers.

'Yeah maybe.' Ben shrugged. Margery scrutinised his face and the thatch of blond hair poking out from under the hat he was wearing. They were truly identical. It was unnerving. 'But we'll cross that bridge when we get there, I suppose. He's not a bad person, you know? He just does stupid things sometimes.'

–

A few hours later and Clementine had been released from hospital. Once she was home all she wanted to do was run around celebrating her near death. Margery managed to force her into the armchair in front of the television, with the threat that she would hide all the Quality Street if she did not calm down. Clementine held court from the chair as she told Pumpkin all about it, though the cat did not look particularly impressed. If anything, she looked more annoyed that Clementine had stolen her seat. No sooner had they settled, there was a knock at the door, shattering the peace. Margery dropped her yarn on the floor, and it bounced merrily underneath the sofa.

'Who the devil could that be?' Clementine said. 'Margery, quick get the door.'

Margery got up and did as she was told. She was startled to see Seren standing on the doorstep in front of her in her big winter anorak and wellington boots, holding a new box of Quality Street and a card in a white envelope.

'What are you doing here?' she asked, her brow furrowed in confusion. Seren grinned at her.

'School's closed!' She beamed much too cheerily for someone who had nearly burnt to death in a room of their colleagues. 'Suspected arson! Just like Ittonvale school!'

'Arson!' Margery cried. 'I thought the tree set on fire because the lights on it were Woolworths own brand and purchased in 1997?' If she was being honest with herself, she had barely given a thought to the cause of the fire, being much more concerned with Clementine's plight than anything else. And after the strange encounter with Benjamin's brother, she had completely forgotten to call the headmaster. She had been meaning to ask him what the police were doing about Matilda.

'Well. That's the thing! They were new, the headmaster said.' Seren nodded seriously. 'Can I come in, Margery? It's freezing out here.'

'Of course.' Margery stood by to let her in. Seren trudged past her, taking off her ginormous men's anorak and chucking it down on the armchair, blowing into her hands to warm them up. Clementine beamed at her arrival, probably glad to have another person to tell the story of her ride in the ambulance and how 'Christmas had nearly killed her'.

'I can't believe it either, the headmaster said he was going to do an assembly about it, but then he remembered he didn't have a hall to do the assembly in,' Seren said, handing Clementine the card. 'Hello Clem, how are you feeling?'

'Very well thank you. Who burnt the school down?' Clementine asked.

Seren shrugged. 'No idea. The police have been and everything.'

'Well,' Clementine said, clapping her hands together, the card falling to the coffee table forgotten, 'this sounds just like a case for the dinner lady detectives. Stupid asthma!'

'We haven't solved the first case yet,' Margery laughed.

'Rose is coming. She's just parking the car,' Seren said, reaching over to the coffee table to grab a toffee penny. Clementine narrowed her eyes at her grasping hands. 'She said to tell you that your driveway is too small.'

'It's a perfectly normal-sized driveway,' Margery said.

'Yes, but it's got your car on it,' Seren said seriously. 'She tried to park on the grass, but she got the car stuck.'

Margery rolled her eyes, dreading to think what their front lawn looked like after Mrs Smith's ginormous truck had been swerving around on it. 'So, what's going to happen with the play?'

'It's off!' Mrs Smith said dramatically from the hallway of the house, where she had appeared silently, her car keys still in her hand. 'We can't go on with nowhere to perform, can we?'

'Come in and sit down, Rose,' Margery said. 'I'll make us all some tea.'

'I've brought my own tea bags.' Mrs Smith sniffed, sliding off her coat and throwing it at Seren, who looked around wildly for a place to hang it. 'Good ones, because you only had own brand tea last time and we might as well have been drinking vinegar.'

'Sarson's or a nice white wine one?' Clementine asked. Rose glared at her.

Margery sighed and went into the kitchen to prepare the tea things, getting the good biscuits down from her secret hiding place. There were only toffee pennies and coconut eclairs left in the Quality Street box now; she thought party rings might raise the mood of the room. She pottered back in with the tea tray, putting it down in the middle of the living room on the coffee table. Seren sat down heavily on the pink crinoline chair and helped herself to another toffee penny from the open tub. Mrs Smith looked around at their small living room, her lip curling in distaste, before finally perching herself delicately in Margery's mother's antique rocking chair by the Christmas tree.

'Party ring, Rose?' Margery offered her a biscuit from the fine china plate.

'Do I look like I eat sugar?' Mrs Smith glowered at her. 'I'll look like the Venus of Willendorf if I eat that processed mess.' But she took a biscuit anyway and crunched away as Margery poured her a cup of tea.

'That reminds me, Margery.' Clementine turned to look up at her. 'What are we going to do with all the food at work?'

'I've been thinking about this, I'm going to have to go in at some point today and sort it.' Margery sighed. 'I mean, I could just freeze all the meat, but it seems like such a waste not to use all the vegetables, and Karen spent so long making the trifles. But I can't well leave you, can I?'

'Don't be silly,' Clementine said, 'I'm fine, perfect health, blah blah blah. You should go. In fact, I'll come with you!'

Margery considered her. 'I'm not sure about that, Clem. You've only just left hospital. I don't think an excursion is the best of ideas.'

'I can stay here with Clem, Margery,' Seren said, ignoring Mrs Smith's glare as she picked up another toffee penny.

'I don't need babysitting!' Clementine scowled at Seren, just as she dropped the teaspoon on the floor again. Mrs Smith chuckled from the corner.

They dwindled off into silence and Margery thought back to the events of the evening before. She was sure it was one of those things that would haunt you for a long time, one that would wake her up in the middle of the night gasping for air. She suddenly felt very tired.

'In all seriousness though, Margery,' Clementine said, 'what will we do about all the food? We can't just leave it in there to rot.'

'No but I'm sure there's a lot going on at the school now,' Margery said, sitting back against the chair. 'The police are probably busy looking for Matilda, and now this fire…'

'What do you mean, Matilda?' Mrs Smith said eyebrows raised, as she took another party ring from the coffee table. 'Tilly, you mean?'

'Yes. The music teacher from Ittonvale.' Margery sighed, folding her arms, and leaning as far back as she could without toppling off the sofa arm.

'She's not their music teacher.' Mrs Smith continued. 'She's science, does chemistry, I think. But she plays the piano for Mrs Blossom, probably because Rhonda is too selfish and terrible to keep a proper member of staff. What has she done? Why're the police looking for her?'

'You really haven't heard?' Margery said curiously. Rose must really not be on proper speaking terms with Mr Barrow if he had not told her. 'We think she was the person who went to the school on that weekend and put the stage up and she was there yesterday in Mrs Large's old office.'

'Good Lord.' Mrs Smith stood and gestured for Seren to pass her coat. 'Well, I'd better get up there and see what's going on.'

'I don't think you should be going anywhere near the school at the moment,' Clementine said. 'Things are only just settling down for you, aren't they? You're lucky the headmaster feels sorry for you for nearly burning to death with the rest of us.'

Mrs Smith glared at her but sat back down in the rocking chair in defeat. The room fell silent once more; only the soft ticking of the numerous carriage clocks could be heard.

'I still can't believe Gloria smashed our cakes,' Seren said, her eyes narrowing at the betrayal. They all hummed in agreement. 'And an Ittonvale teacher put the stage together?' Seren continued, her eyes wide. 'I wonder why they would do that?'

'None of this adds up.' Margery sighed. 'Matilda might have put the stage up, but who helped her, and more to the point, who set fire to both halls?' She suddenly thought back to Mr Daniels in the school hall the afternoon before. She had been so sure that he had left and yet he had appeared outside on the playground with the rest of them.

'All the more reason to go and see what's going on,' Mrs Smith said, standing and pulling her car keys from her handbag. 'Come on, I'll drive.'

Chapter Twenty-Five

'Hello, Margery, how's Clementine?' Mr Barrow smiled weakly as she arrived in the school reception. She had managed finally to constrain Mrs Smith to the car in the car park, though it had taken a lot more effort than she would have liked on so few hours of sleep. She felt like a shrivelled husk of herself today, now that all the adrenaline had worn off.

'Hello, Mr Barrow. Clem's fine.' He did not look happy. Margery supposed that there was not much to be happy about. 'Any news on the fire?'

He shook his head, his mouth set in a grim line. 'Not particularly, no. What are you doing here?'

'I've come to sort out the kitchen,' Margery said. He nodded and folded his arms. He had rolled up his sleeves at some point, his usual tailored jacket nowhere to be seen.

'Oh well, that sounds like a good idea.' Mr Barrow sighed. 'I can't imagine us reopening for a while after all this. The governors are not going to be happy.'

'No, I suppose not,' Margery said. They stood awkwardly for a moment before she decided to take her leave. 'Well, I'd better get going...'

'Those lights were new, Margery.' Mr Barrow turned to her, almost shouting, though Margery knew the aggression was not meant for her. 'How could they have done that? Set alight like that? I changed them myself after the fire Ittonvale had, I thought they'd be safer.'

'What have the fire brigade said?' Margery asked, taking a step back. He had begun to pace up and down the small vestibule.

'They said they'd had been tampered with.' He stared at the school trophy cabinet and Margery wondered what he was thinking; it was hard to tell. Usually, he was so calm and composed, she had never seen him this upset. He was not a person who showed his emotions very much. 'And they found one of the school screwdrivers under the stage.'

'One of the school screwdrivers?' Margery stared at him. 'Not one of the missing ones?'

'Exactly.' Mr Barrow ran his hands through his hair. 'One of the missing ones.'

'What colour was it?' Margery asked, the cogs in her head whirring. 'Did it have a red handle?'

Mr Barrow stared at her for a moment before answering. 'It used to,' he said slowly, peering at her quizzically. 'How did you know that?'

Clarity flooded Margery's brain as things began to click into place.

'Edward Daniels put the stage up,' Margery said, her voice steady and clear even with her nerves. 'I'm sure of it.'

'Edward? Are you sure?' Mr Barrow had stopped pacing. 'What makes you think that?'

'The pliers were found in Mrs Large's office after she died, the office he's been using now she's gone.' Margery explained. 'Mr Daniels had been using that same screwdriver when I saw him yesterday, before the fire happened.' She had been sure she had seen him leave the hall, had been so sure he had left. She had been right. 'He left just before the fire started and didn't show back up until after.'

To his credit Mr Barrow did not look too shocked. He hummed and tapped his chin with one of his long index fingers. 'I did find it strange he looked so clean yesterday on the playground. Everyone else's clothes were dirty from the smoke.'

'Exactly,' Margery said.

–

Margery gathered up the food they had already prepared, and the partridges she had not been able to return to the butcher, intending to get out of the school as quickly as she could. She had told Mr Barrow as much as she could think of Mr Daniels and her suspicions of him. Mr Barrow had rushed off to talk to the police officers still milling around on site, hoping that they might be able to bring him in for questioning before he disappeared like Matilda had. She grabbed the kitchen trolley, wheeling it over to the dry store so she could get all the custard and brandy sauce cartons first. She unlocked the door and wheeled herself in, beginning to grab the cartons.

There was a noise from above, startling her; she dropped a carton on the floor and cursed herself under her breath. The noise was coming from the vent again. She stared up at it, there was someone crashing and bashing around. Who, though? There was no one else here today, there shouldn't be anyway. Maybe the police were doing something somewhere? Though the last time Margery had seen them had been as she arrived at the school. Their focus seemed to be entirely on the school hall.

As soon as she began to think about it too hard, the noise suddenly stopped. She shook the thoughts away, blaming it on the old school plumbing again, which had probably needed replacing decades ago.

Going back out into the kitchen she loaded the trolley completely, then tried to work out how she could get it all out to Mrs Smith's gargantuan car. Sighing, she took her phone from her handbag and began composing a short text, giving up when she remembered how likely Mrs Smith would be to ignore it. In frustration she rang Mrs Smith's number programmed into the phone.

'Hello?' Mrs Smith barked across the line. 'Did you find Matilda, Margery?'

'No,' Margery said. Mrs Smith huffed. 'Can you drive the car around to the kitchen fire escape please? I've got a lot for you to pick up.'

'No,' Mrs Smith said. 'I'm very busy.'

'Yes, I can hear you listening to the new ABBA album,' Margery said, trying not to show the annoyance in her voice. 'I'll leave the fire escape door open.'

There was silence on the other end of the line.

'Hello?' Margery said again, deciding quickly that she was not against using blackmail. 'I think I have a way to save the play.'

'Fine. I'm coming.'

'Okay great, see you in a minute,' Margery said, but Mrs Smith had already hung up on her. She put the phone down on the nearest kitchen counter and heaved the heavy trolley over to the fire door. She jammed it open with one of the boxes of tablecloths she had taken from the storeroom with Clementine, weeks ago now, but it might as well have been years by how much had happened in that time. She pondered as she looked at the pile of food. There was something missing.

'The Christmas crackers!' Margery said to herself. They had not yet managed to drag the box down from the storeroom. She was not a big fan of going up there on her own, the second floor was creepy at the best of times, but needs must today. They could not possibly have a Christmas lunch without them. She left the trolley where it was and wandered down the hallway, up the staircase and through the science block.

It was always too dark in the science block hallways; though the labs were always clean and bright, there was just something dingy about the rest of the place. Margery was usually distracted about kitchen things when she came up to the storeroom, or Clementine was often yapping away as they walked through. She never really took the time to notice how dark it was during school hours when students were inside the classrooms. Now the only light in the corridors was the dim strip bulbs that ran down them, and the dim sunlight beaming in through the windows above each classroom door. Margery reached the storeroom at last, she put her key in the lock and turned it, but the door was already open, and the light inside was already on. Margery pushed it open unthinkingly and then stood still with shock at the sight.

'Mr Daniels?' She could hear the confusion in her own voice. Mr Daniels was kneeling on the floor, the tool kit strewn open in front of him. He was cleaning them viciously with a cloth. Margery stared at the plastic gloves covering his hands. 'What are you doing here?'

'Margery,' he said as he stood, still holding the screwdriver he had been fiddling with, dropping the bag in his hand to the floor. 'This isn't what it looks like.'

'Isn't it?' she said, looking around at the mess. 'Because it looks to me as though you're the one who took the tools and now you're trying to hide it.'

He gave her a long, hard look. 'So what if I am?'

'I can't believe this.' Margery sighed, looking down at where he still crouched on the floor above the tool bag. 'You're the mastermind behind it all.'

'I wouldn't go that far! Mastermind implies intent.' He chuckled, bending back down to pick the bag back up. 'And it was all kind of a mistake to be honest. It just got out of hand.'

'Well, wearing gloves to hide your fingerprints is intent, is it not? Did you let Tilly into the building?' Margery asked. Mr Daniels nodded.

'I did.'

'Why?' Margery asked. Mr Daniels kept tidying up after himself, ignoring her. 'To put the stage up?' He didn't say anything. Margery wanted to kick him, but she could hear her mother's voice in her head telling her not to fight fire with fire. 'Why on earth did you put the stage up? Why not wait for the headmaster to arrange for a maintenance person to do it? Why did Tilly help you?'

Mr Daniels snorted at that, finally acknowledging her. 'Ask her yourself.'

Margery whipped around to find Tilly staring back at her from where she had been hidden behind the door the entire time, Ada Bones in her arms. 'Hello.'

'Hello,' Margery said, her voice felt weak to her own ears. Tilly used her shoulder to nudge the door shut. Margery felt sweat form on her brow and could feel the fear rising in her throat. She looked around at the room. There were dog food cans strewn around everywhere and a pile of tablecloths in the corner had obviously been the poor dog's makeshift bed. She had not noticed before in her surprise at finding Mr Daniels in the room. She turned back to him. 'The headmaster thinks you were at your sister's hen party.'

'I was.' Mr Daniels smirked at the deception. 'That evening. He's not as clever as he thinks.'

'But the police...' Margery began to say; he interrupted with a wave of his hand.

'You should know as well as anyone how useless they are.' Mr Daniels sneered. 'There's no cameras by the school hall, is there? I went in that way. You've probably realised that by now as you're up here asking me loads of questions.' Margery nodded. 'But Matilda hadn't been here before, so she went to the main entrance by mistake, and I ran over and let her in. It was too late to stop her being seen on the camera anyway. I just hoped they'd be blurry enough that they wouldn't see our faces, and honestly, I was counting on them thinking it was Rose.'

He would have known what it would look like on the camera, Margery thought darkly. Must have known that they would assume that Tilly, or Matilda, Margery cursed herself for not realising where she had heard the name from before, with her short, light bob would look like Mrs Smith.

'Well, I suppose you were right there,' Margery agreed, thinking of how many accusations Mrs Smith had had thrown at her since. 'How did you know about the blind spot?'

'I go and chat with Gary quite a lot.' Mr Daniels tied the first bin bag and then began to stuff the empty dog food cans into another. 'He's a nice guy. Bit weird, but aren't we all? Anyway, he's showed me all the cameras and how they work. Interesting stuff.'

'I don't understand,' Margery said, a heavy feeling settling in her stomach. 'Did you know the stage lights weren't set up properly? Why kill Mrs Large? What could she have ever done to you?'

'We did set them up wrong.' He wouldn't look her in the eye, instead piling the bags together and brushing imaginary dirt from his hands. 'But the trap wasn't meant for Mrs Large, we didn't... we never... I didn't think she'd get hurt. It wasn't meant for her.'

'Well, she did,' Margery said angrily. 'Who was it meant for then?'

'Rose, obviously,' Mr Daniels said. 'But not to kill her, just a few broken bones to put her out of the Christmas concert planning stuff.'

'What!'

'We weren't trying to kill her!' Matilda cried from the corner, mirroring Margery's own shout. 'Just stop her from doing the play! Only a little bit of the lights was supposed to fall, not the whole lot.'

'Yeah, we got that wrong.' Mr Daniels winced. 'Didn't read the instructions properly. The stage wasn't from IKEA, was it? Not an easy bit of flat pack furniture.'

'But why?' Margery pleaded. 'Why were you trying to stop Mrs Smith doing her concert?'

'You've said the answer there, Margery.' Mr Daniels poked the closest bin bag with his toe. '*Her* concert.'

'Yes. It is her concert.' Margery looked between them both. Neither of them would look her in the eye. Ada Bones did not seem concerned.

'Thanks for reminding me, Margery.' He finally eyed her carefully, as though deciding how much to say. 'Do you know how disheartening it is to be under Mrs Smith's thumb, day in, day out?'

'I kind of do actually,' Margery said. He huffed at her.

'You don't.' Mr Daniels shook his head. 'Not in the way we do.' He nodded in Tilly's direction. Ada Bones began to growl softly. 'Do you have any idea what it's been like, watching her run the play into the ground every year? A mere assistant to her creative genius.' He scoffed out the last words. 'And Tilly felt the same way about Mrs Blossom.'

'I don't understand,' Margery mumbled. 'Isn't Itton-vale's play really successful every year?'

'Yes,' Tilly finally piped up from the corner. 'But it overtakes everything else. Just when I'm getting my students ready for their mock exams, we have to drop everything and do a play. Science isn't an easy subject to pass, Mrs Butcher-Baker, I need that time. All because she can't find anyone else stupid enough to play piano for her.'

'I don't understand...' Margery began, Mr Daniels cut her off.

'Of course you don't,' he snapped at her. 'How could you?'

'But you stole her dog.' Margery pointed at Ada Bones who looked very small and sad with just a collar and not her usual coordinating outfit on.

'I had to, to blackmail Mrs Blossom.' Tilly looked down at Ada Bones in her arms. 'I look after her a lot, so she went with me easily and we've looked after her well.'

'You've been keeping her in a storeroom.' Margery shook her head. 'Away from her owner. What are you blackmailing her for anyway? I spoke to her yesterday and she never mentioned anything of the sort.'

'I haven't done it yet,' Tilly said, in a tone that implied that Margery would never pass her science class. 'We've got to wait till after we'd got the tools back without anyone suspecting us, and money of course, what else?' Tilly smiled, but there was no happiness in it. 'These things all cost money, and your school has none. Where do you think all the new costumes and stage décor came from? We have to be reimbursed somehow. Edward's and my deal was that I help stop the Dewstow play this year and he'll help me with next year's. That way it would look organic. No one would suspect that we had set it all up.' She and Mr Daniels both nodded, Margery looked between them, at Tilly's blonde bob bouncing.

'Well. I realised, didn't I?' Margery finally said, she put her hand in the pockets of her cardigan so they could not see she was shaking. 'Most of it anyway.'

'And what have you done about it? Told the police, I'm guessing,' Mr Daniels said. 'Well you didn't manage to work it out in time to stop the fire, did you Margery?'

'Mr Daniels, even if the play is terrible, was it worth it? For what, to further your career?' Margery asked, to try and stop Edward from realising that she had done nothing of the sort yet. 'You nearly killed us all the other day, on top of actually killing Mrs Large.'

'It was so easy, that tree never gets watered, it was dry as a bone. I just swapped the new lights for old ones, just like Tilly did at Ittonvale.' He leaned against a pile of boxes. 'I thought it would just be a bit of a shock, scare you all and Rose, and ruin the stage so she couldn't do the play. I wasn't expecting the fire escape to catch fire. That's literally the one thing they aren't supposed to do.'

'You nearly killed my wife!'

He shrugged. 'Sorry. But like I said, it was an accident.'

'So, the Ittonvale school fire was an accident too?' Margery asked.

'That's actually where I got the idea from.' Mr Daniels said, running his hands through his hair as he paced up and down. 'Matilda set Ittonvale on fire. Do you think she enjoys being a dog's babysitter or being bossed around by a random drama teacher? She's the head of science at Ittonvale for Christ's sake. If there's no school hall, then she wouldn't be dragged into doing a play anymore just because she can play the piano!'

Tilly nodded aggressively, moving to stand in front of the storeroom door. Margery stepped back into the room to give her space.

'What! But how, why...?'

'It was quite clever actually as these things go.' Mr Daniels started to ball up the lights on the floor again. 'Did you know that if you put a powerful magnet near to an electrical plug then it will begin to melt? I didn't till then, but it only works on the old ones, so we had to swap the new LED ones out.'

Margery sat down on the nearest box with a thump, flabbergasted by Mr Daniels' revelation. 'How do you even know each other?'

'Tilly and I?' he asked, pointing to Tilly. Margery nodded. 'Oh, she was in my sister's year at school, we go way back.' Mr Daniels dropped the bag of lights on the floor and finally turned to look at her. 'Anyway, Mrs Smith was out of the way because the headmaster thought she put the stage up and we had a real chance of getting somewhere with the show, my show! It was going to be brilliant. But then Rose gets reinstated and ruins all my work. I'd rather destroy it, than let it go ahead as a shambles.' He smiled at her wildly, it was unnerving. 'Then with that success under my belt I could have gone anywhere, out of this awful town at least, got some proper drama work and not been stuck listening to Mrs Smith bang on about how she once nearly went through to the second auditions of *Jesus Christ Superstar*.'

'I don't… I still don't get it. Why set the hall on fire?'

'What's to get, Margery?' Mr Daniels grabbed her hand; she shook it away, staring down at the bin bags he had piled between them.

'I can't believe you. After all the school has done for you, you'd have no career at all if it wasn't for Mrs Smith and the headmaster. You came here straight from university, didn't you?'

'I'm an ambitious man, Mrs Butcher-Baker,' Mr Daniels said. 'This school is too small for me. Anyway, Matilda was sick of them both too and their stupid rivalry. It ruins everything every year. We just wanted Rose out of the way this year. This was all her idea if I'm honest.'

'It's true,' Tilly said. Margery whipped around in time to catch the small smile that flickered over her features.

'Which part of it was her idea? You seem to have had plenty of ideas of your own.'

'Yes, well,' he said, his face darkening. 'The stage was my idea I suppose, though it didn't really go as planned, did it?'

'No, I suppose not.'

'Honestly, I just assumed Rose would be standing on the stage when the lights went, and once Rose was out of the way then normality could ensue. Remember last year? She always shouts all about her play from the stage, doesn't she? But not this time and then!' He slapped his hands together and Margery flinched. 'Mrs Large was under the lights when they fell.'

Tilly put Ada Bones down on the floor next to her. The dog jumped up at her, desperate to be picked up again, but Tilly ignored her.

'Normality.' Margery scoffed. 'That didn't happen, did it?'

'No,' Mr Daniels said, stepping forward towards her. She jumped up from the box she had been sitting on and took a step back instinctively, nearly falling backward over it. 'But you're not going to tell anyone. Are you, Margery?'

She took another step back and then to the side to try and get away from him as he strode towards her. She put her hands up, though she had no hope of defending herself against him. 'What if I already have, what if the police are on their way, then what!'

'They aren't on their way up here, are they?' Mr Daniels said softly. 'I saw your face when you came in, you were as surprised to see me as I was to see you.'

He lurched towards her again; Margery squeaked as she fell into the boxes at the back of the storeroom as he continued his approach. Ada Bones ran around her, barking. Mr Daniels stopped for a moment to consider her. Margery tried desperately to think of a way she could escape his clutches. He was a lot younger and fitter, he would almost certainly catch her if she tried to run. And Tilly was still blocking the exit door. Mr Daniels looked at her as though he might lunge forward again, but instead he walked back across the room, carefully picking his way over the boxes and bags littered everywhere.

'I don't understand why you're here now?' Margery said. 'You could have got away with it.'

'Got to dispose of the evidence haven't I, Margery? Got to clean our fingerprints off these tools and put them all back.' He smiled. 'Anyway don't worry about us, we'll get away with it. Though you might not be around to see.'

Chapter Twenty-Six

Margery tried to stay calm and not panic but it was much easier said than done. She looked around the small room desperately for a way out, not that there was one, she thought bitterly. She sat again down on the nearest box and sighed as it crumpled under her weight. There was no point in wasting energy, she had to get out of here. Ada Bones glared at her from across the room, growling. Margery tried to remember how to calm an angry dog and came up short.

Mr Daniels had seemed slightly apologetic when he locked them in the room, not that it had done her any good. She knew no one would come looking for her, not up here anyway. They would be lucky to be discovered before the end of the Christmas holiday, by which time she would have almost certainly died from dehydration. Ada Bones would probably have eaten her body by then too. She tried not to think about it.

Margery thought about her phone, lying downstairs on the kitchen counter uselessly, and wished she had brought it up with her. All she had on her person was half a packet of Polos in her trouser pocket and a crumpled-up bit of tissue inside the sleeve of her cardigan. She thought briefly about jimmying the door handle off, but Mr Daniels had taken the toolbox with them as he slammed the door behind him. Margery had foolishly left her own key in the door when she had arrived at the storeroom, and she had heard him turn it in the lock. This was not the way she had been planning to go, she had been so looking forward to retiring in a few years and just playing backgammon and crocheting at her leisure all day.

In some ways dying of smoke inhalation during the fire might have been preferable. At least it would have been quicker. Margery wondered what Clementine would think when she didn't return home, and she tried to shake the thought of her all alone in the house, with Pumpkin waiting for her to come home and feed her dinner. Even if Clementine called the police, they would surely not find her here. They would look in the kitchen and the canteen and maybe a few other places, but not here. Mrs Smith would have known she had been in the kitchen of course. But Margery could not see her venturing up to the science block. Mrs Smith had said before that she didn't like to come up to the storeroom at all.

Margery decided that she couldn't keep sitting down and feeling sorry for herself. She had to figure something out. She jumped up and began to search through the piles of objects and boxes of things. There was nothing particularly helpful, though she did find the big box of Christmas crackers from last year, which was of little use to her now. She grasped one and twisted it by both handles till it cracked and pulled apart. There was nothing but a tiny plastic thimble inside. She tried again and again and again until the whole room was beginning to fill with scraps of peeled cardboard, but eventually she had a tiny screwdriver set in her hand.

She held it up and looked at it and realised how ridiculous an idea it was. The screwdrivers were so small she would have had trouble mending a watch with one of them, let alone taking the door from its hinges. She threw it down on the floor and looked around desperately again, sinking down next to the tiny screwdriver set in despair.

Mrs Ada Bones had other plans. She was sniffing her way around the room. Margery watched her for a while. She had nothing better to do. Ada Bones stopped at the back wall and wiggled her way between two boxes, disappearing between them. Margery waited for her to re-emerge. And waited and waited and waited.

'Ada!' she called, wishing she could whistle. She heard the dog bark, but it sounded tremendously far away. Growing concerned she crawled over and began to move the boxes. Ada Bones was nowhere to be found, but at the bottom of the wall was an open vent. She knelt to look at it closer. The vent was half covered by a broken grate, open just enough for a small dog to slide through.

'Why am I always doing the dangerous things?' she muttered to herself as she attempted to fully open the metal grating covering the vent. To her surprise it went easily, swinging back with a creak. She gulped. Leaning forward, she peered into the tunnel that had been revealed; it was very dark inside. Before she could lose her nerve, she went prone and slid down onto her stomach, pulling herself into the vent with her arms. She shuffled into it slowly, hearing her own heavy breathing in the dark tunnel. It was just big enough for her to squeeze into.

Margery hoped with all her might that the vent would not get smaller as she went along. This could end up just as bad an idea as staying locked in the storeroom, but she had to attempt it before she gave up. She tried not to think about the news story she had read once about a man who had got trapped in a cave system upside down, but it came to the forefront of her mind anyway. She dragged herself forward on her elbows, she knew she would have some scrapes tomorrow, but it would be worth it to escape. If she could escape.

It was disgustingly dusty in the vent, how it brought fresh air into the building she did not know, it whined under her weight, and she prayed that she would not suddenly go careening down to the floor. It was so dark she felt her way through with her hands, her own breathing much too fast. Margery tried not to panic as she came to a dead end, her fingers scraping against the metal.

'Ada Bones!' she cried, her voice loud in the tunnel and wobbly with panic. Ada Bones appeared through the darkness, though Margery could hear the tapping of her claws on the metal more than see her. Ada Bones licked her face and pottered back down the tunnel again. Margery grimaced at the dog's smelly breath, wishing she could reach her handkerchief.

Margery could feel herself sweating in the tiny space. She did not think she could push herself backward the way she had come, and the thought was making her panic. She was well and truly stuck. She pushed with all her might and found herself moving an inch back. With the tips of her fingers, she pushed and pushed, and slid and slid back until she felt her feet meet the carpet of the storeroom. She managed somehow to squirm and pull herself out of the vent back into the storeroom, cursing her own stupid idea as she did so and coughing as the dust hit her lungs. She brushed herself off. The relief to be out of the enclosed space was instant, though she was now back in the predicament she had been.

'Ada!' she bellowed into the vent again. Ada Bones trotted back excitedly, and this time Margery lunged forward and grabbed her. She closed the vent for the moment and then let the dog back down on the floor, where she immediately began to rush around sniffing the boxes in the room. Margery had one idea left, though she wasn't sure it would work, and she was terrified that the dog would disappear and leave her all alone.

Margery ripped a chunk of cardboard from the nearest box and then scrabbled around in the pile of trinkets that had been inside the Christmas crackers, finally finding a pen, thanking her lucky stars that this was a new box of Christmas crackers. Clementine had stolen all the pens from the original box. She scrawled a note and attached it to Ada Bones' collar.

'Right, Ada.' Margery addressed the dog, who gazed up at her stupidly. 'Find someone else please. Get them to help us.'

She opened the vent again and Ada went inside once more, sniffing and wagging her tail until she had disappeared around the bend inside. Margery waited, counting down the minutes on her watch. Five went by and then ten and then she heard Ada Bones' claws scraping on the metal of the vent again as she tottered back. Her tiny face arrived back in the storeroom. Margery tried not to seem too disappointed. She sent her again and waited twenty minutes this time, but the dog still returned empty-handed and the storeroom door did not fling open like Margery kept hoping it would.

'No luck then?' Margery asked the dog. She reached for Ada's collar and realised that the note was gone. 'Oh, did you find someone to help us?'

She bent down again and looked in the grate. She could not see anything there, so it hadn't fallen off in the immediate area, but she tried not to get her hopes up too much. She did not know where the vent went, if anywhere. She had read once that the best thing to do if you were lost or in an emergency was to stay where you were and wait for rescue. Margery wondered if this really counted as one of those times. She bent down to look at the vent again and made up her mind as Ada Bones ran back inside it as though this was a fantastic game they were playing together.

She lay flat and dragged herself into the darkness once more, swallowing down her fear. Margery pulled and pulled herself in haste until she reached the bend and then shimmied herself around it, following Ada Bones who had already skipped ahead. There was light at the end of the tunnel. She dragged herself towards it, trying to ignore how tight the passage was becoming, pulling herself over the piece of cardboard that she had written her note on. The dust was so thick, it was as if she was trying to drag herself through dry, dusty mud.

The light was coming from another metal grate. Ada Bones licked her face again, panting, and Margery reached out past her with her fingertips and pushed against the blockage, hard. Nothing happened. She pushed again and again and by some miraculous luck the grate started to move upwards with a squeak, until it clicked into place. Margery pulled herself forward and realised that she could see clearly out into her own dry store. So, this was where the noise had been coming from the entire time. If the situation had not been so dire, she would have laughed and laughed.

Now that they were almost free, she could not see a way to get down without hurting herself. Ada Bones was easy enough to help. She grabbed her by the middle, and reasoning that she had come this far, she said a silent prayer, slid herself out of the tunnel and slithered down head first. She realised her mistake when Ada Bones dropped to safety and her fingertips grazed the top of the chest freezer, leaving her stuck upside-down in a handstand shape, legs in the air. Margery thought she would look hilarious to any passer-by, what with her skirt billowing over her head, and her feet still stuck in the vent. She swung there for a moment as all the blood in her body rushed to her head, making it even harder to think. Ada Bones ran around the dry store in circles barking madly.

Margery rolled herself forward with all her might and felt the vent start to give. There was a terrible crunch and then she was flying to the ground, her shoes coming off as she dropped to the floor in a heap, her arm cracking horribly underneath her as she landed. Her sensible slip-on shoes still stuck in the vent which was now hanging out of the wall. Ada Bones whined.

'Oh God, Margery.' Mrs Smith was suddenly crouching down in her face. In all the drama Margery had completely forgotten that she had asked her to help her with the Christmas food. 'Are you all right? Wait there, I'm going to go get help.'

–

Mr Barrow walked over from where he had been talking to the police and sat down next to Margery at one of the canteen tables where she was perched. She was being monitored by the medical staff who had appeared shortly after Mrs Smith had called them. The headmaster had arrived not long before that.

They had found Mr Daniels and Tilly, not far from the school, and arrested them immediately. Margery waited for the sergeant to arrive back so she could finish giving her statement. He had had to rush off after them. One of the pitfalls of living in such a small town was only having a tiny police force, Margery supposed. Officer Thomas had called for backup from Ittonvale before he left, but they had yet to arrive.

'How's your arm, Margery?' Mr Barrow asked, placing the cup of tea into her good hand.

'It's okay,' Margery said, twisting the arm in the sling to demonstrate how okay it was. 'A little bit sore, but they said it looks like a sprain. I've got to go to the hospital for an X-ray though.'

'Well, it's always good to get these things checked.' Mr Barrow nodded and cleared his throat. 'And Clementine is still fine?'

'Yes, I should think so.' Margery gave him a small smile. 'Looking forward to Christmas now.'

Mr Barrow smiled back at her. 'Of course she is. I would expect nothing else.'

They slipped into an uncomfortable silence. The head-master cleared his throat.

'Look, I'm sorry about… well everything I suppose,' he began softly. 'I'm especially sorry that once again, you've nearly come to harm at the school. I can't believe it, I always thought we had such a good vetting process. Though I suppose Mr Daniels has been here for years.' He sighed. 'I should never have taken so long to let you see the CCTV. You certainly did a better job of it all than the police.'

'It wasn't your fault.' Margery looked down at her arm in the sling.

'I shouldn't have told you not to help. Hopefully there won't be a next time,' Mr Barrow continued, 'but if there is, I promise… you'll have my full attention immediately.'

'Thank you, Mr Barrow,' Margery said. 'I really do appreciate that.'

He nodded in agreement, and they dropped back into silence, both sipping tea from paper cups.

'Sorry about the vent door,' Margery said. 'Is it fixable?'

'Don't be so silly,' he said. 'You were shut in there, what else could you have done? And that trick you performed with the piano the other day, you saved a lot of lives, Margery.'

'I don't know about that…' she began, but he put his hand on her good shoulder to silence her.

'You did. I can't thank you enough.' He nodded at her sincerely. 'It's made me see lots of things in a new perspective, evaluate things differently, see people differently.' He looked over his shoulder at Mrs Smith who was berating poor young Officer Symon about something or other, Mrs Ada Bones safely under her arm. He continued, 'It's just a shame that Mr Daniels was able to get away with his plans for so long, and such a shame about the Christmas lunch!'

'And Mrs Smith's concert,' Margery said.

'Yes, I suppose that as well,' the headmaster said, but he didn't sound as unhappy at all about missing the Christmas play.

'What if I knew of a place we could do the play and have lunch?' Margery asked. 'We could do it for charity, invite all the children from school and their families. I've got all this food left you see, seems a shame to waste it. That's what I was planning on doing.'

He sat back with his cup and considered her. 'I dare say that would be okay, as long as we could get a risk assessment done in time?'

'Of course, I was hoping you'd say that.' She smiled.

'Brilliant.' Mr Barrow smiled back at her. 'You're turning out to be a fantastic manager, Mrs Butcher-Baker. Let me know what I can do to help.'

'Actually, Mr Barrow, I need to speak to you about something else too…' Margery paused, wondering whether or not to continue. 'Someone. Benjamin, one of my kitchen team.'

'Ah yes, I know young Benjamin.' Mr Barrow nodded. 'He's the one who gave the hockey team food poisoning.'

'Yes, that's the one.' Margery smiled weakly. 'Well, I have a proposition for you.'

'All right then,' he said, looking at her curiously. 'Let's have a proper chat, shall we?'

Chapter Twenty-Seven

The next day, bright and early, Margery oversaw the setting up of the church hall; she couldn't do much with her arm still all bandaged up. It was going to be tight, but she was sure they could get everything set up in the tiny backroom kitchen of the building and ready the stage for the school concert. Her eyes kept flitting over in amusement to where Mrs Smith was in full sergeant major mode, bellowing at Seren that they needed more lights. Seren had managed to get herself all tangled up in them and she looked as though she might fall over at any moment. As they finished decorating the hall and the dinner lady team had finally dragged in the chafing dishes and the small electric induction hobs, Margery found herself alone for a moment with Gloria.

'You've done a good job of this, Margery.' Gloria smiled at her awkwardly as she helped her throw tablecloths onto the long plastic tables with her good arm. 'Saved the day. I can't believe you pulled it off, and Clementine seems fine? I'm glad it's all worked out all right in the end.'

Margery looked over to where Clementine was sitting on one of the plastic chairs laughing with Sharon and Karen. They were all supposed to be readying the small church hall oven so they could start cooking, but Margery did not have the heart to go over and tell them to get a move on. It was nearly Christmas after all.

'She's fine,' Margery said, smiling at Gloria. 'She keeps asking me when we're going to do the Secret Santa swap, she has some sort of announcement to make.'

'We'd never do it, if I had my way,' Gloria sighed. Margery laughed. 'I just wanted to apologise, Margery. I shouldn't have got so annoyed before. You are a good manager.'

'It's okay.' Margery smiled. 'I know I still have a lot to learn.'

'Well, I'm sorry I didn't tell you about the cakes before. I was just being selfish,' Gloria said. 'I think I've just been a bit jealous.'

'I've been meaning to tell you,' Margery said. 'I spoke to Mr Barrow and he's going to give you a pay raise for all your hard work.'

'Really? Thank you.'

Margery nodded and they watched the staff members bustling around the hall. Gloria cleared her throat. 'So, how did you manage to get this place at such short notice?'

'My neighbour said we could use it, she's on the church committee.'

In truth Dawn had been livid that Margery hadn't finished crocheting the robins and was still refusing to join the choir, until she had offered the school's Christmas food and service as a peace offering. Though showing up on Dawn's doorstep covered in scratches and with her arm in a sling had probably helped matters along considerably. Dawn had changed her mind when she realised that it meant they could put on a charity event to feed half of the village and have a free show from an award-winning school like Ittonvale. Margery had not told her about the tiny partridges yet, or that Summerview Secondary would also be performing. One thing at a time.

'That was very nice of her.' Gloria smiled even wider. Margery nodded agreeably, smiling back. She supposed it was nice of her, she could have easily told them to get off her property like she usually did when Clementine had been caught stealing flowers from her garden.

Margery turned to watch Ben setting up the sound board for the concert. She reminded herself not to call him Benjamin anymore now that he was going by his real name, Pete. The headmaster had agreed with her that Benjamin was not working out in the kitchen and had given her permission to not continue his probation period. However, Mr Barrow had been very pleased when Margery had assured him that she knew of someone who would be the perfect new caretaker for the building and could start immediately. Pete had jumped at the chance to not only take his dream job, but to stop lying about being his own twin brother. Margery had 'introduced' them, and the headmaster had said he would give him a term's trial to see how he got on. Margery could already see that Pete was going to get on much better than he had as an Education Centre Nourishment Consultant. She felt a tap on her shoulder and turned to look straight into the face of another former kitchen team member.

'Ceri-Ann!' she cried, in genuine surprise. 'What are you doing here?'

'I'm doing the make-up for the play!' Ceri-Ann beamed at her, waving the duffle bag she was holding up. 'And the posters!'

'I saw you'd made the posters.' Margery smiled. 'I didn't realise you'd passed your beauty course so soon?'

'Oh, I haven't.' Ceri-Ann shook her head as though she were bemused Margery would ask. 'I've got a special make-up pass though, don't worry.' She pulled a laminated piece of paper from her pocket and showed it to Margery. It looked suspiciously like the 'detective pass' she had printed for Clementine. Margery tried to hide her laugh with a cough.

'Ooh, before I forget, thank you for making our Christmas cards.' Margery tried to keep a straight face. 'They were… interesting.'

Ceri-Ann beamed at her. Margery had been a bit surprised when she had seen them, there really was no need for Ceri-Ann to have photoshopped their faces onto a pair of snowmen. Clementine, however, had thought they were hilarious and so they had posted them out. They had received several phone calls since from amused and bewildered family members and friends.

'Well. It's been lovely to see you,' Margery said. 'I'm sure I'll see you later when you're doing our make-up.' A sudden thought struck her. Benjamin changing roles was going to leave the kitchen team short-staffed again and she was already dreading sifting through the job applications. 'Wait, how often are you in college? You wouldn't be interested in some part-time work, would you? In the kitchen?'

'Huh. Come back to the school?' Ceri-Ann stroked her chin as she thought about it. Margery worried she might give herself a papercut with the poster still in her hand. 'Well, I am very busy with the health and beauty stuff and that but yeah, I could do a few days a week, I can buy myself a new printer then. You're on, Margery.'

'Brilliant.' Margery beamed at her. 'Can you start after the Christmas holiday?'

'Yeah sure.' Ceri-Ann nodded. 'Oh, by the way I realised the other day that you and Clem haven't used your wedding present from me yet. That voucher expires you know!'

'Oh,' Margery said, the smile on her face becoming forced as she thought of the laminated piece of paper Ceri-Ann had given them on their wedding day. 'Well, we weren't sure how you'd manage a couple's head massage, we didn't want to trouble you with getting another person to help.'

'Don't be silly, Margery.' Ceri-Ann smiled. 'I've got two hands, haven't I?'

She skipped off to set up her things; Margery chuckled to herself as she went.

—

A few hours later and they were all jammed into the tiny church hall kitchen washing up the trays from lunch and picking at the leftovers. Margery was lucky enough to escape this fate with her sling, but she had been left to dry up. Which she did with great difficulty, dabbing at the plates with a tea towel in her good hand. The church hall outside the tiny kitchenette was jam-packed with people of all ages, and the conversation was a low rumble in the room. Margery was amazed how fast they had managed to get the word out. The headmaster must have rung every family from the school. Clementine came bouncing over holding a refill bag of Quality Street chocolates, a crumpled paper hat from a Christmas cracker perched on her head.

'That was fantastic, Margery!' she said. 'Did you see Dawn's face, she loved it!'

Margery had seen her face when the tiny birds and the massive jugs of gravy had arrived on the tables, she smiled. 'She did seem to.'

'Well even if she didn't, it was for free, wasn't it?' Clementine took her good hand and squeezed it. 'How are you getting on?'

'I'm okay.' Margery smiled. 'I'm glad that Mr Daniels and Matilda are getting their comeuppance and I'm glad all their plans didn't go right.'

'Yes, it serves him right,' Mrs Smith said, entering the kitchen through the doorway and looking very out of place among the dinner lady team. 'Imagine if he'd killed me with the lights, we never would have had a play! The world would truly be a darker place.'

'Why are you always sneaking around eavesdropping?' Clementine squawked. 'You'll probably spend your next life as a fly.'

'Well, you shouldn't talk so much with your big mouth,' Mrs Smith snapped and then realised where she was. 'I mean…'

'Where's Seren, Mrs Smith?' Margery asked quickly to change the subject.

'She's around here somewhere,' Mrs Smith said. 'Hopefully getting ready, like you lot should be. We've only got an hour before we go on. I want all of you changed and backstage in the next twenty minutes!'

'Good afternoon, Rose.' Mr Barrow had somehow also found his way into the room. Mrs Smith turned with her eyebrows raised in surprise; Margery noticed that she went red in the face at the sight of him. Clementine nudged her, smirking to herself.

'Hello, Mr Barrow.' Mrs Smith sniffed at him.

'I just wanted to let all of you ladies know that I am dreadfully looking forward to the play,' Mr Barrow said, looking around at them all and then back to Mrs Smith. He did not seem to be able to look her in the eye.

'Well, I should think so,' Mrs Smith said, indignantly. 'We were all nearly killed for it to go ahead, and that's not to mention what happened to poor Elizabeth.'

'Yes.' He nodded awkwardly. 'But Mr Daniels and Miss Jackson are in police custody and so that's the end of that.'

Mrs Smith glared at him. He coughed nervously, covering his mouth.

'Can I talk to you in private, Rosemary?' Mr Barrow asked. Mrs Smith stared up at his face and for a moment Margery thought she might refuse but then she nodded. He left the room, holding the door open for her as she followed. Gloria rolled her eyes at them both as they left.

'Why can't they just get it together?' Clementine said. 'All this dancing about is doing my head in. You'd think one of them had killed the other one's dog they way they've carried on this year.'

'Well actually that's not far off what happened.' Gloria smirked. 'He accidentally shut the cat in her study, and it pulled up all her brand new carpet.'

'That's what they've been arguing about this entire time?' Clementine said, aghast. 'God, they really need to sort their lives out.'

'Maybe they will now,' Margery said, as she watched them through the window of the door. Their conversation seemed to be much more amicable, Mrs Smith was blushing at something he had said to her, her face red against her pale skin and silver hair. 'Shall we go and get changed then?'

'I suppose so,' Clementine said glumly. 'I'm not looking forward to stuffing myself into that costume. Anyway, the church choir are going on in a minute and then Ittonvale, we've got ages.' She took a big spoonful from the bowl on the table in front of her, grimacing as she put it in her mouth. 'Gosh Margery, this yoghurt is very strange.'

'That's left-over brandy sauce, Clem,' Gloria said, shaking her head at her. Clementine shrugged and took another big spoonful.

'Let's get everything packed away properly so we can enjoy it,' Margery said. 'Then we can do our Secret Santa presents.'

'Oh good,' Seren said, arriving through the doorway. Ceri-Ann had obviously got hold of her already, she had a full face of make-up, and a terrible approximation of a snowflake slathered onto her cheek with face paint. 'It wasn't easy, but I managed to get something for three pounds.'

'The budget was five!' Sharon wailed from the sink, her mouth full of pigs in blankets. Karen patted her on the shoulder, and for the fiftieth time this week alone Margery regretted permitting Secret Santa.

'You know that gravy isn't vegetarian, don't you Karen?' Margery said, gesturing at the plate Karen was eating roast potatoes from.

'Yes, don't worry. I'll eat around it,' Karen said as she stuffed another potato into her mouth.

'I have an announcement to make about Secret Santa!' Clementine said, pulling out her notepad. There was a collective groan among the team. 'I've worked out who each of you got and what you got them!'

'You put that away, Clementine Butcher-Baker,' Margery warned. 'Or you might find that your Secret Santa takes away their gift.' She pointed to the pile of wrapped presents in the corner, one of which was very obviously a new cleaver, and winked at her.

'I knew you had me, Margery!' Clementine grinned, flipping the pad around to show her what was written on it. 'Look!' Margery batted her away gently.

'What have you got on your face, Seren?' Gloria asked, eyebrows raised.

'Do you like it?' Seren leaned in so they could all see the glitter on her cheek better.

'No, you'll ruin your skin. I bet you look like a crinkle cut chip under all that face paint.'

'Margery…' Clementine hissed from next to her, dragging her attention away from Gloria and Seren, 'look who it is!'

Margery turned to see where Clementine was pointing. Out through the kitchen door and at the main entrance was a man who they had seen one too many times recently. He looked a bit confused as he peered around the bustling hall, until Mrs Blossom skipped over to him and shook his hand. She held Ada Bones, who was looking rather festive in a Christmas tree outfit, under her arm and a steaming glass of mulled wine in the other. One of the Ittonvale teachers was busily dispensing it from a soup kettle by the stage. Mrs Blossom looked over at the kitchen and then gestured at them. Margery looked at Clementine who shrugged; they both pottered over to her.

'Margery, Clementine,' Mrs Blossom said in her twangy voice, 'This is the gentleman who you stalked like madwomen.'

'Hello,' Margery said weakly. Mr Leith smiled at her and stuck out his hand; they shook. 'Sorry about that.'

'It's quite all right,' he said. 'Mrs Blossom caught me up on what's been going on and I can't say I blame you. Strange man poking about and all that.'

'Michael is here to watch the plays this afternoon and look after Mrs Ada Bones of course, so try not to follow his car home, hmmm?' Mrs Blossom chuckled. Margery and Clementine looked at each other sheepishly. 'I invited him to see which play is the best.'

'That's right.' He smiled again. Margery wondered how she could have ever seen any menace in his face. He was a very normal-looking man, who obviously loved dogs so much he had set up a strange pampering dog kennels. 'What time are you on?'

Margery looked to the stage where the church choir, led by Dawn Simmonds, were beginning to gather. The hall was heavy with anticipated murmuring.

'Not long,' she said to him cheerily. 'Unfortunately, there's not much food left. Can I get you a mince pie instead?'

'Quite all right, I've already had a sandwich at home,' he said cheerily, accepting a glass of wine from the Itton-vale teacher anyway. 'I'll just go and find a place to sit down then, excuse me please, ladies.'

He wandered past them and into the hall. Mrs Blossom grinned at them both. 'See he's lovely! Not a stranger trying to break into your school. Oh, and thank you again Mrs Butcher-Baker for returning Ada Bones. We both appreciate it, don't we Ada?'

She put the dog down on the floor next to her. Ada Bones glared at them all suspiciously. Margery smiled. 'No problem.'

'Gosh, I'd better get up there. I'm supposed to be introducing everyone!' Mrs Blossom clapped her on the shoulder one last time and then went to the stage, tottering up the stairs on her heels; Ada Bones scurried behind her. She approached the microphone that was set up at the front. The waiting audience went quiet.

'Hello all, thank you for coming today. My name is Rhonda Blossom, and I am the musical director of Ittonvale school.' Mrs Blossom looked at the crowd and smiled. 'Before we get going, I just wanted to say a few words about Elizabeth Large, the music teacher for Summerview school.' Margery could see Mr Large and his children sitting over at the far side of the hall. 'Without whom neither of our shows would exist. She was so very talented and I speak for all of us when I say she will be greatly missed, at both Ittonvale and Summerview schools.' There was nodding among the audience. Mr Large put his hands on his youngest son's shoulders. 'So if you have a drink, would you please join me in raising your glass, to Elizabeth Large.' She raised her own glass, so hot still that steam rose from it. Everyone in the hall followed suit.

'To Elizabeth Large!' echoed around the hall.

Mrs Blossom took a sip of her wine and then cleared her throat. 'Well, up first we have the Dewstow church choir, who will be delighting us with some excellent Christmas carols. Please give them a big hand!'

'Oh my God, Margery!' Clementine squealed. 'Look!'

'Clementine, please do not swear!' Margery teased but she looked to see where the woman was pointing. Outside white flecks were pouring from the sky and tumbling majestically to the ground, it was beautiful. Margery couldn't help but step forward so she could see it better. Even the hard concrete of the church hall car park looked strangely wonderous as the flakes fell and covered it in a heavy layer.

'It's snowing!' Clementine bellowed. 'A white Christmas after all!'

'Gosh, what a lovely surprise,' Margery said, looking out through the door. Behind them on the stage, Dawn's choir began to sing angelically. Clementine put her arm around Margery, and she turned to smile at her.

Epilogue

Margery sat happily at the table finishing the smoked salmon and scrambled eggs Clementine had made them both and looked out of the kitchen window into the gloomy garden; the kitchen was gloriously warm and cosy in comparison. The snow had not held for longer than a few days. The neighbourhood had looked as though someone had opened a bag of flour on it for a moment and then it had gone all slushy and horrible. But it had made Clementine's year anyway; it had been the closest snowfall that they had had to Christmas Day for at least a decade.

Margery sat back and smiled to herself. She had never really been a huge fan of Christmas. She was not particularly religious so the whole thing was too much eating for her really, but watching Clementine busy herself in the kitchen she could feel the second-hand excitement pouring off her in waves. Though perhaps it was just the heat radiating from the packed oven and the hob, which was already chock-full of pans bubbling away. Both kitchen counters were smothered with vegetable peelings and assorted seasonings. Margery wondered how Clementine could be so tidy in the kitchen at work and such a disaster at home.

The unfortunate buying of partridge instead of turkey had extended itself to today, as Clementine had done all the holiday food shopping, but Margery thought that perhaps the small bird was a better size for them both. There was still enough room in their small oven to cook roast potatoes and stuffing balls. She could see the bird in the middle of the oven, browning nicely. Pumpkin certainly seemed to think it looked adequate as she sat in the chair nearest the oven. She kept looking between them both with sad doe eyes, as though she had never, ever eaten before and not wolfed down a special holiday tin of tuna for breakfast an hour ago.

Margery hoped they would not forget about the cat in the excitement this year. A few years before, Clementine's mother had been the guest of honour and in the revelry the cat had been shut in the kitchen with the cooked turkey that was resting on top of the oven. That was the only Christmas Day in her living memory that they had eaten oven-cooked fish fingers with all the trimmings instead.

'I hope you're hungry, Margery,' Clementine said as she whisked the Yorkshire pudding batter, another of her non-traditional holiday traditions. 'I've got a full day's schedule planned. Did you get your copy of the itinerary?'

'I did, Clem,' Margery said, thinking of the piece of paper Clementine had thrust into her hands a few days before. It had been a two-page list, front and back. 'I don't know if we'll have time to do it all if you want to open the tree presents before midnight, but we can try.'

They always opened their tree presents one at a time, partly because it was nice to see what each other got and partly to fill up the time in the day. This year was slightly different because, after the success of the last-minute Christmas lunch, Margery and Clementine had found themselves agreeing to cater Mr Barrow and Mrs

Smith's wedding. The planning was already abominable. 'Weddings are easy to plan!' Clementine had said. 'They simply invite 200 people who hate them and then we chuck a bit of chicken on a plate with a couple of potatoes or a piece of quiche for vegetarians. Done!' But she had already been proved horribly, terribly wrong. The only wedding planning experience they had was their own low-key, relaxed wedding day. Not the extravaganza of the year Mrs Smith and Mr Barrow were planning with their numerous dietary requirements and strange requests.

Margery wished she had never answered the phone to Mrs Smith, though her dreamy whisper down the line that their engagement was on had been quite cheering. Clementine had even opened the four pounds ninety-nine bottle of Cava they had been saving for New Year's Eve in celebration.

'Ooh, that reminds me!' Clementine said, putting the bowl of batter down on the kitchen counter. 'I've got a really special present for you! Go and sit in the living room. Quick, before I forget again! My terrible memory and all that, Margery.'

'All right.' Margery did as she was told, wandering into the living room to sit on the old sofa. She wondered what Clementine could have possibly got her and how she had kept it a secret; Clementine was notoriously bad at secrets. Margery already knew what all her other presents under the tree held, because she had told her. The stocking presents they had opened that morning were always the same, a new toothbrush, a bag of chocolate coins, a squashed satsuma, and a year's supply of socks. Margery always had black and Clementine's were always white, Clementine always used to receive navy, but they were far too confusing to pair. It was odd to receive a surprise, and for Clementine to have to run outside into the cold to get it was very strange indeed.

Pumpkin saw an opportunity and came to sit on her lap. She stroked the cat's head idly and relaxed in the pleasant room. The CD player under the television was softly playing carols and soon they would be tuning in to the Queen's speech before they ate dinner. The fringe of tinsel on the mantlepiece blew gently in the breeze from the electric heater, along with the cards that Margery had hung above it on strings. There were so many this year, it made Margery feel truly loved.

Clementine burst back into the house with a cardboard box under one arm, the wreath nearly falling off as she slammed the front door behind her. Her face was the picture of excitement. 'Ready, Margery?'

'Of course!' Margery sat up as Clementine brought the box over and placed it gently on the sofa next to her. Margery took it and peered inside. A pair of big round eyes stared back at her from a small, fluffy face.

'Oh.' Margery stared into the box. 'This is…'

'I know what you're thinking, Margery…' Clementine clapped her hands together in joy. 'But don't worry, I haggled Dawn down to a very good price.'

'I don't think you do know what I'm thinking actually,' Margery said, as she reached into the box with the arm that was not in a sling and pulled out the kitten. It was black and white and very, very fluffy. 'But I suppose Dawn was right about Sprinkles having very cute babies.'

'It's a girl.' Clementine grinned. 'But I thought we'd call her Crinkles, you know after Chris Crinkles, with it being the season and all that.'

'You mean Kris Kringle, Clem.'

'Oh really? Well, Crinkles sounds better.'

Margery smiled and stroked Crinkles on her soft head.

'Look Pumpkin, you've got a sister!' Clementine beamed at her. Pumpkin glared at them all from the arm of the sofa, her round eyes wide and her face raised in alarm.

'Right, better get on with the dinner then.'

Clementine went back into the kitchen, leaving Margery alone with the two cats. She smiled as the kitten bounced out of the box and leapt across the living room carpet. Pumpkin looked on in horror as it rushed immediately to the Christmas tree and began to attack one of the lower branches.

Margery smiled. 'Welcome to the family, Crinkles.'

Acknowledgements

Just like the first book the list of people I must thank is enormous! I have received a tremendous amount of support since the first Dinner Lady Detectives was released, and there are just too many people to give thanks to, but I will try!

Firstly, thank you to my wife Robyn, for everything you do. I love you.

Thank you to the entire team at Canelo – and an especially huge thank you to my editor Siân. Thank you for all your hard work and patience! I know I can't always be an easy author to edit, what with my fondness for adding many needless jokes instead of plot and my complete lack of understanding of punctuation marks.

Thanks to my family and friends as always, especially to Mum and Jim and Dad and Kirstie for buying what seems like most of the first printing of *The Dinner Lady Detectives*. Big thank you also to Auntie's Jenny, Tracey, and Sammy, who brought copies of the book to my sister's wedding for me to sign at the reception, unbeknownst to the bride!

A very special mention must go to Pepper who was a very good kitten and did lots of excellent keyboard typing with her tiny paws.

Also, I owe an apology to Tash McAdam, whose name I misspelt in the first book's acknowledgements – I have double checked your name on Facebook seventy times while writing this and I think I've got it right this time!

Last, but certainly not least, thank you to you! It's bizarre to me sometimes that people would choose to spend their free time reading something I wrote and be interested in what adventures are next for Margery and Clementine. I feel very humbled by it all.

Until the next time…

Do you love crime fiction and are always on the lookout for brilliant authors?

Canelo Crime is home to some of the most exciting novels around. Thousands of readers are already enjoying our compulsive stories. Are you ready to find your new favourite writer?

Find out more and sign up to our newsletter at canelocrime.com